Initiation

In London it was the height of the Edwardian era —but lovely young Levanah Falcon had descended into subterranean depths far below the glowing, gracious surface of that elegant world.

No one would recognize the ladies and gentlemen who surrounded her in this underground chamber. Gone was their elegant attire. Instead they wore primitive gowns and masks, and Levanah felt her own gown being ripped from her body by their eager hands.

Above her Levanah saw the towering figure they called their Master, his great cloak flung open to reveal his rippling, muscular nakedness, his antlers spread gleaming above his black mask. And now she knew this was the moment she had been waiting for so long.

Levanah was about to become a woman—as the fate of the Falcons hung in perilous balance above the flames of hell. . . .

THE FALCON SAGA *by Catherine Darby*

Catherine Darby's
The Falcon Saga - 8
Falcon Rising

POPULAR LIBRARY • NEW YORK

The Falcons

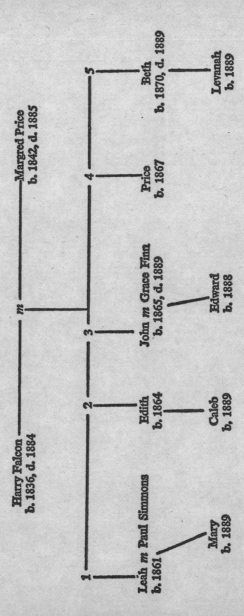

Harry Falcon
b. 1836, d. 1884

m

Margred Price
b. 1842, d. 1885

1   2   3   4   5

Leah *m* Paul Simmons
b. 1861

Edith
b. 1864

John *m* Grace Finn
b. 1865, d. 1889

Price
b. 1867

Beth
b. 1870, d. 1889

Mary
b. 1889

Caleb
b. 1889

Edward
b. 1888

Levanah
b. 1889

Prologue

1901

Levanah Falcon was nearly twelve years old when she discovered she was a witch. She had, from her earliest years, been aware that she was different from other children, but it was not until she disobeyed orders and went to the cottage that she became fully aware of the extent of that difference.

Other children did not have thick, straight hair that was the color of an apple as it ripens, and narrow, amber-colored eyes slanting above high cheekbones, and spindly arms and legs that always seemed to stick out at odd angles to the rest of her thin little body.

Other children were not conscious of forces moving invisibly among the ordinary things of the world, but where they saw leaves and twigs whirled in a gust of wind Levanah glimpsed, out of the corners of her slanting eyes, spirals of light that disturbed the still air into a million ripples.

"Levanah lives in a dream world," Aunt Leah said, half-affectionate, half-excusing.

Aunt Leah had brought up Levanah along with her own daughter, Mary, and Cousin Teddy because both Teddy's parents and Levanah's parents were dead. Teddy's father had been thrown from his horse just after Teddy's mother had died, and Levanah's parents had died when she was a baby too. Or so Aunt Leah said. The trouble with Aunt Leah was her lips often said one thing and her eyes another.

"Teddy's mother was buried among her own family," Aunt Leah said, "and your father, Levanah, was buried among his own people too."

That explained why there was no grave for either of them, but it did not explain why Levanah's mother was buried outside the churchyard nor why her surname should be Falcon. Mary's surname was Simmons, Aunt Leah's husband having been a man called Paul Simmons. So, at Kingsmead, only Mary had a living parent, both Teddy and Levanah being orphans, which sounded pathetic and romantic but actually was quite pleasant and ordinary, with Aunt Leah to take care of the three children and Cousin Wenna to teach them at the school they attended.

The Falcons had lived at Kingsmead in Marie Regina for more than three hundred and fifty years.

"The village took its name from the monastery," Cousin Wenna explained, "but when the monasteries were dissolved the land was given to the king and his courtiers."

Some of that land had gone to the first Sir Harry Falcon and he had built Kingsmead upon it for himself and his descendants. The original house had been a Tudor manor with a great hall that rose up through two stories, a solar and parlor with two bedrooms above on one side, and a kitchen and stillroom with two bedrooms above on the other side. Later owners had added two wings that turned the house into a letter E with the middle bar missing. Levanah and Mary had a room each over the servant's quarters, and in the other wing was a ground floor drawing room with a sitting room over it, though few people ever actually sat there for the apartment had a cool, clammy atmosphere even on the brightest day.

Levanah had gone there one morning, to fetch some sewing silks her aunt had told her to bring, and been surprised as she opened the door to see the pale carpet dyed scarlet in places as if somebody had spilled red wine. But when she had looked again the red patches had gone and the carpet was pale again. She had grabbed the sewing silks and run along the gallery, past the portraits of her ancestors, down the stone stairs into the hall where Aunt Leah sat in a high-backed chair near the fire.

"Do you have to run everywhere, dear?" Aunt Leah had asked in mild reproof.

"The sitting room—" Levanah had stammered. "The carpet—it was red. Great blotches of red."

"That's ridiculous," Aunt Leah had said, but she had gone so white that her eyes looked like black hollows. It was, the child thought uneasily, almost as if Leah were afraid.

The house was a big dwelling for one woman and three children, but Teddy was Lord Edward Falcon and would one day take his seat in the House of Lords and require a grand country residence. More important than that, Aunt Leah had been born at Kingsmead and swore that she would die there. It was not likely to happen soon for Aunt Leah was scarcely past forty, with not a gray hair in her shining black chignon, but she always spoke as if she had never been young.

A thousand acres of rich farming land surrounded Kingsmead, with the river running through it and bisecting the main London road that separated Falcon property from the village. Road and river formed an equal-armed cross, with Kingsmead in the lower left-hand corner and the graveyard wandering down into the village in the lower right-hand corner. On the other side of the river, still on Falcon land, was the school where Cousin Wenna taught selected pupils from the neighboring farms.

Cousin Wenna was actually cousin to Levanah's grandmother, but she had been born to a woman already middle-aged and was younger than Aunt Leah. She had been born in Wales, for there had always been a strain of Celt in the Falcons, and had come to take charge of the school before Levanah was born. The children liked Cousin Wenna, who was firm but kind, with a plain face and plaits wound about her head. Only Levanah noticed that her eyes were the color of grass and full of sleepy awareness of everything that went on around her.

The top right-hand corner of the road-river cross was occupied by the sloping hill crowned by the fragments of the old monastery. Beyond the hill lay Whittle Farm where Aunt Edith lived. Aunt Edith was Aunt Leah's younger sister, but her name was scarcely ever mentioned. There had been a terrible quarrel between the two of them years before, the cause of which was never explained but had something to do with Aunt Edith having a son, but no husband. Cousin Caleb didn't attend the school and Levanah had caught only brief glimpses of him from time to time.

"Cousin Caleb," Teddy explained grandly, "is a bastard. He never had a real father."

"Like Jesus," breathed Mary, who was going through an intense, High Anglican phase.

"No, stupid! Aunt Edith had a lover, but he went away without marrying her," Teddy said.

"But there was another Falcon lady once who had a lover," Levanah said with interest. "Regina Falcon. You know, Mary, the one with red hair, in the gallery. And her son became the master of Kingsmead."

"But Regina Falcon's lover was King Charles II," Teddy said. "Kings don't count."

Levanah didn't agree, but it was useless to argue with Teddy, who always knew better than anybody else.

She thought about Caleb sometimes, wondering what he did with himself all day and who taught him his lessons. Aunt Edith she saw often, wandering about on the hill, a thin woman as fair as Aunt Leah was dark. Levanah was not allowed to talk to her, but the other had stared at her with pale blue eyes in which there was only a queer, pitying expression, and had passed on without greeting.

Apart from Teddy and Mary, Levanah had no friends. She was not even certain if her cousins could be regarded as friends, though the three of them got along without too much quarreling. But the other children at school avoided her, though not so openly as to cause comment from any adult who might be around. She spent a lot of time by herself at playtime, wandering about in the shrubbery at the bottom of the fenced-off garden where the children were allowed to amuse themselves between lessons.

The school had been built on the ruins of another old Falcon house and was officially named "The Lady Margred School" but it was generally called "The Manor School." Lady Margred had been the children's grandmother and her portrait hung also on the wall at the back of the gallery. She had been very pretty, Levanah thought wistfully, with big yellowish eyes and long hair so dark that it had blue lights in it. She had come from Wales to marry her cousin Harry Falcon, and there had been five children.

Sometimes Levanah tried to imagine those five children growing up at Kingsmead. Aunt Leah seldom talked about her childhood except to say that it had been a happy one. Of the others, John, who was Teddy's father, and Beth, who was Levanah's mother, were dead, and Aunt Edith lived at the other side of the hill. There had been a younger brother, too, but Uncle Price had gone out to South Africa years before and they had lost touch with him completely. He had probably died in the war, Aunt Leah said, and when the bonfire was lit to announce the Relief of Mafeking, she took them all to church to pray for his safety.

Levanah tried also to imagine what she and Teddy and Mary would be like in twenty years' time. Teddy would be really important by then, with a seat in the House of Lords and a house in London, and probably a wife and children of his own too. Mary was very pretty and sweet-natured with soft dark hair and long eyelashes, so she would probably have a husband. As for herself, Levanah sighed, wondering if the years might make her prettier. She would have liked to be pretty, but though she looked hopefully in the mirror every day the same pale, pointed face looked back at her.

Meanwhile, life flowed along at Kingsmead as placidly as the river with only the occasional storm to ruffle the surface. There had been such a storm on the day that Levanah went down to the cottage.

It had begun with Teddy as usual. He was no longer at the Manor school but had been at a public school for the last couple of years and, in consequence, thought he had been invested with the right to order his cousins around. Sweet-tempered Mary had submitted. Levanah had not. Aunt Leah, who, if she favored any of the three, favored Teddy, had ordered Levanah either to play chess, as he wanted, or to put on her cloak and take herself out of doors until her temper had cooled.

So, with cape and hood pulled on over her green woolen dress, Levanah had marched through the front door, wishing she dared slam it, across the courtyard and beneath the archway into the main drive that wound between oak and elm to the road. The prospect of walking along the road was not enticing.

Instead she turned, as she usually did, into the meadows that fanned out on every side and were interspersed with apple orchards and stubbled fields that would be sown in spring with wheat and hops. Now they were cropped bare, the furrows muddy after recent rain, the trees a delicate black etching against the pearly sky.

Levanah started to run, partly to get away from the big house which sometimes oppressed her, and partly because she was glad to be outside where she could run and skip without being reminded that she was a little lady.

It was not until she reached the fringe of the woods that bordered the river that she remembered the cottage. The cottage itself was as old as Kingsmead and had been built originally as a dower house for the widows of the owners of the main property. It was known locally as "Witch's Dower," though Aunt Leah frowned with displeasure if that name was dropped in her hearing. She seldom mentioned the place at all and the children were strictly forbidden to go there.

"It's unsafe, and might fall in on you," was all she said, but on her face was the same expression that Levanah had noticed when she had told Aunt Leah about the red patches on the sitting-room carpet.

They had caught brief glimpses of it from time to time when they had wandered in that direction, but over the years the woods had become so thickly laced with creeper that the house itself seemed to have vanished. To go there, when she was already in disgrace, was the most wicked thing that Levanah could think of to do.

Although she was small and slight for her age, it was with considerable difficulty that she forced her way through. Underfoot thistle and nettle and trailing ivy made the ground slippery, and ropes of creeper bound the trees into a maze of bare branches and lichened trunks. Near at hand she could hear the river muttering to itself and, at one instant, glimpsed its rippled brown surface. The trees semicircled a large patch of shoulder-high grass in the midst of which the cottage rose, its windows eyes that kept constant vigil through the foliage of holly and silver wands of birch and willow. Walking through the grass was like wading in a sea of feathery spikes, and the damp earth made little sucking noises under her feet as if it sought to drag her down.

The cottage had been whitewashed once but had faded to a yellowish-gray that showed at intervals between the thick creeper that swarmed up to the roof and fringed the cracked and broken windowpanes. The door was swollen with damp and impossible to open, but rain and wind had denuded one of the lower windows of all but a margin of glass, and it was an easy matter to scramble through.

The room within was dim and green, its floor covered with a thick layer of dust, its walls peeling, its fireplace choked with twigs and bird droppings. A narrow wooden staircase led up to a tiny landing, and at the foot of the staircase a door gave access to another room.

Levanah gazed around with interest, aware not only of the silence but also of a familiarity in the place that puzzled her, for she had never been here before, yet some part of her knew it well.

There was a table at the other end of the room with two high-backed chairs at each side of it and a dresser against the wall. The crockery on the dresser was so black with age that its pattern was obscured and the cutlery in the drawer was green with mold.

Two rocking chairs graced the hearth and in the corner a piece of faded tapestry was stretched tightly across its frame. Cobwebs hanging from the ceiling made veils of lace in the green gloom.

"Poor little house!" Levanah said aloud, and a shower of ash fell into the hearth with a soft, sighing sound as if the house agreed with her.

She went across to the other door and pushed it wide, stepping into the other room, as thick with cobwebs and dust as the first, but containing no furniture beyond a table, a stool, and a chest which, when Levanah lifted the lid, proved to her disappointment to contain nothing more exciting than dust. Shelves ranged along one wall looked more promising. They were packed with dirt-encrusted bottles and jars, but when she uncorked one only a lot of foul-smelling grayish powder tipped out into the palm of her hand. There was a leather bag on a higher shelf. Levanah stood on her toes and pulled it down. Her fingers struggled with the drawstrings and, a moment later, something round and heavy, wrapped in black, lay between her hands. She unwrapped it carefully and blinked at the solid crystal ball, dulled but still retaining points of flashing fire in its depths.

There had been a gypsy with a crystal ball at Maidstone Fair the previous year. Aunt Leah had taken Mary and Levanah and reluctantly allowed them to have their fortunes told. Madame Estella had gazed into her crystal and told Levanah that, when she grew up, she would make a long journey across water and a handsome, dark-haired gentleman would fall in love with her. It had seemed very hopeful until Levanah had found out that she had told Mary exactly the same thing. Aunt Leah had laughed and said it was all nonsense anyway.

Levanah put the ball down on the table and stared at it, but she could see nothing at all in it. Probably Aunt Leah had been right. She rubbed the bridge of her nose irritably, for it had begun to tingle as if she were going to sneeze.

There was a murmuring within the room as if the air was full of tiny bees. Levanah looked again at the shelves. Next to the spot from which she had taken down the crystal something flat and square leaned against the wall.

She reached up again and lifted it down, turning it to face her and blowing the dust away from the surface. The light was dim but, by standing close to the window, she could make out clearly enough that it was a portrait. Not a finished painting, for the background was full of swirling gray, but the face was complete.

It was the face of a young girl, round and fresh

with a half smile on her mouth, a sprinkling of
freckles across her nose, and eyes that dreamed into
the distance. A tail of honey-colored hair softened the
outlines of her face, and lightly indicated beneath the
neck and shoulders an arm bent to display, on the
small hand, a gleaming ring shot with flashes of lilac
and blue.

Levanah's eyes studied the painted eyes. They appeared to be blue, but when she tilted the picture
slightly they shifted to green, and she realized they
were composed of a great variety of colors. The picture was neither finished nor signed, but the eyes told
anyone with the heart to see that the artist had loved
what he painted and painted what he loved.

There was a sound in the doorway behind her and
she spun round in terror clutching the portrait to her.

A boy of about her own age was staring at her, reflecting in his brown face her own surprise. His hair
hung untidily in a blond cowlick over his forehead
and his hands were grimy.

"Cousin Caleb," she said blankly, and reddened as
the thought that she was not allowed to speak to him
passed through her mind.

"Folk call me Cal," he informed her. "You're Levanah, aren't you? Poor Levanah, my mother calls
you."

"Does she indeed! Well, you may tell your mother I
have plenty of money," she retorted, stung.

"So has she," he said.

"Then she ought to spend some of it on clothes for
you." Levanah allowed herself a pointed look at his
torn and grubby breeches.

"These are my everyday things," he returned.
"What are you doing here?"

"I'm playing. And *you're* trespassing, because this is Falcon land."

"I am a Falcon!" Cal said.

"A bastard one!" Levanah said crossly.

"So are you then."

"I am *not!* My mother and father died," Levanah said, her face as red as her hair.

"Your mother killed herself and nobody knew who your father was," Cal told her.

Levanah stared at him in horror, the color ebbing from her cheeks, the pupils of her eyes dilating. When she spoke her voice was a husky whisper.

"That's a wicked lie! I never heard such a wicked lie before!"

"It's not a lie. It's true." He leaned against the doorpost and looked at her with casual contempt. "My mother was your mother's sister, and she told me all about it. My mother said that your mother was betrayed by a man who passed through and then deserted her, and a few days after you were born she cut open her veins and bled to death all over the carpet."

"In the sitting room," Levanah breathed.

"There! You knew all along!"

"No. No, I didn't." Anger forgotten, she whispered, "Is that why she's buried outside the churchyard?"

"I suppose so." The boy's expression became kinder as he saw her stricken little face. "You'd better sit down," he advised.

Levanah, her legs quivering, sat down on the stool. "Did your mother—did she say who my father was?" she asked.

Cal shook his head.

"She said that Beth, that was your mother, had some kind of affair with a stranger who lodged in the cottage here one summer. Then he went away and the following spring you were born and your mother—"

"Yes, you told me."

"I don't know who my father was either," he said. "My mother won't tell me, but she says that Aunt Leah turned her out of Kingsmead and she went to live at Whittle Farm."

"I wonder why she didn't turn my mother out too," Levanah said.

Her first shock over, she could begin to take a detached interest in the affair.

"Perhaps she liked your mother better than my mother," Cal said. "My mother says Beth was very sweet, not like Aunt Leah who's a bitch. I think Aunt Leah should have been the witch, not your mother."

"My mother wasn't a witch," Levanah said indignantly. "There are no such things anyway."

"You don't know anything, do you?" Cal said scornfully. "There've always been witches in the Falcon family, and sooner or later they all come to live here. That's why it's called 'Witch's Dower.' My mother says they weren't all bad either. Some of them were good and used their power well, and some of them live to be very old. Not all of them, though. Have you heard of Willow Falcon?"

"She's buried in the old family tomb. I've seen her name."

"She was a cousin and she married Great-Grandfather Nathan and she was very wicked," Cal said with relish. "She was so wicked that a tree struck by lightning fell upon her, and as she lay dying she said, 'Victory will not come until a Falcon rides upon a moth.' That was a kind of curse, I suppose."

"Well, my mother wasn't like that," Levanah said firmly.

"No, but some of them were. Those who used their power wrongly."

"It's just a story," Levanah said uneasily. "And how did they know they were witches anyway?"

"Because they were born with the mark of the devil high up on their legs," Cal said.

"What's that?"

"A mark shaped like a half moon. It's called the devil's kiss, and it's a sign that the person is a witch. Have you seen that very old grave near your mother's?"

"Catrin Falcon's?" Levanah nodded. "It says that she was drowned."

"Hundreds of years ago," Cal said, "the villagers found the devil's mark on her leg and they drowned her in the village pond. They used to do that in those days."

"I didn't know that," Levanah said.

"Oh, I know lots of things," Cal boasted. "My mother won't let me go to the Manor School because she says Cousin Wenna and Aunt Leah are as thick as thieves, but she teaches me a lot herself. She says she never liked reading when she was a girl, but now she reads all the time so she can keep up with me. Have you been in here before?"

Levanah shook her head.

"I've been up to it," Cal said, "but never inside it before. The place has a funny feeling, don't you think?"

"I like it." She looked about the dim green room.

"Perhaps you're a witch too."

"No, I'm not," she said irritably. "I just like the house, that's all."

"I wonder what's in all these bottles and jars and things?" He wandered over to the shelves. "Poisons, I expect. Have you been upstairs yet? I'm going to explore."

"It's my house!" she cried. "You have to ask my permission, and I won't give it because I haven't been up myself yet!"

"You're a bastard," he reminded her. "We aren't allowed to inherit property unless somebody leaves it to us in a Will. My mother owns Whittle Farm and she's already left it to me."

"I don't care." Levanah's mouth set stubbornly. "The house is still mine."

"Well, I'm sure I don't want it," Cal said. "It's a tumbledown place."

"No, it isn't!" Enthusiasm bubbled up in her voice. "If it was cleaned, and the chimney swept, and the doors and windows mended, it would be lovely, Cal. It would be fit to live in again and proud of itself. I think the girl would like it."

"What girl?"

"I found this picture. I think it's somebody who owned this place once."

"It looks like your mother," Cal said.

"My mother? How do you know?"

"Because I asked my mother once what Beth had looked like, and she said she had yellow-brown hair and dreamy eyes, and she always wore a moonstone ring. That girl is wearing a ring."

"Is it a moonstone?"

Cal shrugged, not much interested in jewelry.

"Anyway, it probably is her," he said. "This house belonged to her. I told you it always belongs to the Falcon witches."

"Then it's mine."

"Because you're a witch. I said so!"

"I'm not, but if it belonged to my mother then it ought to come to me."

"I'll wager you've got the devil's mark!"

"I have not!"

"Show me then!" he demanded.

"It's dreadfully wicked to show your legs," Levanah said primly.

"Show me!" He darted forward and grabbed at her skirt.

"Cal Falcon, you stop that!" she protested, but he was bigger and stronger than she was, and in a moment her skirt had been wrenched up and a thin, black-stockinged leg revealed.

Abruptly she ceased to struggle and stood upright.

"I can't tell," he complained. "Your drawers are too long."

Without speaking she pulled up the white frill to reveal, above the tight-gartered stocking, a crescent moon etched in deep purple on her childish thigh.

Cal took a pace backward and stared at her. The rough teasing had gone out of his face and he ran his tongue round his lips.

"I've had it since I was born," Levanah said. "I thought it was just a birthmark, but after what you said—"

"That was only an old story. I was making fun."

"Then it must mean the story's true," Levanah said sweetly, "for I have the mark, you see."

"I never meant to trespass on Falcon land, Cousin," Cal said hastily.

"I don't really mind," Levanah said graciously. "If you like you can come here again. I'm going to clean everything up and make it nice again. You can help if you've a mind."

"I'm good with my hands." He was anxious to pro-pitiate her. "I'm good at mending things."

"We won't tell anybody; it'll be a secret," she con-tinued. "You'd like to have a secret with me, wouldn't you, Cal?"

"Yes, yes, I would."

"You'd better leave first," she said, very dignified in her new authority. "I don't know how often I'll be able to come, but you can come here alone if you wish. Only don't let anybody see you, and don't go telling your mother."

"I won't say anything to her," he promised. "And I don't talk much to anybody else, except to have a fight sometimes with the village boys. On account of being a bastard, you see."

"I don't think it matters," Levanah said generously. "I think you're a very nice sort of boy, Cousin Cal."

"I think you're a very nice sort of girl, Cousin Le-vanah," he returned, and went through into the other room again where he prepared to climb through the window.

Levanah, following him with the portrait tucked beneath her arm, heard herself say, out of some quaint ancestral instinct, "Blessed be you."

"And you," he said in a slightly startled fashion, and, a moment later, was pushing his way through the long grass again.

She went back into the other room and put back the portrait and the crystal. A mischievous grin lifted the corners of her mouth. He had seemed really frightened when he had seen the mark! Boys, she de-cided, were all stupid, for she had had the mark since she was born and never thought about it.

It was strange, though, that Cal should have heard about such a mark, and that the cottage should be

called "Witch's Dower." What had he said? The
devil's kiss—that was it. It was a strange, unpleasant
name, for the devil, in Levanah's imagination, had
cloven hoofs and a tail and a red-hot pitchfork. She
wrinkled up her nose, and had a sudden mental picture of a young man clad all in green with curly hair
tumbling over a brow from which jutted two silver
horns. The young man was laughing, white teeth
gleaming, his eyes narrowed with mirth. Everything
about him sang of joy and abandon.

The picture lasted for no more than a moment and
was gone, but she touched the side of her leg with
wonder and, for the first time, thought of herself, not
as Levanah Falcon who longed to be pretty, but as
the latest in a long line of women who had borne the
purple crescent and lived in the white cottage.

Everything Cal had talked about was pushing back
into her mind. She sat down again on the stool and
cupped her chin in her hands, brooding.

So she, like her cousin, had an unknown father. In
a way it was as if she had always known it, deep
down inside herself. She wondered who he had been
and if he was still alive. Perhaps he had painted the
picture of her mother, but if that were true, then he
must have loved her and that didn't explain why he
had left her.

Levanah's thoughts moved on to her mother. Aunt
Leah seldom mentioned her and, never having known
her personally, Levanah felt no particular grief. But
to kill oneself was a terrible thing to do. A creeping
horror trembled along her nerves as she imagined the
blood flowing down from slashed veins to the pale
carpet. Her mother had died when she was only nineteen. To be nineteen was within Levanah's imagining,
but to be dead at nineteen was beyond the scope of

her mind. She shivered, clutching her fingers together, watching the thin blue veins in her white wrists, remembering the dreaming eyes in the portrait. There was a great deal she couldn't begin to understand yet, but she knew at least that Aunt Leah had lied, and that the mark on her leg made her different from other girls in a very special way.

The house was silent again, its murmuring stilled, as if for the moment it was satisfied. Levanah got up, took a last look round the room, and made her way out through the window again. The grass had sprung up again in Cal's wake and there was no visible pathway to mark the direction in which he had gone. Back to Whittle Farm, she supposed. It must be lonely without any companions except the strange pale-haired woman who wandered about on the hill.

It was almost dark when she reached the courtyard. It was the hour Levanah loved best when twilight hung like a curtain between day and night and the flowers curled their petals lazily over drowsing bees. At this season there were neither flowers nor bees, and the night unfolded over a barren landscape. It would be sad to die on such a night before the snowdrops came.

"Levanah! Where have you been? It's past suppertime." Aunt Leah had come out and scolded from the front door.

"You sent me out," Levanah said.

"But I didn't intend you to remain out so late," Aunt Leah said. "And your cloak is wet! You've been roaming about in the grass, and with tinkers and vagabonds liable to seize you and carry you off."

"I was playing," Levanah said.

"Well, come in now, do." Aunt Leah gave her niece a small push. "What are you dreaming about?"

"I was thinking that it must be very sad to die."

"Mercy, but what put that idea into your head?" her aunt demanded.

"I was thinking the queen just died," Levanah said.

"Her Majesty is certainly ill," Aunt Leah agreed, "and she is very old, but there is no reason to believe she is in any immediate danger. We have been praying for her recovery these past few weeks."

"Well, I won't pray any more," Levanah said serenely, "because she's already dead."

She walked placidly up the shallow steps into the great hall, leaving her aunt staring after her with something akin to fear on her shallow face.

The hall with its faded tapestries and heavy, dark pieces of furniture had been kept in its original state. Tradition was its keynote. Levanah, without knowing this consciously, had always sensed the harmony of the room, its essential truthfulness, as if, even though the people who lived in it might cheat and lie, its stone and wood and woven fabrics still retained their integrity.

Teddy and Mary, the earlier quarrel forgotten, were sitting by the fire on the high-backed settle. Mary looked sweetly pretty, her dark ringlets drooping over a flame-warmed cheek. At her side Teddy, his fair hair ruffled, was expounding the joys of cricket. Annie bustled in with a dish of buttered turnips, her apron crackling whitely round her ample hips. Annie and Cook and Alice, who did the rough work, were the only indoor servants, for Aunt Leah did not believe in keeping a large staff "to idle and eat their heads off."

In a few minutes they would sit down at the long table where generations of Falcons had supped. The drowned girl had sat there once, and Willow Falcon who had said that victory would not come until the impossible happened, and Beth who had fallen in love and been deserted.

After supper they would go into the parlor for evening prayers, with Aunt Leah reading a psalm or a parable in her clear voice and the three children ranged in front of her on prickly hassocks and, behind them, Cook and Annie and Alice who always had to be prodded to say, "Amen."

Afterward they usually played quietly for a while, or Aunt Leah read aloud, while Teddy whittled at a model ship he was trying to make, and she and Mary pricked their fingers over their samplers The atmosphere would be calm and affectionate and dull, and at nine o'clock Annie would come in with milk and biscuits before they were shooed off to bed.

It would all be the same, and yet nothing would ever be as it was before. Levanah was quite certain of that as she went upstairs to take off her outdoor things.

In her own bedroom she lit the lamp and hung up her cloak and hood. Her shoes were mud-encrusted and the dirt on the carpet would mean a scolding when Aunt Leah noticed it in the morning.

'I could turn her into a toad if I knew how to be a witch,' Levanah thought.

The idea amused her, though she was a little ashamed of herself, because Aunt Leah had always been kind, and she was really not to be blamed for not telling Levanah the truth. It was much nicer to have one's parents safely and respectably dead than to have a mother who had killed herself and an unknown father.

Nicer, but not true. Sitting on the edge of her bed and pulling off her mud-stained shoes, Levanah knew that it was much more important to know the truth than to be fed on lies.

But something good had come out of the day. She had found her cottage, and made a friend, and discovered who she was. Not plain Levanah but Levanah who bore the devil's kiss and had a strange and dramatic background.

"Levanah! Do hurry up or you won't have any supper at all." Aunt Leah's voice echoed up the stairs.

Levanah found her slippers, dragged a comb through her hair, and ran along the gallery. Teddy and Mary were already at the table. Everything looked as it always did, but nothing would ever be the same again.

Chapter I

1906

July flamed in emerald and gold under a canopy of blue. Muslins and parasols were much in evidence among those ladies of Marie Regina who could spare a few hours for leisure out of their daily chores. Those who could not tucked up their sleeves, tied on sunbonnets, and worked, with frequent pauses for lemonade.

At Kingsmead, Leah sat with her daughter, Mary, in the rose arbor at the back of the house. At forty-five Leah was a handsome woman, her youthful plainness transformed into something that in a softer, plumper woman might have been beauty. In Leah it was a subtle dignity that drew eyes when other, prettier women were ignored.

Despite the heat she looked cool in an elegant gown of black silk, its elbow sleeves and neckline trimmed with narrow white ruffles. A straw hat shaded her aquiline features and the small tapestry frame on which she was working.

Mary, her dark curls tied back with a scarf, was sorting silks, her brown eyes narrowed against the glare. In her widespread muslin skirts the varied colors made a rainbow among which her narrow hands darted and swooped like small white birds.

"Do hurry, my dear." Leah smiled across at her daughter. "Sunlight fades the colors so rapidly."

"Yes, Mother." Mary hastened obediently. A strand of scarlet had caught her eye and she looked at it wistfully. Red and lemon were such gay colors. It was a pity they were unsuitable for young girls. A pity too that on such a glorious afternoon she must sit out in weather that demanded picnics down by the river.

"Teddy will be home soon," Leah said. "I wish he had not undertaken to go on a boating trip just before he goes to Cambridge, but we must remember he is a young man and not try to tie him to our apron strings. He is getting very much taller, have you noticed?"

"No, Mother."

"Mary, you must learn to increase your vocabulary a trifle," Leah said in good-humored reproof. "Teddy is not going to find you very amusing when he comes home if all you can say is 'Yes, Mother,' and 'No, Mother.'"

Mary, who cared nothing for Teddy's opinion, bent her head lower over the silks.

"Have you seen Levanah this afternoon?" Leah inquired.

"She went over to the school, I think."

"Levanah might occasionally take it into her head to help at home instead of continually running over to Cousin Wenna." Leah stabbed the tapestry and drew in her lips as the silk hissed through the canvas. "I shall be very pleased when the assistant teacher arrives. Levanah will have no excuse for avoiding her duties then."

"No, Mother." Mary laid aside the red silk, and began to match up two shades of gray.

Levanah, having enjoyed three cups of scalding coffee with Cousin Wenna, rose and stretched. The sunshine pouring through the window made her hair the color of ripe mustard seeds, and sharpened her high cheekbones and pointed chin. At seventeen Levanah was angles of light and shade, moments of sweetness and moments of blazing fury.

Wenna, leaning back and gazing at her, felt a pang of pity. Levanah was still young, still vulnerable, and in the years ahead there would be many to hurt her.

The older woman, remembering that she was in sight of her fortieth birthday, caught herself sighing. She was herself resigned to spinsterhood, but Levanah needed a man to gentle her.

"I have to go," Levanah was saying, reaching for her hat.

"Back to Kingsmead?"

"I might take a walk down by the river," Levanah said, tying the strings under her chin and making a face at herself in the glass.

'That means,' Wenna thought, 'that she is meeting Cal.' From the window it was possible to see first the boy and then the girl slip into the darkness of the woods. It was only surprising that nobody else had noticed and drawn conclusions.

Aloud, she said, "And I have a pile of holiday essays to mark. I'm beginning to wonder if it was such a good idea to get the children to bring work in during the holidays. It keeps up their interest but it does bind me. However!"

"It will be better when Miss What's-her-name comes," Levanah said.

"Miss Bishop. Charlotte Bishop. Yes, I'm looking forward to her arrival. The younger children get restless while I'm setting the older ones work. I thought you were going for a walk."

"Just going." Levanah blew a kiss and whisked through the door.

Wenna's apartment was above the schoolhouse proper, its room cool and always faintly untidy. Bright cushions and vases of dried grasses flavored the surroundings with Wenna's own slightly astringent personality.

In the drive Levanah looked round once to wave, and then plunged into the bright sunshine, her head lowered, her feet hurrying into the main road and over the bridge. The way into the woods was, in contrast, dark and shady, its green depths a refreshment to mind and body.

With luck she would have an hour in which to set the cottage to rights and to talk to Cal. He was working his mother's farm now and increasing the profits. Edith scarcely ever came out these days and rumor in the village had it that she sometimes took a drop too much. Cal seldom spoke of her and Levanah seldom mentioned Leah. It was as if by unspoken consent she and Cal confined themselves to their interest in the cottage. This was their bond, and away from "Witch's Dower" their lives were quite separate.

The cottage looked very different from the cobweb-shrouded building she had explored five years before. Cal had scythed the tall grass in the clearing, but left the creeper-bound trees to form a screen from prying eyes. The ivy clinging to the walls had been trimmed back from the windows, and glass now sparkled in the frames.

As usual Levanah entered with a feeling of possession. This was her house in a very special way.

Cal was already there. His broad shoulders and untidy fair head were hunched over a carving. His hands, just emerging from the gangling clumsiness of boyhood, held the wood tenderly and firmly. He looked up at Levanah as she stepped into the living room and grinned, the mantle of the dedicated artist slipping from him as he exclaimed, "You look like a wet turnip in that hat!"

"At least I don't sweat!" she retorted. "How is it coming?"

"Slowly." He held it out for her to see. The figure was taking shape, the legs ending in cloven hoofs, the head crowned with tiny horns, the face still blank but with the indentations for eyes and mouth already grooved.

"You are good with your hands," she approved.

"It's rough," he said.

"It will do for what I want," Levanah told him.

"Why do you want it?" he inquired curiously.

"As a . . . guardian," she said hesitatingly. " 'Witch's Dower' needs a guardian, for when we're not here. Even woodland gods need shelter in winter."

"You're an odd girl." He sat back in his chair and gazed at her. "I can't understand half you say and I don't believe the other half."

"Perhaps it's as well sometimes. Have you had any blackberry cordial yet? It's about ready for drinking."

"Are you sure," he inquired cautiously, "that you know what you're doing? I'm afraid you'll end up poisoning somebody if you're not careful."

"As you're the only one who tries out my brews,"

she teased, going through into the other room, "then you don't need to worry about the rest of the neighborhood."

The other room had been scrubbed and aired, and shutters fixed to the windows. Cal had whitewashed the walls and mended the shelves, and the jars and bottles, having been scoured, now contained a variety of roots and powders and syrups that Levanah had concocted partly out of old recipe books borrowed from the library, partly out of her own head.

Pouring the blackberry cordial, she looked as usual toward the wall. The portrait hung there now, and on a ledge beneath it was the crystal wrapped up in black silk and a vase of wild flowers. The little woodland god would stand there too when he was complete.

"I'll guarantee," said Cal, lunging through the door, "that this cordial is sour."

"Drink it and stop complaining!" Watching the muscles contract in his brown throat, Levanah was conscious of a feeling in her own body that she had experienced before. It was a sensation that both frightened her and made her feel as if she were on the edge of some tremendous discovery about herself.

"It's not bad." He put down the glass and nodded.

"You'd better get back to the carving." Her breath came thick and fast. "I don't suppose you have much time, and I'm supposed to be with Cousin Wenna."

"She's a nice-looking woman," Cal said.

"Cousin Wenna!" She followed him back into the other room. "Why, she's old!"

"Not so old. She has lovely eyes." He looked up again from his carving and said, as if he had discovered something, "You have beautiful eyes too."

"Have I?" Pleasure lit her face.

"Pity the rest of you doesn't match up," he said sadly.

"Cal." Levanah sat down opposite him. "Cal, do you believe I am what I say I am?"

"A carrot top?"

"No, be serious! Do you truly believe that I am . . . ?"

"Yes." He spoke flatly, his hand stilled on the knife. "Yes, I've always believed that. Not just the mark on your leg, but the way you look sometimes, the way you often say things that are in my own mind just before *I* say them. Yes, I believe it."

"I've found something out, Cal." She clasped her hands together tightly. "Going to church and Ladies Aid Bazaars with Aunt Leah and Mary is my—my outside self. But here, in this place, where the small creatures move and the grass grows high, this is my—inside self. And it's free and joyful and has nothing to do with charity work, or sewing for the Jews Basket, or tight corsets. Can you understand that?"

"I think so, but I'm not sure. What use will it all be?"

"Use? Everybody talks about usefulness!" she exclaimed. "Cal, listen! I'll tell you something! At night sometimes, when everyone is asleep, I go out of the house and across the fields into the woods. You'd think them silent, but they're full of rustlings and creakings and flutterings. I come down here to the cottage and light a candle and sit, just sit and let the night wash over me. It's exciting, Cal. You can't guess how exciting it is."

"But what do you think about when you sit?" he asked puzzled.

"About my mother," she said softly. "My father too. I wonder who he was, and if he was the one who painted the picture, and why he left her. And I try to make things happen, not big, important things but little things, to see if I can. I stare at the candle flame and will it to grow smaller or to stream upward and it dwindles or grows as I will it."

"I believe it," Cal said somberly.

"If only there were some way I could do more," Levanah said wistfully. "If there were two of us . . ."

"You want me to sneak out in the middle of the night and sit looking at candles, is that it?"

"You make it sound ridiculous," she said laughing. "But something might happen. I don't know exactly what, but something!"

"If you and I met in the middle of the night something might very well happen," he agreed, "and it wouldn't be candle flames."

"Don't be coarse!" she rebuked.

"I am coarse," he said serenely. "I'm a bastard, remember. Bastards are not gentlemen."

"Don't you ever wonder about your father?" she asked.

"Why should I? I don't suppose he ever wondered about me." Cal shrugged and returned to his carving, but as she was leaving he said, "Can you get out tonight? I might stroll over, around midnight. You might need a fresh supply of candles."

It was always the same. Cal teased her and made fun of her, but in the end he did what she wanted him to do, as if, deep inside himself, he was afraid.

Hurrying back across the fields Levanah wished she could make Aunt Leah do as she wanted. Unfortunately Aunt Leah spent a great deal of her time trying to make everybody else do as *she* wished. With Mary she had succeeded, although Teddy sometimes defied her. Levanah simply went on her own way, lying only when it was necessary. At least she could be thankful that her aunt never went near the cottage. Indeed, she avoided the woods as much as she avoided the upstairs sitting room.

Mary came to meet her as Levanah approached the garden at the back of the house. The two projecting wings gave shelter to the rosebushes and herb borders and, with the windows open and the long curtains stirring in the slight breeze, Kingsmead presented a picture of summer tranquility.

"Mother is absolutely furious," Mary said in her sweet worried voice. "She declares that you spend far too much time over at the school, and that it's time you grew up and became a young lady."

"I'll leave that to you. You're much better at it than I am."

Levanah gave her cousin an affectionate kiss as they stepped through the French windows into the long apartment with its hangings of rose and apricot. The elegance of the room suited Leah, who presided over the tea table, her skin unflushed by her afternoon in the sunshine.

"Mary and I have had our tea," was her greeting. "I really must insist on punctuality, my dear Levanah. It is very unfair to the servants to keep them waiting for the dishes."

"I don't want any tea," Levanah said.

"And you have surely not run back from the school looking like that! Your hair is like a bird's nest and you have dust on your skirt. No, pray don't tidy yourself here. Go upstairs and attend to it properly," Leah said wearily. "If only you took a little trouble you would be a very attractive girl."

"As attractive as my mother?" Levanah asked.

"Your mother? What put your mother into your mind?" Leah said.

"I wondered if she was pretty," Levanah said. "Was she, Aunt?"

"Well enough," Leah said shortly. "She had taking ways."

"And my father? What was he like? You never have described him to me."

"It's all such a long time ago," Leah said vaguely. "Do run along, child. I want to read you both Teddy's latest letter before supper."

'But I'm not a child,' Levanah thought resentfully. 'I'm past seventeen and one day Aunt Leah is going to have to find out that I already know about my mother and her lover and the way she died.'

"Mother is disappointed that Teddy went on a boating holiday," Mary confided, when the two girls reached Levanah's room. "She wanted him to come home."

"If Aunt Leah had her way we'd none of us ever leave home." Levanah dragged her skirt over her head and splashed cold water on her face from the flowered pitcher. Her bedroom was furnished, like Mary's next door, in the style that Aunt Leah considered suitable for young girls. Blue chintz curtains and covers and carpets of deeper blue with touches of lemon in the borders were repeated in pink and white in Mary's room.

"Teddy prefers to be with his own friends," Mary said. "One can't blame him for he is quite a young gentleman now."

"Don't you find Marie Regina dull sometimes?" Levanah inquired.

"Dull? No, why should I? You don't."

"Well, I go where I choose," Levanah said, toweling her face. "But you're pretty. You ought to have a London season. Young men ought to come calling with bouquets and flowers."

"I'd love to go to a ball," Mary said wistfully. "I'd like to be presented at Court, too. They say Queen Alexandra is charming but terribly unpunctual."

"Then she wouldn't suit Aunt Leah," Levanah said dryly.

"Anyway, Mother disapproves of the vulgarity of modern society," Mary said, "so I'll never be allowed to go. And I think . . ."

"Think what?" Levanah, catching the hesitation in her cousin's voice, looked at her.

"I think Mother intends me to marry Teddy," Mary said in a low voice.

"Marry Teddy? But you're cousins and she never has approved of cousins marrying."

"She says they did it too often in the past, but Uncle John's wife wasn't from these parts and neither was my father, so Teddy and I are cousins on one side only, so to speak."

"Would you want to marry Teddy?" Levanah asked curiously, fastening her white blouse and stepping into a brown velvet skirt.

"I always think of him as just one of the family," Mary said thoughtfully. "But Mother keeps hinting how pleasant it would be if one day . . . you know."

"She can't make you marry anybody if you don't want to," Levanah said, "and Teddy will certainly choose his own bride."

"I know that too, but Mother usually gets what she wants," Mary said in resignation. "Sometimes I'm afraid I'll wake up one day and find myself married to Teddy without ever having had any fun at all!"

"Is that what you want?" Levanah asked. "Some fun?"

"I don't really want to leave Kingsmead," Mary said, "but I do wish sometimes that something exciting would happen. The days do get terribly long."

"I shall make a wish," Levanah said flippantly, "and send you a handsome lover, though I'm not certain where he'll come from because I've not found one myself yet."

"Then where do you go in the middle of the night?" Mary asked and put her hand up to her mouth as Levanah swung round, eyes narrowing in temper. "I'm sorry," she said contritely. "I'm truly sorry, and I don't mean to pry into your business, but I've heard you open your bedroom door, and the board by the gallery door creaks a bit when you tread on it. It woke me up once and I've heard it two or three times since, and last week I went into your room and your bed was empty."

"Have you chattered about this?" Levanah demanded.

"I've not said anything to anybody," Mary protested, tears filling her brown eyes. "I was pleased for your sake, Levanah, if you had somebody. I was a little hurt that you hadn't said anything about it to me, but I decided it was your own affair."

"I'm not stealing out in the middle of the night to meet a lover," Levanah said, annoyance turning to amusement. "Would you like to know where I go? I go down into the woods, Mary, down to 'Witch's Dower.'"

"To that old cottage that used to be there? Surely it's tumbled down by now? And we've never been allowed to go there anyway."

"I've been going there for years," Levanah said.

"We mended everything and cleaned up everywhere, but the wood around is grown so thick you can't see the cottage from the road, and nobody ever goes near that part of the estate anyway."

"We?" Mary looked at her in question.

"Cousin Cal and I tidied it all up together."

"Cal Falcon and you? But we're not allowed to have anything to do with anybody from Whittle Farm," Mary said in alarm. "Aunt Edith was never married and that makes Cal a . . . you know. Mother would be furious if ever she found out. You know how much she values the good name of the family."

"It's a silly feud anyway," Levanah said. "Even if Aunt Leah and Aunt Edith did quarrel all those years ago it has nothing to do with any of us. It's not Cal's fault that his parents were never wed. Neither were mine."

"Levanah! That's a dreadful thing to say!"

"It's true," Levanah insisted. "I thought for years how odd it is that my surname should be Falcon. After all, you're Mary Simmons because Aunt Leah is Mrs. Simmons. But my mother was always Beth Falcon. It was Cal who told me."

"Told you that your mother was never married?"

"He said my mother had a lover who deserted her, and she was so brokenhearted that after I was born she killed herself. That's why she's buried outside the churchyard. So I'm like Cal, but for some reason Aunt Leah kept me and brought me up along with you and Teddy."

"Does my mother know that you know about this?" Mary asked.

Levanah shook her head. "The cottage belonged to my mother," she said. "I found a portrait in the place and I'm certain it's a portrait of her. I've made the place my own now. If it belonged to my mother then by rights it ought to be mine now. It's always belonged to the Falcon witches."

"Do you believe that old story?" the other asked.

"I have the mark," Levanah told her. "You've seen it on my leg And I can do things, Mary. Remember when I was a child how I told Aunt Leah the old queen had just died, and she scolded me, and then we heard later that she had died at the time I said?"

"That was a coincidence," Mary said uneasily.

"Perhaps, but I can do other things too," Levanah said tensely. "I really can, Mary. That's why I go down to the cottage at night. I like to practice making things happen. It's fun."

"I wish I could come with you," Mary said wistfully. "I'm not saying I believe in any of it, but I'd like to come. It would be exciting."

"You don't like going down into the woods at any time," Levanah objected. "You'd not like it in the dark. And Cal is coming tonight."

"Tonight? Are you going down to the cottage tonight?"

"You'd not stay awake long enough to come with me."

"I would, I would!" Mary insisted. "Do let me come with you. I'd not fall asleep or make a fuss about the dark woods. And I'd not mind Cal being there. I've seen him once or twice about the village. He looks rough, but one ought not to blame him for that, I suppose. Do let me come."

Levanah hesitated and then nodded. Mary, she considered, needed a little entertainment, and it had been good of her not to say anything to Aunt Leah.

"We'll go together," she said at last. "More things might happen if there are three of us!"

She broke off as Aunt Leah's voice sounded from the gallery.

"Levanah! If you hurry, dear, you'll have time to work on the new cushion cover before supper."

Chapter II

The household seemed to take longer than usual that evening to settle down. Aunt Leah, who usually retired shortly after ten, kept the girls in the solar until past that hour, reading Teddy's letter to them two or three times over and discussing his future.

"Not that he will need to take his degree, but two or three years at Cambridge will give him a certain polish. When he's twenty-one he will naturally take his seat in the Lords and be expected to maintain an apartment in town, but his duties ought not to occupy too much of his time. His main responsibility will still lie here at Kingsmead. Fortunately he's always taken an interest in the running of the estate."

"In two or three years' time Teddy will probably want to get married," Levanah said, glancing toward Mary.

"Time enough for that," Aunt Leah said.

"If he goes to London," the girl persisted, "he'll probably find a wife there."

"That must be Teddy's decision," said Aunt Leah, "but it often happens, you know, that when a young man does choose a bride he chooses one from the same background as himself. I cannot see Teddy ranging very far afield for his wife."

When the girls were finally dismissed, Aunt Leah spent ages in the kitchen, instructing Cook in the mysteries of the new range, and it was past eleven when they heard the firm closing of the door at the other end of the gallery.

Mary was not undressed when soon after midnight Levanah tapped on her bedroom door. She had had the sense to change into an old riding habit and to tie back her curls, but Levanah shook her head over the high-heeled boots and small hat.

"Put on your old boots and that woolen scarf that Annie knitted you for Christmas," she advised. "And pull up your collar. It can get very cold at this hour."

"How will we find the way? I'm not very good at seeing in the dark," Mary asked.

"I take a lantern. We can uncover it when we are out of sight of the house," Levanah explained. "With the servants sleeping at the back and Aunt Leah at the front, we strike out across the fields. If anyone from the village did happen to see the light they'd think it was a poacher and look the other way."

"Will Cal be there?"

"He said he'd be there. We'll wait another ten minutes and then go. And walk as quietly as you can. Boots make an awful noise on those stone stairs."

"Do you start making things happen at once?" Mary asked.

"Nothing might happen at all," Levanah said. "I've never tried making things happen when other people were there before. Are you sure that you really want to come, Mary?"

"Oh, yes. I'm looking forward to it," Mary assured her. "It will be interesting to meet Cal Falcon. He looks a sullen kind of boy."

"He's all right," Levanah said casually. "He works hard, you know. He hires a couple of men at the Summer Fair every year to help out at the farm, and they only keep one house servant."

"Because Aunt Edith drinks," Mary said.

"How did— Who told you that?" Levanah asked sharply.

"I heard Cook talking to Annie," Mary confessed. "She said, 'I heard that Miss Edith is on a jag again,' and Annie said, 'Ah, poor Miss Edith! There's a lot I could say if I'd a mind, but Miss Leah's been good to me and a nod is as good as a wink to a blind horse.' Is it true, Levanah? Does she drink?"

"Cal doesn't talk much about his mother," Levanah said, "and I don't talk much about what happens here at Kingsmead. The cottage and the woods are separate from everything else. There's a magic about them."

"Do let's go now," Mary begged. "I'm sure that Mother will be asleep."

"Don't make a noise then," Levanah warned.

The lantern lit, they came out to the shadowed gallery and began the slow, cautious descent to the great hall below. Levanah had often regretted that no pets were kept at Kingsmead, the dogs being kenneled away from the house and kept only for hunting, but their absence made it easier for her to come and go as she liked.

"It's creepy isn't it?" Mary whispered, as they reached the bottom step.

Levanah looked round at the dark tapestries and the looming pieces of furniture. Rectangles of moonlight lit the stone floor from the uncurtained windows, and on the dresser a Tudor christening cup, given by the first Elizabeth to a long-dead Falcon, gleamed.

"I like it," she breathed back, and pressed her cousin's arm warningly as they tiptoed toward the baize-covered door that led to the kitchen. The back door was fastened but it was a simple matter to slide the bolts cautiously back, and within a moment they stood outside.

"The moon is up. We may not need the lantern," Levanah whispered. "We'll have to hurry, else we'll not be back by five when Cook and Annie rise. You don't have to cling to me, Mary. It's quite bright."

"Everything looks different," Mary faltered.

"It always does at night. Do come on!"

Levanah set off at her usual brisk pace, with Mary panting behind her. It was an unusually clear night with a pleasant breeze and a silver sheen over the landscape. She would have preferred to be alone, to fill herself with the sounds and scents of night, but Mary was at her heels, emitting occasional shrieks as she caught her foot in tussocks of grass.

As they reached the wood the world darkened abruptly, the sky blotted out by a canopy of shivering leaves. Underfoot the ground was deep in long grass and littered branches.

"Do uncover the lantern," Mary begged.

Levanah obediently uncovered the low-burning flame and a narrow shaft of light winged its way between the close-growing trunks.

"Keep behind me," she said, "and do try not to squeal. You must move with the lie of the land and not against it. And look out for rabbit holes."

Mary, hearing the suppressed irritation in the other's voice, fell silent and plodded along behind.

As they came into the clearing, however, she could not hold back an exclamation of surprise.

"Levanah! It looks like something out of a fairy tale!"

"It's an old cottage," Levanah said briefly, wishing that Mary would not try to limit things by describing them. "Cal and I have worked hard to make it nice."

"I saw a light in one of the windows," Mary said.

"Then Cal is already here. I knew we ought to make better time across the fields. Come on."

Levanah hurried to the front door and lifted the latch. Cal was sitting on the stool by the table munching a hunk of bread and cheese. His hunched shadow dominated the white walls, and for an instant the girl hesitated, aware of something dark and primitive in the crouching figure. The illusion was gone directly as Cal spoke, his tone one of good-humored raillery.

"I've been staring at this flame for ages and it's not going up or down."

"You don't bear the mark," Levanah said serenely. "Come in, Mary. Cal, you haven't met Mary, have you?"

"I've seen her about. Why did you have to bring her? I thought this was our private secret." He scowled at Mary, who stood timidly within the door.

"She won't say anything," Levanah promised. "And the magic will work better with three."

"As long as something happens," he complained. "I'm not fond of losing a night's sleep for a load of nothing."

"Watch the candle flame," Levanah said.

Her own eyes were narrowed upon it and her hair,

freed from its scarf, fell thickly about her narrow face. In her thin little body there was a coiled concentration and her hands, slightly raised, made black swans on the pale wall.

The flame was streamed upward and then dwindled down, its yellow darkening to blue, the corners of the room retreating into blackness.

"Do stop it," Mary said in a high nervous gasp. "Please stop it."

Levanah smiled, flicking her fingers, and the candle burned steadily again.

"You really can do it," Cal said.

He too spoke uneasily and his glance was wary.

"I told you I could. If you're not polite to me," she threatened playfully, "I'll put a curse on your well-water."

"I've got something for you," he said quickly. "Light some more candles and I'll show it."

"Help me, Mary." Levanah, who had extinguished the lantern as they entered the clearing, now re-kindled it and indicated several candles stuck onto saucers.

"I can't," Mary said. "My hands are trembling."

"Baby!" Levanah lit the candles herself and fastened the shutters across the windows The room looked cheerful now, and a little of the color came back into Mary's face.

"Here it is." Cal put the little wooden figure into Levanah's hands. "I finished the face off after you'd gone this afternoon."

It was small and crude, but there was still a joyfulness in the slanting eyes and mouth and tiny up-turned nose. The little god sat on a base of wood, his smile mocking their grossness.

"It's very clever," Mary said. "I didn't know you could make things like that, Cal."

"You didn't know anything about me at all," he retorted. "You've never even passed the time of day."

"Only because Mother forbade it," she said.

"Well, my mother always forbade me to have anything to do with my cousins at Kingsmead, so we start even," Cal told her. "I'm happy to meet you, Cousin Mary."

"And I you, Cousin Cal." Her hand in his was light and delicate as a bird's foot.

"He is perfect," Levanah said. "I shall call him Lob, guardian of 'Witch's Dower,' and we will have a ceremony right now, to install him in his place. We must make him feel welcome and then he will bring us great good luck."

"What do we have to do?" Mary inquired.

Levanah, having not the faintest idea, but confident of her powers of invention, stared down at the wooden figure.

"We will each take a candle," she said slowly, "and go into the other room. We'll leave the shutters unfastened, so that the rays of the moon will shed a blessing. I will carry Lob, and we must take off our shoes."

"Why?" Mary wanted to know.

"To get closer to the earth," Levanah said. "Come on, let's not be too long. Half the night is gone and the dawn comes early in summer."

She was tingling with excitement and the top of her nose was itching again. It often did when she was in the cottage, though the dust had long since been banished.

Mary gave another stifled exclamation as they entered the other room.

"Is that your mother?" she breathed, staring at the portrait. "Is that Aunt Beth?"

"I'm sure of it. Do stop chattering, Mary," Levanah said, wishing her cousin would learn the value of silence. "Did you bring any candles?"

"I'll get some." Cal dived back into the other room and returned with three.

"I will make a speech," Levanah said, "and then we will each of us make a wish out loud, and set a candle in front of Lob. We'll put him in the middle of the ledge with the picture on his right and the crystal on his left."

The others stood at each side of her, candles in their hands. Mary looked wrought up to the point of tears; Cal had a sheepish grin on his face. Her own fingers and toes quivered.

"The floor is cold. Do hurry up," Mary complained.

"Friends, help me to make the circle," Levanah said.

"How? What circle?" Cal looked round.

"The circle of enchantment, stupid," Levanah said testily. "We'll walk three times round the room."

"Like a fairy ring," Mary said.

They set off, slowly treading out the circle. The moon rayed the three young figures and in the light of the candles the eyes of the portrait shifted and grew aware.

"Now I'll make the speech," Levanah said. Her voice was husky with excitement, but her hands were steady as she set the carved figure on the ledge.

"Hail, Lob," she said, and suddenly the words poured out of her in a steady stream. "Hail, Lob, guardian of 'Witch's Dower.' I set you here to protect my place and to do my bidding, to grant my wishes, to will what I will and bind what I bind. I set you under the care of the sun that burns by day, and the moon that shines by night. I set you over the creeping elements of earth, the spirits of fire and air and water. Amen."

"I'm sure she shouldn't have said 'Amen,'" Mary whispered.

"Mary, make a wish out loud and put your candle there," Levanah ordered.

Mary timidly put her candle on the ledge, stepped back, and said in a nervous mumble, "If you please, I wish a nice young gentleman would fall in love with me."

"One will anyway, because you're so pretty," Levanah said. "Now you, Cal."

"I wish for a good sensible wife with a cheerful nature," Cal said, promptly putting up his own candle.

"You've neither of you got a particle of imagination," Levanah complained.

"You make a better wish then," Cal challenged.

Levanah took a step forward and held up her candle.

"I wish," she said slowly, "to discover the truth about my mother and father. I command you, Lob, to open the way."

"What do we do now?" Cal inquired.

"We close the circle," said Levanah.

Again they trod the circle. The moon was obscured briefly by a cloud and beyond the window a screech owl sent up its complaint.

"Cal, did you bring anything to eat?" Levanah asked.

"Some bread and cheese. I've eaten some of it."

"We'll eat the rest, and have some of the cider I

made," Levanah decided. "We have to pledge our friendship and make plans to meet again."

"When?"

"At the next new moon," she told them. "We'll come here at every new moon to tread the circle and offer praise to Lob."

"It seems a bit blasphemous to me," Mary said diffidently. "I'm sure the vicar wouldn't approve."

"You needn't bother to come if you don't want to," Levanah said huffily.

"Oh, I do!" Mary said hastily. "It's only that . . . you talk as if that little thing was alive. It's only a piece of wood that Cal shaped."

"But the idea behind it is real," Levanah insisted. "Don't you see? The picture of my mother isn't really my mother, but it looks like her, and she was real enough. And the little statue is like that."

"But your mother was a live human being," Mary objected. "Lob never existed."

"He existed in my mind," Levanah said firmly. "Everything in the world begins as a thought."

"Are we going to eat or argue?" Cal, weary of metaphysical discussion, broke in.

"We'll eat. I'll get the cider."

"Not in here." Mary gave a timid look at the candlelit ledge. "I'd like to go back into the other room now."

"Help Cal lay out the food then." Levanah went over to the shelves and took down the small flagon of cider.

"Come on, Mary." Cal took his cousin's hand and they went out together.

It was a pleasure to be alone for a few minutes. The room closed round her as if it were a shell and she was the small, pale oyster at its heart. The sky was already fading from black to gray. She went back to the ledge and stood, looking at the picture of her mother. The gathering dawn drained the portrait of color but the eyes were still compelling.

"Why?" Levanah whispered. "Why did he leave you? What was his name?"

Her eyes shifted to the crystal, but there would be no answer there, for she had looked in it many times and seen only the reflection of her own face.

"Lob?" Her lips shaped the name with pleading, but the little figure sat laughing at her.

She uncorked the flagon and poured a few drops of cider onto the ledge in front of the figure.

Some waft of air from her sleeve must have caught the candle flames for they flickered and died. Thin spirals of blue smoke snaked upward.

Levanah sighed. She was weary and the power had gone out of her. It was also getting perilously near the hour when Alice got up to stoke the range.

Cal and Mary were already eating. Mary looked tired, the skin beneath her eyes dark-stained, her face too pale. Against the white flesh her ringlets looked darker, their glossiness unimpaired. She ate daintily, nibbling the bread and cheese like a small, tired mouse.

"Did you blow out the candles?" Cal asked.

"They went out." Levanah poured the cider.

"It was exciting," Mary said. "There was a strangeness in the room, as if something were about to happen that had never happened before. Didn't you feel it, Levanah?"

"It's over," Levanah said shortly, "and I'm tired. I'm ready for home. Cal, will you clear away here?"

"And we'll come back at next new moon," Mary said, looking about for her boots.

Levanah, draining her mug of cider, saw Cal kneel down to help Mary pull them on. The sight of his untidy head so close to her cousin's knee irritated her, though she could not have given a reason for it. She pulled on her own boots without any help, and tugged the long scarf about her hair.

"Goodbye then, Cousin." Mary gave the boy her hand and smiled up at him.

"Until new moon," Cal said.

"Are you coming or not, Mary?" Levanah pulled open the front door.

Outside, the first twittering of birds filled the clearing. Insects rose and hovered above the long grass.

"We'll never be back in time!" Mary said in alarm.

"We'll tell Alice we went for an early morning walk," Levanah said, "but do come on now."

As they threaded their way between the trees, Mary said, "I like Cousin Cal. I think he's what they call a rough diamond. I wonder why Mother has been so adamant about our not speaking to him."

"Because of her quarrel with Aunt Edith, I suppose."

"And Cal says that his mother has always forbidden him to speak to us. It's rather romantic, isn't it?"

"I think it's childish and silly," Levanah said dampeningly. "I never could stand those silly feuds."

"Like in *Romeo and Juliet*," Mary said dreamily.

"With me as the Nurse, I suppose? You can be sillier than anyone else I know sometimes!" Levanah said in exasperation.

"That wish you made? Do you really want to know all about your father?" Mary asked.

"I wouldn't have made it otherwise, would I?"

"But I never knew my father either," Mary said. "I don't know what he looked like, or what he did."

"At least you know that he was married to your mother," Levanah said, disentangling herself from a trailing bramble. "Their names are in the Parish Register, and we know he died when he was visiting some friends in London and was buried there."

"That's what mother told me," Mary said, "but I've never seen his grave. Mother told you that both your parents had died but she never said your mother had killed herself or your father deserted her."

"You just want a bit of mystery in your background," Levanah said, scrambling out of the last fringe of trees and setting off at a brisk pace through the dew-damp meadow.

"One day I'm going to ask Mother to take me to London so that I can pay my respects at Father's tomb," Mary said, panting after her.

"If you do that, you might not be at home when that handsome man comes courting," Levanah teased.

The exercise and the fresh breeze had restored her good spirits.

"Do you think he will come?" Mary's face was eager. "Oh, I do hope it doesn't turn out to be Cousin Teddy, but I could never endure being married to him, and Mother means it to happen. I know she does."

"You'll have to stand up to her," Levanah said, but her glance was doubtful.

There was a fragility about Mary that was more of the spirit than of the body. Looking at the weakness of her cousin's pretty mouth Levanah shrewdly surmised that Mary would be easily coaxed or bullied into submission.

They were within sight of Kingsmead now and she broke into a run, anxious to be done with conversation.

By great good fortune Alice had overslept, and they were able to rebolt the back door and gain their own bedrooms without discovery. On the threshold of her room, Mary said in her gently impulsive way, "I am truly grateful to you for letting me share the secret. And I think your Lob is sweet."

"You're sweet-natured yourself," Levanah told her.

"And it was interesting to meet Cousin Cal," Mary said. "He is a very agreeable young man, and he really was most attentive to me."

"Was he? I didn't notice."

Levanah wondered if she really liked Mary as much as she thought she did.

"I'll see you at breakfast," Mary said. "I'm so tired I could sleep for a week!"

Levanah nodded and went into her own room. She was free to be alone now until the breakfast gong went at eight-thirty. Later on she had promised to help Mary write out the cards for the stalls at the Church Fête. She made a face at herself in the mirror and sat down to pull off her boots. The long, dutiful day yawned ahead.

Chapter III

The woman driving the pony trap had alighted at the station just as the train drew in. Charlotte Bishop, surmising correctly that this was Mrs. Wenna Davis, strode forward with outstretched hand.

"Mrs. Davies? Charlotte Bishop. Glad to meet you." She was an attractive young woman, Wenna thought, wincing slightly from the strength of the handshake. Hair so pale it was almost white was plaited at the nape of her neck. Eyes of a clear, cool gray beneath down-slanting lids gave her a long, appraising stare.

"As we are to spend so much of our time together," Wenna said kindly, "let us dispense with formality. In private, at least, do please call me Wenna."

"And I liked to be called Charlie," the other informed her, slinging a portmanteau into the trap with scant regard for anything breakable that might be in it.

"Oh, Charlie. How pleasant," Wenna said idiotically, giving the newcomer a startled look.

"Charlotte is such a dead name," Charlie said, hitching up her skirt and clambering into the high seat.

"It's rather a pretty name," Wenna objected.

"It ought to have been Charles. Papa was heartbroken when his only child turned out to be a girl," Charlie said.

"And your mother?"

"She died when I was born. Papa never married again. There were just him and me, until he took himself off to the Alps on a climbing holiday," Charlie said. "He ought not to have attempted the north face—the guide warned against it, but Papa always knew better than anybody else, and down he went."

"My dear, how dreadful for you!"

"It hit me hard," Charlie admitted, "but I was too busy clearing up his affairs to have time for brooding."

"From your letter of application I gathered there were financial difficulties."

"Financial chaos!" Charlie exclaimed. "Papa's special subject was botany, but lecturing fees barely financed his expeditions, and there was my education to consider as well. By the time I'd sold the house to pay off the creditors there wasn't anything left, so I went into teaching. That was four years ago."

"And you've had two posts since."

"Neither of them congenial," said Charlie. "I'm not cut out for private governessing and my last school was run by a fiend of a woman who believed the pittance she doled out bought souls as well as service."

"I don't think you'll find me a fiend," Wenna told her. "And Mrs. Simmons who engaged you is not one to interfere in school matters."

"I expected a personal interview," Charlie said.

"Your letter of application was very sensible and literate, and the two references you gave were impeccable. Leah—Mrs. Simmons—backed her own judgment."

"She is a relation of Lord Falcon, isn't she?"

"His aunt." Wenna gave her companion a sideways glance, wondering how much to confide. "She was Miss Leah Falcon before her marriage. Teddy, the present Lord Falcon, is her brother's son. His parents died when he was a baby and Leah brought him up with her own daughter."

"And Mrs. Simmons is also a widow."

"Yes." Wenna hurried on. "There is another niece at Kingsmead—Levanah. Her parents also died. Leah reared the three children, and she administers the estate until Teddy comes of age. We are passing the main gates of Kingsmead now, but you cannot see the house from the road. The school entrance is three miles farther, at the other side of the bridge. The village proper lies in a hollow on the right. You can see the spire of the church below the graveyard."

"It's a large one," Charlie exclaimed, staring.

"The folk of Marie Regina seldom venture far afield," Wenna explained. "You'll find the same names cropping up again and again—Stone, Fiske, Whittle. And with the railway looping around the area it's remaining virtually unspoiled. Ah! here are Mary and Levanah now."

She reined in the pony as two young girls approached, and called, "Come and meet my new assistant, Miss Bishop."

"Charlie. I like to be called Charlie." The young woman leaned from her seat to shake hands.

The delicately pretty girl, with the dark ringlets and pink parasol that matched her dress, said in a low sweet voice, "I am Mary Simmons, Miss Bishop. This is my cousin Levanah."

The other girl, whose light red hair was cut in bangs across her forehead and swung, thick and straight, at each side of her narrow face, nodded politely. Her eyes, of a curious yellow shade, were unsmiling

"Levanah is an unusual name," the newcomer said.

"It means moon child," the girl said.

"How quaint!" the young woman said, a little taken aback by the hostility in the husky voice.

"We Falcons are very quaint," Levanah said, with a curious little grimace. "You must tell her about us, Cousin Wenna."

"What a disconcerting young person!" Charlotte exclaimed, as the trap bowled on over the bridge.

"Levanah is at a difficult age," Wenna excused. "If you look to your right, you can see the ruins of the old monastery up on the hill. The village takes its name from the monastery."

"She and the other young lady are cousins, you say?"

"Yes, and cousins to young Lord Falcon."

"To Teddy?"

"That is what they call him." Wenna spoke repressively, swinging the trap left through the open gates of the Manor School.

"Families fascinate me," Charlotte said. "It's never having belonged to one myself, I suppose."

"You had your father."

"Who thought more of flowers and weeds than of me. But you're a Falcon yourself."

"My mother was an aunt to Leah's mother. That makes me a sort of cousin, I suppose."

"Is your mother still alive?"

"She's very old," Wenna said. "She still lives up in Wales. I've not been home for years. This is the school."

"It's a handsome building," Charlotte said.

"It's suited me for nearly twenty years," Wenna said dryly. "If you'd like to come upstairs I'll make some tea. There are two bedrooms, but we'll share the sitting room."

"I won't get in your way," Charlotte said, jumping down from her seat and hauling her bag to the ground.

'She certainly seems eager to please,' Wenna thought. The bedroom she pronounced "very nice," and when they had eaten their tea, she stacked the dishes and helped to wash them up. Her questions about the Falcons continued unabated, however. There was something unpleasant in her probing, as if she sought an identity for herself among them.

"They don't go often into Society then?" Charlotte was saying.

"They're a close-knit family." Wenna wished she didn't sound as if she were making excuses.

"But surely there are balls and parties—" Charlotte broke off, staring through the window.

"What is it?" Wenna asked.

"A young man. Fair-haired. A laborer, I think. I glimpsed him among the trees at the other side of the river."

"That'll be Cal Falcon," Wenna said incautiously.

"Another Falcon! Is he a cousin too?"

Wenna hesitated and then made up her mind. It was better that Charlotte should hear the truth from her than echoes of distorted village gossip.

"Leah—that is Mrs. Simmons—had two younger sisters," she said slowly. "Both had children out of wedlock. Beth-Beth died and her child, Levanah, was reared at Kingsmead. The other, Cal's mother, is still alive. She lives with her son on Whittle Farm at the other side of the hill. They have no contact with the rest of the family and Edith's name is never mentioned at Kingsmead."

"And the two mothers were never married?"

"No, but the subject is not referred to, as I said."

"No, of course not." Charlotte's down-slanting eyes were alight with interest. "And you have never married yourself?" she queried after a moment.

"I'm an old maid," Wenna said lightly.

"I don't intend to marry either," Charlotte informed her. "Men are of very little use. My father is a splendid example of that."

"But surely you were proud of his journeyings," Wenna said.

"He fed, clothed, and educated me," Charlotte said, a harsh note coloring her voice. "Beyond that the only thing of note he ever did was to kill my mother."

"My dear!" Wenna stared at her in horror.

"Oh, not literally," Charlotte said impatiently. "She died when I was born, so he did kill her indirectly, though he never blamed himself for it. Men never do blame themselves, you know."

"But you were fond of your father, surely?"

"Fond enough." Charlotte rose and paced the room. "Had I been a boy he'd have allowed me to accompany him on some of his expeditions. As I was disobliging enough to be born a female—" She shrugged her shoulders and paused by the window, drumming her fingers lightly on the sill. When she spoke again her voice was casual, almost disinterested. "The two young ladies, Mary and Levanah, are not engaged, I suppose?"

"Neither of them is 'out,'" Wenna said. "They are both very much attached to their home."

"Mary is very pretty," Charlotte said.

"She's a sweet girl," Wenna agreed. "We'd best discuss the way in which we intend to divide the work. To begin with, you can take charge of the little ones. I'll show you some of the books, if you'll come over here."

She went on talking, and after a moment the younger girl joined her at the table.

At Kingsmead, Leah was reading a letter from Teddy. She read with less than her usual pleasure, her nephew having written to inform her that he was extending his holiday. He gave no reason, but his mention of a friend's sister as being a "ripping sport" was sufficient hint. Her brow creased, for Teddy was developing an independent streak. Best, however, to let him have his head for a while. He had sent his love to Mary and to Levanah, as if they were equal in his cousinly affections. It was time for him to come home and see for himself how pretty Mary was grown, but it was of no use to force his issue. The girls' voices sounded in the hall and a moment later they came in together. As usual, Leah's glance softened imperceptibly when it fell on her daughter, but her voice was sharp.

"You've been dawdling down in the village again, I suppose."

"If we'd hurried, you'd have complained about that," Levanah said, pulling off her straw hat and flopping down on the sofa.

"Don't be insolent!" Leah said.

"I'm not, just stating a fact," the girl said lazily. Mary, the peacemaker, said, "We saw the new teacher. Cousin Wenna was driving her from the station."

"What is she like?" Leah asked.

"Pleasant-looking," Mary said. "She has very fair hair."

"I didn't like her," Levanah said flatly "I didn't like her at all."

"She seemed anxious to be friendly," Mary said, faintly reproving.

"Not pushing, I hope," Leah said. "I dislike pushing young women intensely, and her letter of application gave no such indication."

"She wasn't pushing," Mary said. "She was very polite and respectful."

"I didn't like her," Levanah said again.

"You are too apt to jump to conclusions about people," Leah chided, "and you express yourself more forcibly than a young girl should."

"You asked what she was like," Levanah muttered. Between the curtains of light red hair her narrow face was sullen.

"Is that a letter from Teddy?" Mary inquired hastily. "Is he enjoying his boating trip?"

"So much that he plans to extend it." Leah glanced at her daughter, but Mary's face remained sweet and indifferent. A trifle irritably, she said, "Are you not sorry to miss him?"

"Oh, yes, indeed," Mary assured her, "but he is probably having a good time with his friends."

Leah, her glance sliding to Levanah, saw that the sullen expression had given place to a mirthful grin. Her irritation spilled over into annoyance.

"Now that Cousin Wenna has an assistant," she said, "you will have no need to go running over to the Manor School at all hours of the day."

"I don't go just to help," Levanah said. "Cousin Wenna enjoys my company, you know."

"I cannot imagine why," Leah said tartly, "for in this house your conversation is hardly sparkling."

"Ah, but I always display the better part of my nature to Cousin Wenna," Levanah said serenely. "Shall we go up and try your hair in the new style, Mary?"

"I want Mary to write a letter to Teddy," Leah said.

"To Teddy? Whatever for?" Mary asked in surprise

"Because you have not written to him for months. He will begin to think his cousin has forgotten him."

"Oh, Mother, must I? I can never think of anything to say," Mary was beginning, but Levanah interrupted, yellow eyes demure, the corner of her mouth twitching.

"We must both write to Teddy," she said. "Then he will know that neither of his cousins has forgotten him. Shall I get the writing paper, Aunt Leah?"

Her sweetly helpful voice challenged and defeated the older woman.

Later that evening Edith Falcon lay in bed and listened to her son going out. He had looked in on her earlier as she lay with closed eyes and cheek pillowed on her hand, and now, believing her to be fast asleep, he was not too cautious about the noise he made. She could hear the scrape of his boots on the tiled floor of the kitchen, his gruff whisper to the dog as he secured the chain that would prevent the animal from following him. Then came the closing of the door and the sound of him walking across the cobbled yard.

When she was quite certain that he had gone she risked lighting a candle and getting out of bed, padded over to the bureau. Cal kept strict watch on the other cupboards, but at the back of the bureau a small bottle of brandy fitted nicely.

She took a satisfying pull and replaced the stopper. The liquor warmed her veins, the pit of her stomach relaxing as the warmth spread, the tight band around her head and her heart expanding. It was not, she thought, putting back the bottle, that she was a drunkard. She could stop drinking whenever she chose. A nip of brandy sufficed to put her in a better humor, to keep at bay the loneliness of the night.

After a few moments, she lit another candle and got back into bed, reaching for the novel she had had Cal bring her from the Circulating Library that week. As a girl she had disliked reading, but in the years since, books had become a solace, and she had lived vicariously to a hundred happy endings. Tonight the printed romance had no power to move her. She let the pages flutter idly through her fingers and looked across to the shadowed mirror where her reflection wavered.

She had been the most beautiful of the three Falcon girls, the one who had longed most passionately to be married and to have children. Well, she had the one son, and Cal was a good boy. He was worth half-a-dozen Teddy Falcons, she decided, and the reflection in the mirror smiled palely like the ghost of the beautiful girl she had been.

In daylight there was little trace of that beauty. Nothing could spoil the delicate bone structure, but the hair was more gray than gold, the blue eyes faded, a network of tiny red lines marring the skin.

"Nobody would marry me now," Edith said aloud, with bitter humor.

Of her brief love affair she never allowed herself to think. It had given her Cal, and for that she was grateful. And her own stubbornness kept her at the farm when others in her situation might have left the district. But it gave her a dismal pleasure to know how her presence in Marie Regina shamed Leah. In the years of their estrangement she had seen her sister only a few times, and on each occasion Leah had turned her back, but Edith had noticed the deep flush in the elder woman's cheeks and the contempt in her eyes. Beth would never have acted in such a fashion, but sweet Beth had possessed neither Leah's vengeful nature nor Edith's stubbornness.

Edith wondered where Cal went in the middle of the night. She supposed he had a girl somewhere, but she had never asked him. Leah had always poked and pried into the affairs of her relatives. Edith had such a horror of seeming possessive that she sometimes gave the impression of indifference.

It would be pleasant, she decided, sliding farther down the bed, if Cal fell in love and brought home a nice, respectable girl. It would mean a bit of company in the evenings.

She debated with herself whether or not to have another nip of brandy, but her eyelids were drooping and she was too sleepy to make the effort to get out of bed again.

In the cottage Levanah put on her shoes again and went into the living room where Cal was sharing out a cold, roast chicken. Mary, perched on a stool, lashes thick above sleepy blue eyes, yawned like a kitten. As Levanah came in, she said, with a hint of petulance, "Nothing very exciting is happening at these meetings. You said we would be able to do all kinds of things."

"You've seen the candle flames change," Levanah

said, taking her portion of chicken and sinking her sharp white teeth into it.

"That's not much," Mary said. "It doesn't do much good, making flames go up and down."

"What do you want?" Levanah demanded. "Earthquakes?"

"Something more exciting," Mary insisted.

"We'll have to wait until All Souls' Night for that," Levanah said.

"When's that?" Cal inquired, spearing a chunk of bread on the point of his knife.

"On the second of November. If you ever came to church you'd know these things," Levanah said severely.

"What will happen on All Souls' Night?" Mary wanted to know.

"That's when it's possible to raise the spirits of the dead," Levanah said. "I want to raise the spirit of the first witch who lived here."

"You're joking!" Cal said incredulously. "Such things aren't possible."

"Wait until All Souls' Night then, and see," Levanah returned.

"But wouldn't it be terribly wicked even to try?" Mary ventured.

"Don't come then, if you're afraid." Levanah took another bite out of her piece of chicken.

"I'll look after you, Mary," Cal said.

"Then I won't mind." She gave him a timid, grateful glance.

"You can hold her hand," Levanah said, smiling, "in case the bogeyman comes."

"But what might come?" Mary asked nervously.

"The witch, I suppose. They say she came out of Wales and bequeathed her mark to those of her descendants chosen to have the power. Can you imagine her, Mary? Small and black-haired with yellow eyes like mine? Can you imagine her fingers making strange patterns in the air and her lips opening and closing because, after so long in the grave, she has forgotten how to speak. And in the green gloom her fingers creep out to fasten on your neck?"

"Levanah, stop it!" Cal exclaimed. "You're frightening Mary to death!"

He had his arm around the trembling girl and his eyes were indignant. A small, lonely pain tore at Levanah's heart.

"I was only building up a bit of atmosphere," she said casually. "But we might be able to raise the witch for all that. We ought to be getting back soon, Mary. Aunt Leah was saying you always look half asleep these days."

She was pulling on her cloak, pretending not to notice how Cal, helping Mary, let his hands linger on her shoulders. The closeness between the two of them was growing, but if she thought about it too clearly her loneliness would increase.

In the sittingroom of the schoolhouse Wenna sat by the darkened window, looking out across the smooth lawns to the river. She had finally persuaded Charlotte Bishop to retire to bed. The younger woman had temporarily exhausted her stock of questions and was now, Wenna obviously hoped, peacefully asleep. This sharing of her living quarters with her new assistant was not going to be easy. Yet Charlie—a ridiculous nickname!—seemed a pleasant, capable young woman, if a trifle overanxious to fling herself into the private concerns of the family. There was no reason in the world for Wenna to feel a slight shrinking from her.

Wenna herself, hair unbraided, pulled a strand of it

between her teeth. Sometimes she felt a faint surprise in herself at the thought that she was still a virgin at forty. Once, years ago, she had allowed herself to grow fond of Teddy's father, had suspected that he was growing fond of her, but John Falcon had been killed in a fall from his horse, and in the years since she had been too busy with her duties at the school to have time for memories.

Across the river a light flickered and was gone. Cal and Levanah on their midnight prowls again, she supposed, having glimpsed them once or twice before. Perhaps she ought to have dropped a word in Leah's ear, but that would have been to invite trouble. Leah hated even to admit the fact of Cal's existence. And that, Wenna thought, was plain foolishness. Cal was a fine young man—oh, not a gentleman like Teddy, but strong and attractive in a roughhewn way, with that blond cowlick and big, sunburnt hands. Thinking of those hands Wenna shivered a little and her face grew warm in the darkness.

Chapter IV

November had thinned the leaves and the bare branches reached up imploringly into a darkening sky. The two girls, muffled in thick capes and wearing woolen mittens, sat on the edge of Levanah's bed and waited for Leah and the rest of the household to fall asleep.

"Do you really think that something might happen?" Mary was asking.

"You'll have to wait and see," Levanah said. She was growing a little tired of the constant question, and of Mary's half-delighted terror at the prospect of things unseen. "I've told you over and over that you don't have to come."

"But Cal will be there," Mary said. "Cal will know how to deal with anything frightening."

"You're in love with him, aren't you?" Levanah said abruptly.

"I'm not certain." Mary's delicate face was troubled.

"I think about him a lot, and when I'm with him I feel at ease, safe."

"He's falling in love with you," Levanah said. "You'll have to decide what you're going to do about it."

"Mother would never permit an engagement," Mary said. "You know how we have never been allowed to mix with Aunt Edith or Cal, not even allowed to mention their names or talk about them as members of the family."

"Would you let that stop you?" Levanah asked with faint scorn. "I'm sure if I loved someone I'd defy the world for him."

"I don't mind the whole world. It's Mother who bothers me," Mary said with a glint of humor, but immediately her face grew serious again. "You've always been strong," she said. "I've seen you look Mother straight in the eye and give as good as you get. I can't do that. My knees start shaking and all the words I meant to say fly out of my head."

"You'll have to do better than that if matters get serious between you and Cal," Levanah said.

"He's not even kissed me yet," Mary said, "not that I'd allow him to do so if he tried, of course. And I'm far too young. Mother wouldn't let me marry anybody until I was at least eighteen."

"She wouldn't agree to you marrying Cal at any age," Levanah said. "You'd have to elope."

"I'd never dare!" Mary said faintly.

Levanah shrugged, abandoning the subject. What was to happen would happen, she supposed. There was nothing else she could do but watch the progress of the affair, and hide her own lonely little pain when her cousins looked at each other or touched hands in passing.

"It'll be safe now," she said. "Aunt Leah will be asleep by now, I'm sure. Cover the lantern, Mary."

They moved more surely down the stairs and out into the dark wood, habit making a pathway for their feet. It had rained earlier and the bushes showered them with drops as they pushed by them into the clearing. The lamp in the cottage was already lit and Cal had kindled a fire in the hearth.

"It's not likely the smoke will be noticed. We'd freeze without a fire," he said by way of greeting.

"It was thoughtful of you." Mary began to remove her outer garments, and Cal hastened to help her.

Levanah took off her own cloak and went into the other room, holding up the lantern so that its gleam fell upon the shelf where the picture, the crystal, and the carved figure were ranged. The painted eyes of the girl in the portrait seemed to move as if a living spirit were imprisoned in the canvas.

"He must have loved you, to paint you so," Levanah whispered. "I wish he had signed his name. I wish you could tell me why he deserted you."

"Are we going to raise the witch then?" Mary asked from the doorway.

Levanah gave a little start of anoyance. Her impulsive boast that she could bring back the dead seemed childish and silly now, but when she turned round Mary was gazing at her eagerly.

"If you're sure you want it." She spoke briskly, putting her own thoughts away. They were private thoughts, not to be shared with Mary or Cal.

"Do we have anything special?" Mary asked.

Cal, at her elbow, said, "Shall I set an extra place for the witch?"

Levanah felt a spurt of anger. They regarded it as

an adventure, a kind of joke. Cal had a teasing grin on his face as if he were humoring her.

"The dead don't eat," she said shortly. "We'll leave our shoes on tonight, because of the cold. And we'll not use the lamps, only the candles."

"Do we have to make a circle?" Mary asked.

"Not tonight. Put out the lamp and light a candle each," Levanah ordered. "It must be nearly midnight."

"A few minutes to twelve. Is that when the dead walk?" Cal inquired.

"We'll have to see." She watched as Cal lit three candles and extinguished the lamp.

Abruptly the room changed, their shadows growing tall against the white walls, their features sharpening in the candlelight, the black clouds scudding past the unshuttered window. On the shelf the crystal glinted faintly and the bottles ranged along the walls were shot with silver.

Mary moved nearer to Cal and her fingers gripped his hand. The candle she was holding shook violently.

Levanah, noticing, was filled with an energy born of hysterical mirth and spite. So Mary crept close to Cal, and they pretended to be afraid as an excuse for holding hands. On this night then she would give them something to fear.

"Spirits of earth," she said in a low, chanting voice, "you who dwell in the dark places, you who whisper the secrets of the living to the dead, creep now into the witch's tomb. Flesh her bones and fill the sockets of her eyes, and bring her back to this place where she once wove her spells. Tell her that I, Levanah, have need of her skills, must borrow of her power. Bring her back to us on this night when the dead walk free. With this candle I summon her from the land of shades to the world of the living With this candle I light her pathway."

She swung round toward the window, lifting the candle high, and was frozen into immobility. Beyond the black panes a goblin face was pressed with open mouth and elflocks of tattered hair.

It was there for a moment and then Mary screamed, her candle spinning from her hand, and flung herself into Cal's arms, sobbing wildly.

"She was here," Levanah said. "She came when I called and you frightened her away. You frightened her away, you stupid idiot!"

"I want to go home," Mary whimpered. "Please, let me go home!"

"You're in no state to go anywhere. Come into the other room," Cal said. His voice was young and scared, and the arm holding Mary trembled perceptibly.

"You frightened her away," Levanah said again. Her voice was tight with fury. "She came when I summoned her, and you frightened her away!"

She went to the window, pressing her hand against the cold glass, peering out into the darkness. There was nothing to be seen but the tossing arms of the trees under a rising wind.

Mary and Cal had gone into the other room together. She could hear Mary's weeping and Cal's deeper voice soothing her. The loneliness rose up in her again. Before, there had been only Cal and herself, making the house ready, coming in secret to exchange confidences. It was all different now. Mary was with them and Cal had eyes only for her. It was not that she begrudged Mary the attention she received, any more than she begrudged her the dark curls and pretty face with which she had been favored. It was simply that the old times were changing, and it seemed to Levanah that they were all growing up too quickly.

She turned again to the portrait, but the room had grown darker, and the eyes could no longer be discerned. Even the tiny carved figure was no more than a lump of wood. She nodded her head briefly and went into the other room.

The wind, moaning through the trees, tugged at the ends of Edith Falcon's cloak as she ran up the long drive toward Kingsmead. On a more leisurely occasion she might have reflected on the fact that she had not come home since before the birth of her child, and yet so unchanged was the great house that time might have stood still.

Stumbling up the steps she reached for the thick bell rope and pulled on it. A strident clamor woke within the darkened building, and a few moments later the heavy bolts were drawn back and the door opened a few inches. In the aperture Leah's nightcapped head appeared. In one hand she bore a candle, the other clutched a shawl about her.

"Who in God's name is making all this— Edith!" The annoyed, questioning tone changed into one of outraged consternation as she recognized her visitor.

"Don't shut the door!" Edith panted. "Please, Leah! Something so dreadful, Leah! Please let me come in and explain."

"You walked out of here with your shame years ago," Leah said low and shaking. "How dare you come back in the middle of the night? You'll find no gin or brandy here."

"I've not been drinking," Edith said. "Let me come in, Leah!"

"If I don't, you'll have the neighborhood awake," Leah said tightly, opening the door wider.

At the kitchen door Annie stood, timid and startled, her mouth a circle of astonishment. Leah, seeing her, called irritably, "Go back to bed, Annie! No need to stand there gaping, girl!"

"No, Miss Leah." Annie scuttled back into the kitchen thankfully.

Edith stepped into the hall and stood, nervously pulling and patting at the long tresses of windblown hair that straggled over the high collar of her cape. Leah bolted the door again and said coldly over her shoulder, "You'd best come into the solar. We can talk there without rousing the entire household."

The tapestries, stirred by the draft through the open door, whispered against the stone walls as they went through to the solar. A low fire still glowed in the hearth, its dim light reddening the panels. Leah poked it into a blaze, lit the lamp from the flame of the candle she carried and set the candle in its sconce. Only then did she look at her sister, and in her gaze was both the contempt of years and the shock of realization that so many years had passed since they had stood face to face.

"You've changed," she said.

"And you have hardly changed at all," Edith said bitterly. "Life has treated you kindly."

"I have worked very hard. It's not easy to rear three children."

"I too have reared a child." Edith's panting breath was slowing down and there was a certain dignity in her bearing.

"Do you imagine that I could forget that?" Leah asked. "Do you imagine I could forget it for one moment? For years you've flaunted your bastard in the face of the whole village. For years you've lived at that farm our poor brother was fool enough to give to you."

"You've lived safe here, on the estate."

"Managing it for Teddy, for John's heir. I've brought up three children."

"And gloried in the possession of them! You'd have had Cal too, my Cal, but I kept him away from you, so you pretended that he didn't exist, that you were ashamed to own him as a nephew. What you can't have, you hate, Leah."

"Your child is a bastard."

"So is Levanah, so is Beth's child," Edith said.

"The case is different. Beth was gentle, sweet. She died young . . ."

"And bore the witch mark as I'll swear her daughter does!"

"That old superstition!" Leah spoke with weary scorn.

"It's true! Down the centuries it's been true," Edith said. "Since the witch came out of Wales in Tudor times, certain women in our family have borne the mark and had the power to curse or to do well. Mam told us the stories when we were children, and I paid no heed, but I've thought of them since. I've had time for thinking since."

"This is the twentieth century!" Leah cried out.

"And so the old truths must be swept aside? They *are* truths, Leah. Remember how Mam talked of Willow Falcon, who swore as she died that victory would not come until a Falcon rode upon a moth? Mam had the devil's kiss on her thigh. Beth had it too, and she could see things, far into the future sometimes. And Levanah—I have seen with my own eyes—"

"I'll not listen!" Leah said vehemently. "Levanah is as dear to me as my own daughter, Mary."

"It is with Mary we are concerned," said Edith.

"With Mary? What of her?"

"What of her indeed? And what of my son? What of them both, eh?"

"I was stupid to let you in," Leah said. "Drink has addled your wits."

"I saw them," Edith said. "At 'Witch's Dower.' "

"That old cottage must be a ruin by now. Nobody goes to that part of the wood anymore."

"Mary and Cal go there," Edith said. She had dropped her voice and her face in the glowing firelight had an eerie quality. "Levanah goes there too. She with her wild prancing, her face sly as a fox, and candles lit, and your Mary and my Cal . . ."

"Doing what?"

"Embracing," Edith whispered. "Lovers already, perhaps. I saw them not an hour since."

"Dear God, not that!" Leah's face was white, the lines on it etched deeply.

"I tell you I saw them, and Levanah urging them. I knew Cal had a girl. I wondered where he went at night when he thought I was asleep, so tonight I followed him."

"You're lying." Leah spoke tonelessly, her eyes fixed upon Edith's face.

"I could see candles flickering through the windows. I hid in the bushes, not certain what to do. Mary and Levanah came a little later. I saw them, Leah. I watched them go into the cottage. It's not a ruin. The windows and doors are mended and there was smoke coming from the chimney."

"Mary and Levanah are asleep in their beds."

"Mary and Levanah are down at 'Witch's Dower,' "

Edith contradicted. "I crept up to the window and saw them. There's a kind of altar set up with a picture on it, and Levanah was doing some kind of dance, raising her arms high. Mary and Cal were embracing. I looked through the window and saw them, Leah!"

"I'll prove you wrong. I'll call them down."

Leah took up the candle again and went purposefully into the hall and up the stairs. Edith was at her heels, but she took no more notice of her sister than of the painted ancestors ranged along the back wall of the gallery. The door to the girls' wing opened with an almost imperceptible squeak, but the doors to their rooms stood open, and the neatly made beds had not been occupied.

Leah went down again into the hall and through to the solar. Her hand, putting the candle back into its sconce, was perfectly steady but her mouth was working violently.

"My daughter and your son," she said at last. "God in Heaven, is there to be no end to it? If you had gone away before your bastard was born— You have much to answer!"

"I had a right to stay. Marie Regina is my home," Edith said. "And you need not seek to blame me. If you had not prevented my marrying when I was a girl—"

"I did nothing to prevent it. Is it my fault if you were not able to catch a husband?"

"Because you always put some impediment in the way. You were jealous, Leah. Always jealous because I was prettier than you and people loved me more."

"If-if-if," Leah said restlessly. "If you had wed, if I had not wed, if you had not stayed at the farm—what is the point of going over that now? There are the children to be considered."

"They're not children," Edith said. "You think of everyone as an inferior, don't you? An inferior or a child, to be ordered about or possessed. Cal is a young man."

"Uncouth and uneducated from all reports!"

"As you've never spoken to him, how can you tell?"

"And he is with my daughter! While we sit here, arguing about issues past, your son is with my daughter. It's horrible! Horrible!"

"What are we going to do?" Edith whispered. "Leah, what are we going to do?"

"And Levanah was there? You say that Levanah was there?"

"Encouraging them. Twisting and turning, rising and falling on her toes. I tell you, there was something evil in that girl tonight. You may see poor Beth when you look into Levanah's face. I see corruption there. Evil and corruption, and my son holding Mary in his arms!"

"Do you think I can't picture that?" Leah asked bitterly. "Be still a moment, Edith! I want to think. We have to deal with this carefully."

"We have to tell them the truth," Edith said.

"There must be some other way."

"The truth, Leah! The truth!"

"If I forbid Mary—"

"Forbid her whatever you please. I shall tell Cal the truth."

"And shame yourself all over again?"

"I ought to have told him years ago," Edith said. "We both ought to have told them. It would have been easier when they were small."

"But you can't tell them everything," Leah said.

"There's Teddy to consider. We can't tell them the whole truth. Don't you see, Edith? Teddy has never done any harm to anybody. He is in his first year at University. A shock like this . . . Teddy is a sensitive boy."

"As he's never been allowed to speak to me," Edith said resentfully, "I'll have to take your word for that."

"Please, Edith! I'll never ask anything of you again, but not the whole truth!"

"I'll tell Cal that his father died," Edith said at last. "Will that make you happy?"

"Happiness is not an emotion I feel very often," Leah said. The pleading in her voice had hardened to ice again.

"'As ye sow, so shall ye reap,'" Edith said. "I've not been to church since Cal was baptized, but I can still quote the Scriptures."

"So can the devil." Leah's face was hard.

"You are the devil in this family," Edith said. "You always were, Leah. You and that piece of corruption that Beth spawned. Poor Beth! It's as well she killed herself before you took her and twisted her as you've twisted her child. Do you ever think about her, Leah? Do you ever turn your head at a quiet moment in the hall? If I were you I'd see Beth in every corner of this house."

"You'd best get back to the farm." Leah's lips still shook, but there was something in her eyes that cut short the younger woman's tirade. "Get back to the farm and make your son understand how the sins of the fathers are visited upon the children!"

"Why Leah, you can quote the Bible too," Edith said softly. In her ravaged face a bitter amusement woke some semblance of her youthful beauty. Then she went swiftly ahead of her sister out into the piercing wind of the November night.

Leah bolted the door again and stood for a moment in the shadowed hall. For her, Kingsmead had always been a refuge against the outside world. Her brief excursions to London disappointed and irritated her and the return to her home was the best part of any journey. All her life she had existed within the stone walls of the ancient house like a crab in its shell. Now the shell was beginning to crack as if the waves of some alien sea beat against it.

"It was not my fault," she said aloud to the whispering tapestries. "I always did everything for the best. I devoted myself to those three children."

But they were no longer children. In that, at least, Edith had been right. They were young men and women now, with all the passions and appetites of youth. And Mary was an extraordinarily pretty girl.

"But she is for Teddy," Leah muttered. "From the time that she was born I planned that."

It was all going wrong just as it had before. Teddy showed no more than a cousinly interest in Mary, and Mary was dabbling fingers with Cal. The cottage that should have fallen into ruin apparently still stood, and Levanah danced and chanted in candlelight.

Something rustled behind the wainscoting and was still. It was a mouse, Leah knew, but she felt an instant's alarm as if someone had trailed a silk skirt across the floor. Beth had had a dress with a bustle, a flowered dress in springtime shades, and she had not lived into the summer of her life.

"It was not my fault," Leah said again. "I did it for the best, I have always considered the family first."

There was an answering rustle behind the tapestries, and in sudden panic she ran through to the solar again and began to pile wood on the fire.

It was still dark, though a faint grayness betokened a false dawn, but the solar was becoming bright and warm. This room had been Leah's special place since her childhood. She had often come here to learn her lessons or work at her sampler. She could see herself, a plain sallow child with tightly braided hair, and none of Edith's blond beauty, or Beth's quick-silver charm. Edith had been her father's pet; Beth had never been too far from Mam. The boys, John and Price, had generally played together.

Five children, and now they were gone. John killed in a fall from his horse. Price, emigrated and probably dead. Beth, bleeding her young life away on the sitting room carpet. And Edith was a haggard woman with the shaking hands and slightly defiant stare of someone who drinks more than they should.

'At least, I have never let myself deteriorate,' Leah thought. 'I have managed the estate, and reared Teddy and Mary and Levanah, and lived in such a fashion that the old scandals are almost forgotten. At least I can never blame myself for the sins of others.'

Comforted by this, she sat down by the newly kindled fire, wrapping her shawl more securely round her slim frame, her ears pricked for the sound of footsteps in the hall beyond.

Rain pattered abruptly against the window. Edith had a long walk back to the farm, and would be soaked to the skin. Leah, thinking of this, felt a fierce and joyful satisfaction.

Chapter V

Levanah and Mary, moving quietly across the kitchen into the hall, were transfixed by the sudden emergence of the slim, nightcapped figure. Leah was fully in command of herself. She was even able to summon an inward gleam of amusement, for the girls clung together as if some ghost had risen to confront them. Both were wet and Mary's face, even in the dimness, was drawn with fatigue.

"Both of you," Leah said, each word a sliver of ice, "had better come into the solar."

"We're very damp," Levanah began, but her aunt interrupted.

"You can take off your outer garments in the solar. Come."

She turned her back and went briskly through the door again, aware of them trailing miserably behind her. The unpleasantness of her task was not something on which she allowed herself to dwell.

In the solar she sat in the high-backed chair near

the writing bureau and watched coldly as they removed their cloaks. The rain had tangled Mary's hair into a riot of curls. Levanah's red tresses hung limply at each side of her narrow face and her amber eyes were slitted.

"You need not bother to invent excuses or to deny anything," Leah began, "for I know exactly where you've been, and what wickedness you've been inciting. To sneak out of the house in the middle of the night is, in itself, reprehensible. Silly children might be expected to behave in such a fashion, but not responsible young ladies."

"If this is going to be a long lecture," Levanah said impertinently, "we may as well sit down."

She pulled at Mary's sleeve and the two of them sat side by side on the sofa, Mary clasping her hands nervously, Levanah leaning back with an assumption of indifference.

"You went to the old cottage," Leah said. "I suspect it was not the first time. You have always been strictly forbidden to go into that part of the estate. The building is very old and probably unsafe, and the ground near the river is very treacherous. However, I am not obliged to give you reasons for my prohibition. It is sufficient that I forbade it."

"For children, yes," Levanah said, "but you have just told us we are not children."

"Levanah, be silent!" Leah's voice, crackling with suppressed rage, made Mary jump.

"You went to the cottage tonight," Leah continued. "The two of you there would have been bad enough, but Caleb Falcon was there too. I have never permitted any contact between the three of you and my sister's son, for reasons that go back to before any of you were born. Yet he was there tonight, holding hands with you, Mary. Embracing you."

"Oh, Mother, please!" Mary put out her hands in a little troubled gesture.

"That a daughter of mine should so forget her modesty and good breeding as to allow such intimacies shocks me," Leah went on relentlessly. "It appalls me that the ... person in question should be Caleb Falcon."

"You don't understand," Mary said, her lips trembling. "There's been nothing wrong between Cal and me. I swear it. It's not as you think, not as you make it sound!"

"How is it then?" Leah asked with delicate sarcasm. "How is it? Do enlighten me."

"I think I'm in love with him," Mary said. "I truly believe that, Mother. And he is beginning to love me too. I know you won't be pleased, but you don't know Cal at all. He's a fine young man and he'd make me a good husband. Please, don't judge until you've met him."

"You and Caleb Falcon? The mere notion is monstrous," Leah said.

"I know he's a—was born out of wedlock. That wasn't his fault. If you would only agree to invite him here."

"Caleb Falcon will never set foot under the roof of Kingsmead," Leah said. "Understand this, Mary, for I mean to be obeyed. You are never to speak to that—person again. I want your solemn word of honor on that."

There was a long silence. Then Mary raised her head and spoke in a voice that shook perilously.

"I can't do that, Mother. I'm sorry to disobey, but I can't give you such a promise. I know I'm very young and nothing is settled, but it's my life and I have a right to lead it as I choose."

"Are you defying me?" Leah too had reared her head.

"I don't mean to defy you," Mary said. "I don't want to rush off and wed Cal tomorrow. He's not asked me yet, not even told me that he loves me. These feelings have to grow. And I want to go on seeing him, to find out if they do grow into something strong. I intend to go on seeing him, Mother."

"You will never see him again," Leah repeated.

"But why? Why? I've a right to know why," Mary cried. "Why must we never speak to our cousin? Is it because you want me to marry Teddy one day? I never will, you know. Even if I don't marry Cal, I'll not have Teddy."

"Who is a fine young man worthy of you in every way."

"So is Cal a fine young man," Mary choked.

"But not for you." Leah's voice had softened and there was concern in her face. "Apart from my own hopes for your future, apart from anything I might dislike about him, that boy is not for you."

"Then tell me why," Mary begged.

"I was married once," Leah said. "Your father's name was Simmons. Paul Simmons. He was a Londoner, a journalist by profession, though not a very good one. We were married and I was a good wife to him. Anyone would tell you that."

"I don't see," Levanah drawled, "what that has to do with any of us."

Leah ignored her and went on talking, her voice even, her eyes fixed compellingly upon her daughter.

"I was very happy with Paul. I was delighted when I learned I was to have a child of my own. Teddy's mother had died and I'd the rearing of him, but I've always been good with babies. I looked forward to having a child of my own. I didn't tell Paul at once, because I wanted it to be a surprise. A surprise!"

For a moment bitterness flooded her face and voice. Then she controlled herself and went on steadily.

"I was the one who received the surprise. My sister Edith came to me and confessed she was with child. With child by my husband, by Paul. She left Kingsmead at once and went to Whittle Farm. The property has been in the family for years, but John made it over to her as a deed of gift. My brother was always good-hearted."

"Are you— I don't understand what you're saying," Mary said in a small, tight voice.

"I'm saying that your father was Caleb Falcon's father too. I'm saying that Caleb Falcon is your half brother. Is that plain enough?"

"Cal and— Are you sure? Are you quite sure? There could be a mistake."

"There's no mistake," Leah said shortly. "My sister and my husband betrayed me. And she went on living in Marie Regina, living here with her bastard! The most she would agree to was not to reveal the name of her child's father. But I swore never to speak to her again, never to acknowledge her boy as my nephew."

"What happened to him?" Levanah asked. "To your husband, I mean. What happened to him?"

"He left," her aunt said. "I heard later that he'd died. It didn't seem so important by then. John was killed in a riding accident and I had the estate to manage on Teddy's behalf. And you were born. Another love child!"

Her mouth twisted and in the growing light her face was haggard.

"Cal is my half brother," Mary whispered. "Dear Lord, oh, dear God! We can never be wed, never fall in love."

"I'm sorry," Leah said. "I'm so very sorry, my dear, but you are young, and the young forget. In years to come, when you have Teddy's children—"

"Don't!" Mary, her face anguished, sprang to her feet. "How can you be so cruel as to think I could consider Teddy, or anyone, so soon! If I can't wed Cal I don't want anybody! I shall never love anybody again!"

Sobbing wildly, she looked about as if for rescue and then ran out of the solar. Her footsteps echoed on the stone stairs and a door above slammed violently.

Levanah had also risen but Leah's sharp voice halted her.

"Sit down! I have something more to say to you!"

"Are you going to tell me that Mary's father is my father too?" Levanah inquired insolently.

"Your father—"

"Never married my mother, and after I was born she killed herself. I've known that for years," Levanah interrupted. "I want to know if your husband was my father too."

"I have no idea of your father's name," Leah said coldly. "Beth was a very foolish girl, very trusting. She owned the cottage. Mam left it to her when she died. I always hated the place, but Beth liked it. One summer she rented it to a traveler. He was married, that much I know. When he went away he left Beth with child. She hoped he'd come back, but she'd no address where she could send any letters and, to do him justice, he probably never guessed her condition.

After you were born she became very depressed, and then she killed herself. And I did my duty and reared you."

"It isn't that I'm not grateful," Levanah said uncomfortably.

"You have a strange way of showing it," Leah said. "I blame you for this entire affair, Levanah. Mary is a good, obedient girl but you were always defiant and strong-willed. Candles and altars indeed ... what I heard tonight shocked me to the soul!"

"How did you hear?" her niece asked suddenly. "How did you know we were at 'Witch's Dower'?"

"My sister followed her son and watched what went on. She had the good sense to come straight to me."

"Then that was the face at the window," Levanah said slowly. "Not the witch but poor old Aunt Edith!"

Unexpectedly she began to laugh, her sharp little teeth gleaming between her parted lips, her slim white throat swelling.

"What witch? What childish nonsense is this about a witch?" Leah demanded.

"No nonsense, Aunt," Levanah said. Her eyes, between fringes of golden lash, glinted. "You know as well as I do that for centuries women bearing a certain mark and having certain powers have been born into the family. You know it's true, though you pretend not to believe in such things. But my mother had the mark, didn't she? That was why Grandmother left her 'Witch's Dower,' and I have the mark too."

"A birthmark!"

"And the power," said Levanah. "It's true, Aunt. I can make things happen, you know, by willing them to happen, and sometimes I know what people are going to say before they put their thoughts into words."

"That's superstitious nonsense," Leah said, her eyes uneasy.

"Watch," said Levanah.

Her eyes were fixed upon the candles, her narrow hands curved as if in prayer. Abruptly the flames streamed up, then dwindled down into points of fire. The room was growing colder, so cold that Leah felt the skin of her hands shriveling as if she were fading into bones.

"You see, Aunt, I can do it," Levanah said.

She made a little flickering motion with her hands and the flames burned steadily again.

"A draft from the hall," Leah said.

"You know it wasn't that," Levanah said gently. "Oh, I admit it isn't much, but it's a beginning. I'm getting stronger, Aunt. Day after day I practice and concentrate and grow stronger."

"Is that what you do at the cottage? Silly conjuring tricks?"

"I use my mind," said Levanah, "to make things happen. There are forces all about us, and we can learn the secrets, we can make them obey us. But I need to learn more, much much more. The first witch who ever married into the Falcons and brought the power with her, she knew the secrets. I tried to raise her tonight, to call her back through time, so that I could learn those secrets. She didn't come, but then I suppose if I was strong enough to be able to do that I wouldn't need her help anyway."

"Edith said that you were evil," Leah said. "I am beginning to believe that she spoke the truth. Have you no sense of shame or decency?"

"I meant no harm," Levanah said. "To know how to

do things is all I want. The cottage is full of memories, Aunt. The walls are soaked in memory. That's why I persuaded Cousin Cal to mend and paint the place. I've been going there for years, sometimes alone when the moon is full and all the little night creatures rustle around. There's no harm in it, Aunt."

"No harm in taking Mary down there!"

"She found out I was going to the cottage," Levanah said. "I let her go with me, that's all."

"To prance about in front of a heathen altar."

"It's a shelf," Levanah said. "Cal put it up for me and he carved a little goblin god, with cloven hooves. I call him Lob, and he is the guardian spirit of the cottage. We light candles in his honor, and I brew wine, and Cal brings food. There's no harm in it."

"Stop saying that!" Leah exclaimed, fury breaking out. "You sit there, innocence in your face, and prate of corruption as if it were child's play! Have you no conscience at all? To disobey me and to lead Mary to disobey me is bad enough. You make it ten times worse by dabbling in devil's mischief. Making heathen idols, trying to raise the dead! In olden days you'd have been swum as a witch."

"Like Catrin Falcon, who was buried outside the churchyard? But this is the twentieth century, Aunt, and you don't believe in witches."

"I believe in wickedness," Leah said. "I've seen too much of it in my life to have any false illusions. I can see it in you, Levanah. I can see wickedness in you."

"That's not true," Levanah said. "I'm not wicked! But I have a right to do as I please on my own property."

"Your property! What gives you that notion?"

" 'Witch's Dower' has always been handed down from one woman who bears the mark to the next. It belonged to my mother and so it belongs to me now."

"Is that what you think?" Mockery replaced anger in the older woman's face. "That cottage and the acre of woodland that surrounds it was never part of the original entail. Whoever owns it may leave it to whomever they choose, but if they die intestate it reverts to the original estate again. Your mother died without making a Will. She died intestate."

"But she left a daughter. I am entitled to inherit her property."

"She left a bastard daughter. You are entitled to inherit nothing!"

"But the cottage is mine," Levanah said. "The very first time I entered it I knew it was mine. We belonged together. It was so neglected, Aunt. It needed care and attention, and I gave it that. And Cal helped me. He mended the roof and the door and put in new windows, and I cleaned and polished. We worked on it bit by bit for years, Aunt. It's a happy place now. If you would only come down to see it—"

"I don't intend to go anywhere near the place." Leah ignored the pleading in her niece's voice. "I don't intend to allow you to go anywhere near it either. No, I'm not going to forbid you, and neither am I going to ask for your promise. You would only break it, for I can no longer trust you. So 'Witch's Dower' will be destroyed."

"Destroyed? You can't do that," Levanah said.

"Indeed I can," Leah said calmly. "I will have the trees felled and the building pulled down. It's unsafe and should have been done years ago."

"If the cottage isn't mine, but part of the main estate now, then it belongs to Teddy," Levanah said gaspingly. "You can't destroy Teddy's property!"

"Until your cousin comes of age I have power of attorney," Leah said. "I can do whatever I please, if I consider it to be in the interest of the family. The cottage is unsafe and will be pulled down. I'll have the men over to do it before the end of the week. In the meantime you are forbidden to go anywhere near the place. If you disobey me then I'll take steps to have you sent so far away from Kingsmead that you'll never find your way home."

"If you touch the cottage," the girl whispered, "you'll die, Aunt Leah. I promise that I'll wish you to death."

"Hysterical threats don't make the slightest impression on me," Leah said, rising.

"I'm not hysterical," Levanah said, "but I mean what I say. If you touch 'Witch's Dower,' I'll not make candle flames dwindle. I'll do nothing but send out black hatred to you. And hate is a powerful emotion. It eats you up, and in the end you'll die. You'll die, Aunt."

"Go to your room and stay there!" Leah's face in the gathering light was gray and old. She looked much more than her forty-five years.

"Do you mean to lock me up on bread and water?" Levanah asked. "This is the twentieth century."

"Go to your room," Leah repeated. "I will have to think of some way of dealing with your wickedness."

"It's you who are wicked!" Levanah cried. "Wicked to tear down a place that belongs to me, and wicked to try and make Mary wed Teddy, and wicked never to speak to Cousin Cal. And I'm glad your husband made love to Aunt Edith. I hope they both laughed at you while they were doing it."

She stopped, panting, her lips drawn back over her teeth, feathers of red hair clinging to the high white cheekbones. Then she whirled about and sped into the hall. The bolt of the front door was wrenched back and as she tugged open the door a gust of wind set the tapestries whispering again.

Leah, for the first time in her life, was not at ease in the solar. It was as if some of her niece's passionate hatred had disturbed the harmony of the centuries. In the half light the furniture assumed threatening shapes.

She went swiftly into the hall, stared for a moment at the gaping door before closing it, and, picking up the long skirts of her nightgown, climbed the stairs. There was no sound from behind the door leading to the girls' apartments. Mary, she guessed, would by now have cried herself to sleep. Poor, silly Mary, fancying herself in love with Cal Falcon! Thank God, Edith had seen them and come to tell her before the affair had gone any further. As it was, no great harm had been done. Mary would believe her heart was broken, but Teddy would be home for Christmas, and by then the girl would be ready to be consoled.

At the door to her own rooms Leah hesitated. She was so weary after an almost sleepless night that she longed to throw herself down on her bed and let oblivion overwhelm her, but some compulsion drew her into the big room opposite.

The upstairs sitting room was seldom used. It had been a bedroom once but the bed had been removed after Beth's suicide. Not that Beth had died in the four-poster; she had died leaning against it with the blood from the severed arteries in her wrists pumping out onto the carpet.

Leah had gone in and found her there. She had only to glance at the spot to remember that huddled figure, that curling tail of hair that was the color of dark honey with the sun on it, the eyes that were all shades and yet none.

There had been time to save her, time to staunch the flow of blood. Her sister had still been alive, with an imploring expression in her eyes as if she regretted her moment of despair. Leah, looking at her, had seen only Mam's favorite, the one who had always been considered special because she had a birthmark on her thigh. And she had gone out of the room and quietly down the stairs again, leaving Beth, at nineteen, to die in an utter absence of hope.

"But I took care of your bastard!" Leah whispered now to the chill apartment. "I reared her with Teddy and my own daughter. I even kept all word of her bastardy and of your suicide from her. I was like a mother to her, Beth, and this is how she repays me! She disobeys me, and lends her soul to evil, and corrupts Mary, who is sweet-natured and stupid. She's evil, Beth."

Beth had not been evil. She had been gentle and never harmed anybody, and her occasional moods of strangeness had disturbed her as much as they disturbed other people.

"But if you had lived," Leah whispered, "you would have grown evil too. You were born with the devil's kiss on your thigh, with generations of wickedness behind you. It was best that you should die young."

There remained Levanah and she was a problem that must be solved.

"She can't stay here," Leah said. "I can't let her stay here at Kingsmead. She will spoil everything for Mary and Teddy. She will continue to spread her corruption in the family, in our beautiful home. I will have to send her away, for Mary's sake."

That she herself was afraid of the girl was a black shame at the back of her mind.

She was conscious of the emptiness of the long apartment. In the kitchen below, the maids would be stirring, raking out the grate, putting the kettles on to boil for the early morning tea. Across the river Cousin Wenna and Charlotte Bishop would still be asleep, with no thought in their minds beyond the day's work ahead. And Edith, having told Cal the ugly truth, would, Leah guessed, have drunk herself into a stupor. For a moment she envied her sister. Then cool determination rushed over her. All her life she had devoted herself to the family. She had kept scandal to a murmur instead of a shout, had efficiently managed the estate on Teddy's behalf, had reared the girls as ladies, had seen that the school was well run. A tumbledown cottage and a girl with evil yellow eyes were joined together to threaten everything she had achieved.

The cottage would be torn down and its contents burned. Levanah would have to go away for a time. She needed discipline, something to cleanse the wickedness from her soul. A position as companion to some self-indulgent old lady might curb her sharp tongue.

Leah went back to her own room. It was cool here too and the drawn shutters made it dim, but her head had begun to throb and the skin at her temples was stretched tight. She went over to the bed and lay down, neglecting, for once in her life, to take off her slippers.

After a few seconds her eyelids drooped down and faint, blurred images moved across the surface of her mind. She could recognize none of them, for she was very tired and Beth had died a long time ago.

Chapter VI

Levanah had not returned by midmorning, and Mary sent down a message by Anne that she had a sick headache and wished to remain in her room.

Leah, breakfasting late in her own room, made her plans. A short sleep had banished her weariness, and there was a sparkle in her eyes as she contemplated the fitting together again of her secure, ordered world. Challenge was something from which she had never shrunk, and something in her nature rose to meet it.

Having drunk her second cup of tea, she slipped a long coat over her dress and pinned a small toque of tiny mauve flowers on her smooth black head. The white wings at her temples were growing wider and the network of lines about her eyes was deeper, but her figure was still trim, her teeth excellent. She had been a clumsy child and a plain girl, but in middle life she flattered herself that she had acquired a certain distinction.

She picked up her gloves and went serenely down the stairs. One of the grooms had brought round the pony trap, and she nodded her thanks as he helped her up to the driving seat.

"I'm going over to see Mrs. Davies at the school, so I may not be back until later this afternoon," she told him. "If the rain begins again I may stay later."

"Yes, Miss Leah." He touched his forelock and backed away.

There had been talk among the maids of Miss Edith having arrived at Kingsmead in the middle of the night, but Miss Leah looked as calmly efficient as usual, and he was apt to discount the rumors.

The rain had ceased but the lowering skies threatened more. Leah held the pony on a tight rein, negotiating the turn into the main road with skill. There was a subtle pleasure in handling a skittish animal. She wished that human beings were as amenable as beasts.

As she neared the tangled bridle path that dipped down into the woods, she looked deliberately in the opposite direction, toward the high spire and huddled roofs of church and village. There was security and common sense and kindliness in the village, but what lay hidden in the rain-drenched wood was a reminder of past evil. Soon it would be demolished and the trees cut down, and the evil would be gone.

The voices of children chanting their alphabet flowed sweetly through the open windows. She alighted from the trap and stood for a few moments, listening with pleasure. Children were so innocent, so eager for love, so grateful for protection. It was a pity they had to grow up.

She pushed open the door and waited, smiling, as the heads turned toward her and the chanting voices trailed into silence. Charlotte Bishop, pointer upraised, hesitated, with a question in her face.

"Do forgive this interruption," Leah said charmingly. "I'm sure Miss Bishop will excuse you for the rest of the day. This can be a holiday, a treat to reward you for all the hard work you've done this term. Hurry home in good order. Miss Bishop."

She bowed slightly but the teacher's voice rose above the clamor of the departing children.

"Mrs. Simmons, something must be wrong! Is there anything I can do?"

"Where is Mrs. Davies?" Leah asked.

"Upstairs, with your niece. She asked me to take all the classes this morning."

"I thought Levanah might have come here." Leah frowned, tapping her teeth with the handle of her whip.

"Something *is* wrong. Do let me help."

The young woman's eyes were full of eager curiosity.

Leah made up her mind swiftly. If Levanah had already chattered, it was likely that Charlotte Bishop had gleaned some distorted version of the truth. It might be better to allow her to learn the full story.

"There has indeed been some—family upset," she said cautiously. "I hope I can rely on your discretion, Miss Bishop?"

"Oh, indeed. Yes, indeed," the other breathed.

"My daughter, Mary, received a very severe shock early this morning," Leah said. "She is quite prostrate, poor child. I am of the opinion that she needs a—confidante, a sympathetic ear."

"Is there anything I can do, in any way?"

"If you could ride over to Kingsmead and talk to her, or let her talk to you?"

It might be a good idea for Mary to make another friend apart from Levanah. Miss Bishop was sensible and practical, an excellent teacher who, in being permitted to learn more of the Falcons, would be more closely bound to the school.

"I'll go at once, Mrs. Simmons. Had I better inform Mrs. Davies?"

"Inform me of what? What on earth is happening? Why are all the children going home?" Wenna, looking distinctly annoyed, swept in.

"I gave them a day's holiday," Leah said calmly. "You'd best be leaving for Kingsmead, Miss Bishop."

"Yes, Mrs. Simmons." Charlotte Bishop whisked through the door.

"I would like to know by what authority you undermine my position," Wenna said, low and furious.

"I built the school and engaged both you and Miss Bishop," Leah said coldly. "I don't owe you any explanation for whatever I may choose to do. Where is Levanah?"

"Upstairs. I made her change her clothes and rest for a while."

"She told you everything, I suppose? Her version of it?"

"Wasn't it true, then, about your husband and your sister?"

"Perfectly true. I've lived with the humiliation for many years. You can understand that any thought of a . . . union between my daughter and Caleb Falcon is horrible, morally and legally?"

"Yes. Of course, I do." Wenna's voice softened slightly. "It must have been very distressing for you."

"Levanah is at the bottom of it," Leah said. "If she had never gone to that wretched cottage— She told you that she worships idols, I suppose, and believes herself possessed of extraordinary powers."

"She's an unusual girl," Wenna admitted. "I remember her mother."

"Beth was slightly unbalanced," Leah said sharply. "It is not something I would admit to anyone else, but she was always strange. One has only to remember the way in which she died. And I fear—I very much fear—"

"There is nothing wrong with Levanah's mind," Wenna interrupted. "She's an intelligent girl."

"An evil girl," Leah said, her knuckles clenching on the whip. "She is wicked, Cousin, as her mother was never wicked."

"Surely not! What occurred at 'Witch's Dower' was no more than a little superstitious nonsense, a youthful craving for excitement."

"It will not happen again," Leah said. "There will be no repetition of such—obscenity."

"Levanah said you'd threatened to destroy the cottage. I couldn't believe—"

"It was no threat. I intend to have the place pulled down and the wood destroyed."

"But you have such a respect for tradition!" Wenna exclaimed. "You never would have anything changed at Kingsmead."

"Some traditions are best rooted out like poisonous weeds, as 'Witch's Dower' will be."

"But the cottage belonged to Beth, and she loved it so!"

"Beth is dead and left no legitimate heir. I'll go up to Levanah now."

Leah began to ascend the narrow stairs that led to the apartment. Behind her, Wenna said, "I do urge you not to act hastily. Young girls are so vunerable."

"I think you can trust me to deal with family matters as I see fit," Leah returned, gaining the landing and opening the door to the sitting room.

It was in its usual state of faintly Bohemian disorder, with books piled high on the shelves and multihued cushions brightening the somber décor. Leah's eyes went straight to her niece, who stood with her back to the fire and her legs apart as if she were about to repel an attack.

"So you followed me," she said bitterly. "You'd have done better to stay home and comfort your daughter."

"Mary is young and will get over her disappointment," Leah said.

"Leah, I have told Levanah that it was very wrong of her to disobey you," Wenna said. "I begged her to apologize."

"And I refused," Levanah said proudly. "I've every right to visit my own property, and you have no right to think of destroying it."

"The property is not yours, and I will do as I please with it," Leah said. "There is not the slightest good in your arguing or threatening. The matter is closed."

"But it isn't," said Wenna. Her expression was a mixture of regret and relief, as if she disliked thwarting Leah but felt a certain satisfaction at having attracted her cousin's attention.

"Are you presuming to contradict me?" Leah's smooth dark brows raised in faint surprise.

"Beth left a Will," Wenna said.

There was a long silence during which aunt and niece, united in astonishment, stared at her. Then Leah said flatly, "Don't be ridiculous. Beth died intestate when Levanah was a few days old."

"I went to see her after the child was born," Wenna

said. "The day afterward. You were a tiny scrap of a thing in your cradle, Levanah. Did your aunt tell you the circumstances of your birth?"

"I found out long ago that my mother wasn't married," Levanah said.

"Your mother was sweet and gentle," Wenna said. "I had come from Wales to teach at the school here. Teddy's father, your Uncle John, was still alive. He was thrown from his horse and killed, right in front of Beth. We didn't know until later how it had been. John was found by the servants, and it wasn't until much later that we found Beth. She had panicked, you see, and run down to the cottage. She always went there when she was very happy or very sad."

"Did you find her?" Levanah asked.

"I had a feeling something was wrong," Wenna said. "Something drew me to the cottage, and Beth was there. You were born at 'Witch's Dower.' Two months too soon, with no more flesh on you than a plucked chicken, but you and she were alive."

"And John was dead," Leah said hoarsely. "He swerved to avoid Beth as he galloped down the drive and crashed against the tree. She told us about it when we got her into bed. John died to save her, and she ran away!"

"She was not a strong character," Wenna said. "She couldn't stand up to life like other people, but she cared about you, Levanah. When I was sitting with her she asked for pen and paper and made her Will. I witnessed it and so did one of the maids. It was very short. I can remember it. 'I, Elizabeth Falcon, being of sound mind, do bequeath the house known as "Witch's Dower" and the land belonging to it to my natural daughter, Levanah.' And then the date."

"You're lying," Leah said. "You're lying!"

"She asked me not to tell anybody," Wenna said. "She wanted everything legal, you see."

"Where is this Will?" Leah demanded. "Where is this so-called Will?"

"I took it to the solicitor in Maidstone after Beth— died," Wenna said. "I didn't think it necessary to mention its existence at the time. I suppose I assumed that the cottage would be regarded as Levanah's. I didn't envisage any trouble."

"But you kept that Will in a safe place. I suppose so that you could hold it over my head when the time was ripe."

Leah's face was white with passion. Her hands twisted together over and over.

"I never thought it would be necessary to tell you about it," Wenna said miserably. "I thought that in common justice—"

"Justice! What justice was there for me?" Leah shrilled. "My own sister betraying me with my husband! My own brother dying young and leaving me with the responsibility of the estate! And Beth, whom I never blamed for having an illegitimate child, makes a Will and gives it to you. Why to you? Why not to me?"

"Perhaps she didn't trust you, Aunt," Levanah said in a small, clear voice. "Perhaps, deep down, she knew that one day you'd try to cheat me out of what was mine."

"I'm sure Beth told me about the Will because Cousin Leah was fully taken up with all the arrangements for John's funeral," Wenna said quickly. "And there had to be an inquest on him. 'Accidental death.'"

"My sister said she was of sound mind?" Leah's face was suddenly thoughtful. "And a week later she killed herself. If I were to contest on Teddy's behalf—"

"I would feel it my duty to testify that when Beth made that Will she seemed perfectly sane. Shocked and depressed over her brother's death, weakened by her own ordeal, but quite sane," Wenna said. "It was not in her mind to kill herself then. I know it."

"If you were to quarrel with me in Court over a tiny cottage," Levanah said, "you'd be the laughing-stock of the county."

"So the property is yours," Leah said slowly. "I wouldn't insult you, Cousin Wenna, by asking to see the Will. You have always impressed me as a truthful person, and I've no doubt that it's worded as you remember, and kept exactly where you say it is."

"So you can't destroy my property," Levanah said triumphantly. "*My* property! Because if you do I'll take *you* to Court."

"I'm sorry," Wenna said.

"Not at all." Leah had drawn herself up and her voice was rigidly controlled. "I have no desire to break the law by destroying property that doesn't belong to me. 'Witch's Dower' belongs to my niece and when she is of age she will be perfectly entitled to live there or dispose of it as she chooses. In the meantime I will act as seems to me to be most fitting. Levanah, you will return with me to Kingsmead."

The girl opened her mouth in protest, but Wenna stepped forward and laid a warning hand on her arm.

"Best go home, dear," she said.

"You will stay within the house," Leah went on as if Wenna had not spoken. "I will not allow you to communicate in any way with Mary. You may think you can defy me, but in this matter I intend to be obeyed. Do I make myself clear?"

"Yes, Aunt." Levanah spoke meekly, her yellow eyes downcast.

"Go down to the trap and wait for me there," Leah said. "Cousin Wenna, I am ... hurt that you didn't see fit to confide in me about this matter before. I do not enjoy being made to look a fool."

"It slipped my mind," Wenna said honestly.

"Then I'll say no more, for the present." Leah, her mouth tight, bowed and followed Levanah downstairs. When the front door closed, Wenna relaxed for the first time since Levanah had burst in earlier that morning. Her forehead was damp with sweat and her legs trembled violently. In a few brief hours the unhappiness of past years had risen up to confront her and make a mockery of the quiet teaching and solitary walks that had filled her life since.

She had been ready to love John Falcon when the accident that killed him had blighted her chance of marriage. The Manor School had become her life, its pupils her children, and in Levanah and Mary she had seen the daughters she would never conceive.

She felt an unwilling admiration for Leah, who went so ruthlessly toward her goal with no thought for the people she might hurt. Respectability was Leah's god and in its worship she would sacrifice everything else and pay no heed to other people's feelings. Yet, learning of the situation between Mary and Cal, there was little else she could have done.

In the trap Levanah cast a sideways look at her aunt. Leah sat bolt upright, her lips thinned to a narrow line, her face without color.

"Aunt, why did my mother kill herself?" Levanah asked.

"A fit of depression," Leah said curtly.

"But what made her depressed?" the girl persisted.

"If she'd be going to kill herself she'd surely have done it before, when she knew she was with child, or when Uncle John was killed trying to avoid her. Why wait and then do it?"

"She was unbalanced."

Leah thought of the portrait at the cottage. That girl had looked sweet and gentle, a little lost perhaps, but quite sane.

"I think something happened," she said slowly. "I think something else happened; something so terrible that she didn't want to go on living."

"Beth is dead. Let her rest," Leah said.

"After she made her Will, if it had been in her mind to do it she'd have done it then. She'd not have waited a week. Something else must have happened."

"I forbid any further discussion," Leah said. Two spots of scarlet darkened her cheekbones and her voice shook.

"I'll find out," Levanah said softly. "I'll find out why my mother died. I know something happened." She was guessing, seeking by any means to upset her aunt, in which she was apparently successful, for Leah laid her whip so viciously across the pony's broad back that the animal plunged forward at breakneck speed.

"You had best go straight up to your room," Leah said, as they alighted in the courtyard. "You may come downstairs for your meals, and if you desire exercise then you may take a walk. Where you go is your own affair. I intend to send you away as soon as possible, but in the meantime you will not associate with Mary."

Levanah, beyond a long, insolent look, gave no sign of having heard, but walked into the house and ascended the stairs without a backward glance.

As Leah entered the hall Charlotte Bishop strode forward.

"Mrs. Simmons, I persuaded Mary to tell me the whole story." Her voice was low and thrilled. "You can certainly rely on me to say absolutely nothing to anybody."

"Thank you, Miss Bishop."

"I took the liberty of suggesting a little jaunt into Maidstone, if it meets with your approval. Fresh air, tea out, a look at the shops."

"An excellent idea." Leah looked at her slightly more kindly. The young woman might, as she had hoped, prove a suitable friend for Mary.

"May I be permitted to say," the other said breathlessly, "how very much I feel for you. To have stood alone all these years is a marvelous achievement, so typical of the strength of character one finds in modern woman."

"Is it?" Leah, who thought of modern woman in terms of divided skirts and loud voices, was uninterested.

Her attention was diverted by Mary, who drifted in, subdued and pale with red-rimmed eyes.

"Miss Bishop tells me that you and she are to spend the rest of the day in Maidstone," Leah said brightly. "That will be much better for you than moping in your room."

"Yes. Charlie has been very kind," Mary said, giving her mother a wavering smile.

"Well, run along then." The words, after the trauma of the night, sounded false and trite. Half-hearing their effect, Leah added, "I am so very sorry you are unhappy, my dear. I know how painful these things can be, but I know too that disappointment can be

healed, and you do understand how such a relationship would be . . . quite unspeakable."

"If we had known the truth from the beginning,"
Mary said, raising heavy eyes, "I never would have
begun to think of Cal in such a way."

"May we use the pony trap, Mrs. Simmons?" Charlotte Bishop put in.

"Yes. Yes, of course." Leah watched the two young
women cross the threshold. Mary was graceful and
pretty even after weeping, her dark curls a contrast to
the pale plaits twisted around her companion's head.
At the steps the teacher put her hand lightly, with no
more than the faintest suggestion of possession, on
Mary's arm.

Leah went into the solar. It seemed an age since
Edith had stood there, rain dripping from her thin
cloak, and told her of looking through the cottage
window. Yet only a few hours had passed. Well, it
was out now. The secret of her husband's desertion
and of Cal's parentage was known to the girls, to
Cousin Wenna, and to Charlotte Bishop. At least
Teddy's name had been kept out of it.

She allowed herself a small sigh. Then her face
hardened again as she thought of Levanah. The girl
was a viper, a sly fox who had corrupted Mary's innocence. She would have to be sent away as soon as
possible.

Leah reached out for the newspaper and began to
scan the columns attentively. It would have given her
infinite satisfaction to place her niece in service in
some bleak charitable institution, but such a proceed-
ing would cause comment. Levanah, whatever her
sins, was still a Falcon and Beth's daughter. A post as
companion to some rich and disagreeable old woman
would be the very thing to humble that defiant spirit.

There was one such advertisement here. A Mrs. Varney, living in London, required a young girl as companion-help. London was less than a half day's journey away, but it was smoky and noisy. Country-bred Levanah would hate it.

Leah went over to the writing bureau and took out paper and pen. In a few minutes she was writing in the elegant copperplate hand instilled into her by a childhood governess and never forgotten.

Up in her room Levanah sat, sullen and triumphant. "Witch's Dower" was hers and nobody could ever take it away from her. The look on her aunt's face as Cousin Wenna had related her information had been something to see! Thinking of it Levanah's own face broke into a gleeful smile. When she was of age she could live in her own property. Mary would be married off to Teddy by then. Aunt Leah would see to that. And Cal ... the girl's hard little face softened as her cousin's name came into her mind. With Mary out of the way the old comradeship between him and herself would revive, might turn into something sweeter and stronger.

'But first,' Levanah thought, 'I must find out exactly who my father was, and why my mother killed herself. I must have everything clear in my own mind before I can contemplate marriage.'

She nodded toward he. reflection in the mirror, pleased with her own decision. The face in the glass was, though she didn't realize it, much more like the face of Leah Falcon than that of the gentle-eyed girl in the portrait.

Charlotte Bishop held the reins efficiently and kept up a running monologue of trivial remarks as they drove along the Maidstone road. She seemed not to expect any answers, but her voice was pleasant and soothing.

Mary, dabbing her eyes as they passed Whittle Farm, was grateful for the other's undemanding company. She had poured out her woes to Charlotte Bishop and the telling of them had brought a certain relief.

Imperceptibly her spirits began to rise a little. She was still desperately unhappy, and she was determined never to be pushed into marriage with Teddy, but the rain was still holding off, and it was a long time since she had been into town, and the ritual at "Witch's Dower" had really frightened her. She dabbed her eyes again and, at her side, Charlotte Bishop went on talking, pleasantly, soothingly.

Chapter VII

"So you'll be leaving for London soon, Miss Levanah?" Hattie Jenks, who had officiated at the village Post Office for nearly thirty years, gave her customer a brightly inquisitive smile.

"To stay with friends for several months." Levanah repeated the lie on which she and Leah had agreed. No sense in telling the whole village that she was being sent away in disgrace. No sense either in allowing Leah to see how much she minded going. She had received word of her banishment in dry-eyed indifference, only remarking, "The cottage is mine, and one day I'll come home again, Aunt."

Hattie Jenks, aware that the Falcons were the most clannish family in the district, raised her sandy eyebrows and pursed her lips slightly.

"Bit near Christmas for going away on a visit, isn't it?" she ventured.

"Mrs. Varney is a widow and rather lonely. And I

shall probably be thoroughly spoiled," Levanah said. "I'll have some of those licorice sticks too, please."

Leah wanted her out of the way before Teddy came home. She wanted Mary and Teddy to be alone together.

"Your mother always liked licorice sticks," Hattie said, filling a twist of paper. "She used to come in once or twice a week."

"You knew my mother. But, yes, you must have done. Levanah stared at the plump sagging face of the woman behind the counter.

"I knew her all her life," Hattie said. "A happy creature, always ready for a word. Poor soul!"

She shook her head and added another licorice stick to the bag.

Levanah bit her lip, considering. It was likely that Hattie Jenks knew the name of her mother's lover, too, but she couldn't stoop to the asking ot it. Instead she asked, "You must have been upset when you heard of her—suicide?"

"You know about that?" Hattie looked surprised. "Miss Leah made it very plain there was to be no talk, and we respected her wishes."

"My aunt considered I was old enough to know," Levanah said vaguely.

"It's still a stigma," Hattie Jenks said, shaking her head again. "I've blamed myself since. If I'd said something to her on that last afternoon, she might have— Oh, who knows? But it was a week later that she— Why, I wasn't to know, was I?"

"You saw my mother? When?"

"On the day Lord John was thrown from his horse and killed," Hattie said. "She came into the shop here that very afternoon. I can see her now."

Beth Falcon had worn a cotton dress that clearly

outlined her pregnancy and her hair had rippled down her back. Hattie had considered her shameless then, but time had softened the older woman's moral strictures.

"She came in here?" Levanah said.

"Walking very stiff," Hattie said, "with a frozen look on her face. She asked for an envelope and the use of pen and ink."

"To write a letter?"

"She never wrote any letter," Hattie said. "She turned her back and put something in the envelope. A ring, I think. And she addressed it and told me to post it. I'd not thought of that for years, not until this minute. What she said as she was going out—that put everything else out of my head."

"What did she say?"

"She said, 'Tell the Vicar he'll be needed up at Kingsmead. There's been an accident and my brother John is lying dead in the drive.' Words like that. And then she went out, running up the street toward the main road. She was going over to 'Witch's Dower,' I suppose."

"The letter? The envelope, I mean—did you post it?"

"I put it with the rest to be collected." Hattie bridled slightly.

"The address? Do you remember the address on the envelope?" Levanah's voice was tense.

"I'm not in the habit of reading other people's letters," Hattie said virtuously. "And with everything that went on that day, with what she said to me, I never thought of looking. But it would have been to that artist who lodged at 'Witch's Dower' in the summer."

"You knew him too?"

"He came in here once or twice did Mr. Shaw. Pleasant gentleman, older than she was. Left suddently."

"Why to him?"

"Stands to reason," Hattie said. "They'd been thick as thieves the summer before. Going everywhere together, and then he leaves, and she never wrote any other letters to anyone. None to him either, come to that. But the last afternoon—perhaps I did glance at the name. I can't remember now, but it came back to me. Miss Leah was particular that nothing should be said, but as she's told you—it was a terrible time for everybody."

"Yes. Indeed it must have been." Levanah had never really thought of affairs at Kingsmead as having repercussions over at the village. Her aunt had always forbidden them to gossip with the local people, and it was obvious that they, out of awed respect for Miss Leah, had kept many matters to themselves.

"Will there be anything else, Miss Levanah?" Hattie Jenks cocked her head to one side, hoping that she had not said too much. The girl had a queer, waking look on her face, as if she were coming out of a dream.

"Nothing else." Levanah paid, deposited her few purchases in her bag, and went out. The name "Shaw" lodged in her mind. "Levanah Shaw." That might have been her name if the mysterious Mr. Shaw had come back to marry her mother.

It was all so simple that she stopped dead, bag dangling from her hand. Her mother, terrified by the accident that had killed her brother, had run to the village and sent some kind of message to her lover. Some prearranged signal, perhaps? Hattie Jenks had mentioned a ring. The girl in the portrait had worn a moonstone ring. Beth had sent the token and fled to "Witch's Dower" to bear her child, and when a week later her lover had not come she had killed herself.

"Levanah, good morning! You're in a brown study, aren't you?"

Cousin Wenna stood smiling in front of her. The older woman looked smart in a tiered coat of light golden-brown tweed, her head covered by a small bowler of matching velour. Under its rolled brim her face was pink and serene.

"I've been buying licorice. Do you want some?" Levanah rummaged in her bag.

"No, thank you. I'm past the age when I can make a pig of myself in public." Wenna grinned ruefully, her eyes kind. Levanah looked very childish and vulnerable in her hooded cape. "Were you going to come over and say goodbye to me, dear?"

"Yes, of course. I wanted to ask you if you'd look after 'Witch's Dower' for me," Levanah said eagerly. "I went down there to collect one or two things that belong to me, but I need the cottage to be aired and fires lit there from time to time. It would mean a lot to me."

"I'll go over regularly and keep everything spick-and-span," Wenna promised. "How are—matters at Kingsmead? Cousin Leah told me that you are to go to London."

"As a companion to a Mrs. Sarah Varney. My aunt hopes that an inferior position will 'curb my proud spirit.'" The girl made a small grimace.

"I'm sorry," Wenna said, "but it may be better for you to go away for a time. Leah was very angry and the story she had to reveal distressed her very much. You must try to see it from her point of view."

"I don't mind going away," Levanah said surprisingly. "It will be interesting to visit London and live in a different house. And one day I will come back. Aunt Leah can't make me stay away forever."

"Try not to bear resentment," Wenna urged. "Your aunt may seem harsh to you, but you were wrong to disobey her. Even though I'm aware you meant no harm, such goings on are very shocking."

"Oh, I'm still in deep disgrace," Levanah said lightly. "I am not allowed to speak to Mary at all, but you probably know that already. Miss Bishop is over at Kingsmead nearly every evening."

"I know." Wenna hesitated, then hurried on, "And Teddy will be home for Christmas."

"In time to mend Mary's broken heart," Levanah said ironically. "But she has no wish to marry Teddy, and I don't think that Teddy has any interest in her. Aunt Leah has a hard task ahead."

"And Caleb? Have you seen him?"

Levanah shook her head. She had not laid eyes on her cousin since she and Mary left "Witch's Dower" after trying to raise the witch.

"He'll make out," she said. "I'd better be on my way, Cousin Wenna. If I don't see you again before I leave, you'll remember about the cottage?"

"Yes, of course, but you'll be home for holidays."

"I'll come home when I'm ready," Levanah smiled, and for an instant her eyes glittered, amber slits in her pale, young face.

Wenna made her own few purchases and retraced her steps to the main highway. Charlotte Bishop was taking classes this afternoon. Wenna frowned slightly as she thought of her assistant. Charlie—as she insisted on being called—was cheerful and helpful. Leah was certainly encouraging her friendship with Mary, and no doubt the girl needed somebody outside the family in whom to confide, but there was something in Charlotte Bishop that set Wenna's teeth on edge.

Dismissing the teacher from her mind, Wenna walked on briskly over the bridge. On her right the ruins of the old monastery crowned the slopes of the hill. Edith Falcon often wandered there, but Wenna had not caught sight of her for weeks. Instead of turning into the school drive she continued walking, past the hill to where the land, becoming level again, was bounded by the high walls of Whittle Farm.

It was none of her business, of course, and Leah would be angry if she were to find out, but it was only charity to try and help. Without giving herself any more time to consider the matter Wenna pushed open the gate and went into the yard.

The solidly built Tudor manor was nowhere near as large or imposing as Kingsmead, but it had weathered the generations spendidly, only sinking a trifle more firmly into the earth. It reminded Wenna of the little stone house where she had been born and bred. Saron Farm had been tiny in comparison, but both had the same aura of permanency.

Wenna had not returned home for years. Sometimes she promised herself that she would go back some day, but she never had, for her roots were now too firmly entrenched in Marie Regina. To return home would be to bring back memories of her brief, youthful marriage. Her husband had been killed in a quarry accident, and she had not allowed herself to think of any man since, except for John Falcon, and his death had happened when she had scarcely begun to care for him.

"Mrs. Davies? What are you doing here?"

The voice, hostile and surprised, startled her. Cal Falcon, shoulders hunched against the cold, had come around the corner of the house and was staring at her.

Her mouth dried a little. He looked older than his years, and in his face was something of the same tenacity she had glimpsed in the farmhouse.

"I came—that is, I wondered how your mother was . . ." She hesitated.

"After eighteen years," he said slowly, "you begin to wonder how my mother is. That's generous of you, Mrs. Davies."

"Cousin Wenna," she said swiftly. "My mother was your grandmother's aunt. That makes me a relative."

"It also makes you dependent on Leah Simmons for your post at the Manor. You'd best be getting back there."

"I came to make a civil inquiry," Wenna said. "This isn't the first time that I've inquired after her. I always stop and speak whenever I see her."

"Very noble and self-sacrificing of you," he mocked. "I hope nobody saw you associating with a fallen woman."

"You're abominably rude!" she exclaimed, anger flashing in her.

"That's because I'm a bastard and haven't had the advantages of a gentlemanly upbringing," he retorted.

"You're bitter, for one so young," she said sadly.

"And you're stupid, for one so—" He had been going to say, "old," but looking at her he was aware of the clarity of her skin and the beautiful greenish color of her eyes.

"Yes. Perhaps I am." Anger fading, she stared at him with compassion. "I ought to have come long ago. It was foolish and selfish of me not to have come before, not to have made a friend of Edith, but I cast her off. I chose to live comfortably, to ignore what might offend Cousin Leah."

He said nothing but went on staring at her. After a moment she raised her hand in a gesture of defeat and turned away.

Her hand was on the latch of the gate when he said, "My mother has been drinking steadily for weeks. I try to prevent her but she hides bottles everywhere, and as she has control of her own money, she can buy where she chooses."

"I wish I could help," she said impulsively.

"Come in, if you like." He sounded indifferent, but she followed him round to the back door where a few hens scratched in the dirt.

She stepped into a low-ceilinged kitchen, neither dirty nor cluttered but subtly shabby. The fireplace was covered by a fine film of ash, plants on the sill drooped for lack of water, greasy dishes were piled neatly in the sink.

"The maids gave notice," Cal said, holding open the door. "I've tried to keep the house clean, but I've the animals to tend and I'm not much of a cook."

"I am an excellent cook," Wenna said, removing her hat and beginning to unfasten her coat. "Have you ham? Eggs? Lard for frying?"

"In the pantry."

"Get them for me. I'll light the range, and you can mend the fire while I prepare your meal."

"My mother is in her room."

"Then she can stay there for the moment. We'll eat together first and then I'll see what can be done for Edith."

She was tying an apron about her waist, her movements smooth, controlled. The boy watched her for a moment, fascinated by the curve of her breasts above the neat waistline, the shape of her hands.

"Go on, then," she said, without looking at him. "I'm hungry too."

Within half an hour the fire blazed brightly, and hot dishes steamed on the table. Cal, scrubbing his hands over the sink, sniffed appreciatively and enjoyed the sensation of hunger.

"Come and eat." Wenna was pouring tea with the absorbed air of a child playing hostess. "A man needs food."

"You know what happened?" He dried his hands roughly and came to sit at the table.

"I heard it from Levanah, but I'd often wondered. In the years since you were born ... I've suspected that Edith's lover might have been Leah's husband."

"I don't want to know anything about him. I don't want to hear what he was like, or why my mother did what she did." He speared bread on his knife and stared at her.

"Then we'll not talk about him," Wenna said calmly. "I fried some potatoes. Will you have some?"

"Was Mary—?" He hesitated.

"She knows that you're her half brother," she said. "It upset her, naturally."

"Naturally." He nodded gravely and then said, in a rush, "There was never anything between us, you know. If we had never discovered the truth, something might have happened, but as it is—"

"Mary's feelings were not deep," Wenna said with brutal kindness. "She will get over them quickly. And so will you."

"I always knew," Cal said slowly, "that my mother was unmarried. I grew up knowing that I couldn't play with the Falcons. Knowing that my mother

couldn't go to Kingsmead. My mother told me about
Levanah, told me that she was a bastard too. I used
to wonder sometimes why she was brought up with
Mary and Teddy when I wasn't allowed to go on
Falcon land, and yet my name is Falcon too. It
seemed wrong, unfair, but a child gets used to situa-
tions, gets accustomed to them."

"Levanah is going away," Wenna said. "She is going as companion to a Mrs. Varney in London."

"Because of what she did in the cottage?"

"Partly."

"I'm glad," he said unexpectedly. "I'm glad she's going. Ever since the very beginning, ever since we
started making the cottage fit to live in, I've been
afraid of her. It sounds so silly, so silly."

"She's a strange girl, but a lovable one. A sweet
girl."

"Sweet!" He gave a brief snort of laughter. "She has
the devil's kiss on her thigh. My mother told me the
old stories about the family. The witch who was
drowned in the pond. The one who was killed by
lightning. And Levanah has the mark. I saw it years
ago when she was little."

"Have another cup of tea."

She refilled his cup and rose neatly, untying the
apron. As she went toward the door she laid her hand
briefly on his shoulder.

Edith was propped on a pile of pillows with the
counterpane tossed over her legs. Wenna was shocked
at the change in the beautiful girl she had known.
The years had treated Leah more kindly, but Edith's
clear complexion was blotched with tiny-thread veins,
her blue eyes filmy, her hair lank with gray salting
the gold. She looked up from beneath her lashes with
a half-sullen, half-belligerent stare.

"Playing the Lady Bountiful, Cousin Wenna?" she inquired. "I thought that was Leah's chosen task."

"How are you, Cousin Edith?" Wenna came over and sat down on a chair near the bed.

The room was stuffy, dust-laden and untidy. Items of clothing were flung carelessly across the furniture, a row of empty bottles lined the windowsill, a tray of half-eaten food had been left on the floor.

"It is not much like Kingsmead, is it?" Edith said, her own eyes following the direction of the other's gaze. "And I am changed, am I not?"

"You are not well," Wenna excused.

"I am slightly drunk," Edith said. "Not completely so; that comes later. But I am not sober. To be sober is almost unbearable. Cal looks at me as if I were—dirty."

"You imagine it, surely!" Wenna exclaimed. "He thinks as much of you as he ever did."

"He knows that I made love to my sister's husband," Edith said. "He knows it now."

"He has always known that he is a—love child," Wenna soothed. "He cares nothing about his father. He has no interest in him at all."

"But he despises me now," Edith said. "He despises me because, if I had not made love to my sister's husband, he and Mary might have—"

"A childish infatuation. No more than that," Wenna said.

"I failed him," Edith said. "I failed everyone! I let Paul seduce me. I let him seduce me."

"And now you will stay here for the rest of your life, repenting what happened nearly twenty years ago!" Wenna said scornfully. "That's a fine end for a Falcon!"

"I wish I had been born into some other family,"

Edith said in maudlin fashion. "There is a curse on us all. I know it."

"I'll give you ten minutes," Wenna said, putting on her most schoolmistressy voice. "That will give you time to put on a fresh gown and comb the tangles out of your hair. I'll bring some fresh water."

"My head aches," Edith moaned.

"With the reek of brandy in here, I'm not surprised." Wenna went over to the window and pushed it wide.

"I need a drink," Edith said. "A small one, to steady my nerves. Look how my hands shake!"

"I'll make you some tea and some toast."

"I need a tot of brandy, not tea," Edith said pettishly.

"Tea will be better for you," Wenna said firmly. "And don't go sneaking any liquor out of your cupboards."

"There's none left. I'll have to send one of the maids over to Maidstone to buy more. Cal has stopped them from selling me any in the local inn."

"The maids have given notice." Wenna picked up a wastepaper basket and began to thrust the empty bottles into it. "If you want any brandy you'll have to go out and buy it yourself."

"That Levanah!" Edith cried. "It was her fault. I saw them in the old cottage through the window. She was chanting and dancing up and down. Evil! It was evil, Wenna."

"Levanah is going away," Wenna said shortly. "It's better if you put out of your mind what you saw at the cottage, and stop thinking about Cal's father."

"You needn't talk to me as if I were a child," Edith said irritably, pushing the hair out of her eyes.

"Then stop acting like one." Wenna opened the

door wider with her foot and carried the clinking
bottles through.

In the kitchen Cal sat, elbows on the table, another
cup of tea between his hands. A lock of fair hair
flopped over his brow. As Wenna entered he looked
up and gave her a tired grin.

"Your mother is getting up," Wenna said. "She's
suffering from guilt and self-pity, and that's an unpleasant combination. She'll get over it, but I'm afraid
you'll have to expect—"

"Bouts of drinking? They've been going on for
years, but they've gone worse recently. Even before
she came to the cottage she was drinking more heavily."

"I'll do what I can." She touched his shoulder again
and began to cut bread. The discarded basket of
empty bottles stood on the floor between them.

"I wish you could stay here," Cal said abruptly.

"To cook and clean? My job is teaching."

"You ought to have married," Cal said.

"I did," she said lightly.

"But you were widowed after a few months,
weren't you? You ought to have married again."

"I must pin an official complaint to the church
door," she joked.

"I mean it," he insisted. "You ought to have had a
husband and children."

"Must you talk as if I were senile?" she inquired.
"I'm only—well, never mind, but I'm not ready for a
wheelchair yet! If you've finished, watch the toast
while I take some hot water to your mother."

"I was rude when you came," he said, his glance
detaining her. "I'm sorry about that."

She nodded, accepting the apology, and poured
water from the kettle into a large enamel jug.

"And you don't look—whatever age you won't tell me," he blundered on.

"That's very nice of you," Wenna said gravely. "Watch the toast."

In the hall she paused for a moment, a smile curving her mouth. The temptation to throw back her head and laugh aloud for the sheer joy in living had not been so strong in years. And there was no reason for her not to visit the farm again. Leah might pay her salary, but she didn't own her body and soul.

She composed her mouth into its usual firm composure and went briskly up the stairs, the steam from the jug reddening her face.

Chapter VIII

The leaving had not been so bad. Mary had been permitted, under Leah's watchful eye, to say goodbye, but Charlotte Bishop had been waiting to go riding, and Mary had seemed embarrassed and resentful, as if she blamed her cousin for having taken her to "Witch's Dower" in the first place.

"You are to receive fifty pounds a year as Mrs. Varney's paid companion," Leah had said. "Also your keep. I wrote, on your behalf, telling her that you desired a change. I did not, of course, mention your disgraceful behavior at the cottage."

"You'll remember, Aunt, that my mother left the cottage to me?" Levanah had said softly. "I'd not want to come back and find that anything had ... happened to it."

"The wretched cottage will still be here," Leah had said. "But you need not hope to come back here for many months. Paid companions do not expect frequent or lengthy holidays."

She had given no more than the briefest goodbye, and one of the grooms had driven her to the station to catch her train. Teddy was expected home the following day and an orgy of polishing and cooking had begun. Mary had been bidden to hurry back from her ride so that her hair could be washed. Levanah, listening, caught a flash of something dark in Charlotte Bishop's face. It was gone in a moment, and then the teacher bowed coldly, wished Levanah a pleasant journey, and whisked Mary away as if she were protecting her from some infection.

It had been a wet month and rain still dripped from the trees and hedgerows as they drove to the station. Levanah had taken the picture, the crystal, and the little wooden statue from the cottage, and they now reposed at the bottom of one of her two suitcases. She herself, in brown coat and skirt and small green hat, looked, with her heavy red hair, like a fugitive leaf blown from one of the branches.

At the station she had been surprised to see Wenna. The older woman looked fresh and pleasant as she kissed her cheek.

"I thought I'd come and see you off," she said by way of greeting. "I had an idea that nobody would come."

"They're preparing for Teddy's arrival," Levanah said.

"And preparing Mary, no doubt." Wenna gave her a wry look. "This will be your first visit to London won't it?"

"Hardly a visit." Levanah grimaced slightly.

"An experience, anyway," Wenna corrected herself. "It will give you an opportunity to see that Marie Regina is not the whole world and what happens here is not a matter of great concern to the rest of the human race. And when you come back, 'Witch's Dower' will still be here."

"And so will my Aunt Leah," Levanah said, smiling.

"Cal sends you his best wishes," Wenna remembered as they stepped onto the platform to meet the approaching train.

"You've seen him?"

"Now and then." Wenna's face was hidden as she bent to lift one of the cases. "His mother is ... not very well. I've been helping out."

"I'm sorry not to have seen him," Levanah said. "Goodbye, Cousin Wenna."

"God bless you, my dear." Wenna stood for a moment and then walked swiftly away.

Now, with early afternoon darkened into evening, Levanah sat primly in the back of the cab she had hired at the station, and looked with interest at the hurrying crowds, and flaring gas jets of the city. The streets were narrower than she had pictured them, the buildings grimier, and the people seemed intent on their own business. Skirts, she noticed, were narrower than ladies wore them in Marie Regina, and many women carried large fur muffs. Hair, too, was looped and puffed with elaborate coils and ringlets with tiny hats perched dangerously over their eyes. There were gentlemen with opera capes flung back over one shoulder to display red silk linings. With several of the gentlemen were women in vividly flounced dresses with long embroidered coats and feather boas twisted around their necks. Their voices, coming to her through the partly open windows, were shrill and nasal.

They were leaving the city behind and rattling over cobbles to an arch in a wall that reminded her so much of Kingsmead that she felt an unexpected surge of homesickness.

"This is Varney House, Miss," the driver informed her, peering through a small trap in the roof.

"Oh, thank you." She alighted, paid the fare, and received her two suitcases as they were handed down. The cab rattled off, and she stood alone, conscious of the darkness, of the quiet street that stretched behind her, its gas lamps diminishing into glowworms of sparkling brilliance. After the warmth of the cab the air struck chill on her face, and she could hear the noises of the city faint and far off, muffled by the high houses and tall roofs.

For a moment she longed passionately to be at home again in her own room with the meadows and the woods of the estate around and the cottage hidden deep in its clearing. Then she remembered that her mother had sent a message of some kind to the man called Shaw who had rented the cottage for a brief summer. A man who, she was certain, had painted the picture of the girl with the moonstone ring. And the man had been a Londoner. It was as if she had seized the end of a thin and tangled skein of facts that would lead her, in the end, to the truth.

She picked up her two suitcases and went resolutely through the archway up to the house. It was a large building with shuttered windows and a dim glow coming from the fanlight above the front door. The yard was enclosed by high walls, and not a bush or tree softened the stark outlines of stone and brick.

The bell pealed briskly, a daytime sound that was unexpectedly cheering. Only a moment elapsed before bolts were drawn and the door opened to the length of a chain.

"Yes?" The voice was sharp, female, and unfriendly.

"Miss Levanah Falcon, to see Mrs. Varney." The girl drew herself up in unconscious defiance. If they expected a companion to come to the back door like a servant they could think again.

"She's expecting you." The chain was unhooked and the door opened by a thin woman in the garb of a parlormaid.

The hall was long and narrow, widening into a larger one from which doors led off in all directions. A graceful staircase curved to an upper landing. Thick carpets and velvet drapes gave an impression of luxury and a rather conservative formality of taste.

"Leave the suitcases, Miss. This way."

The maid tapped on one of the doors, opened it a little way, announced Levanah's name, and indicated to the girl that she was to go in.

The apartment was obviously a drawing room, furnished in the same heavy elegance as the hall. She had no time to take in more than a glimpse when a tall woman in a loosely flowing garment raised herself on the cushions of the sofa on which she was reclining and said, "Come and take off your things and sit by the fire, my dear. This is an ordeal for you, I'm sure."

"Mrs. Varney?" Levanah wondered if she were expected to curtsey or shake hands.

"Sarah. Call me Sarah. I detest formality."

"Sarah," Levanah said and sat down, unfastening her coat. Her eyes were fixed with intense curiosity on her employer.

Sarah Varney could have been any age between thirty and fifty. The olive tint of her skin, her blue-black hair, hinted at Italian or Spanish descent, but her eyes were a light, hard blue, her voice precise and unaccented.

"Did you have a pleasant journey?" she was inquiring. "My health is not good so I never travel these days. In my youth I did a great deal. My late husband was a colonel in the Indian Army, and I spent many years out east with him. Your aunt tells me you are an orphan."

"Yes, ma'am—Sarah."

"And the rest of your family? Tell me about them."

"I was brought up with my cousins, Mary and Teddy."

"Ah, yes! Young Lord Falcon! No, I don't know him personally, but after receiving your aunt's letter I did a little checking."

'If you know, then why ask me?' Levanah thought. Aloud she said, "I am not certain what my duties are. Your advertisement said 'companion,' but that . . ."

"Could cover a multitude of sins?" Sarah Varney laughed. "Or did you expect a fat old lady with two lapdogs? I wished for a companion, my dear, because I enjoy youthful company. You will find your duties very light. All I require is that you deal with some of my correspondence, undertake small shopping expeditions on my behalf, help me to entertain guests from time to time. You are discreet, I take it?"

"Yes." Levanah looked slightly surprised.

"I dislike gossip," Sarah Varney said briefly. "Yes, Mathilde, what is it?"

The thin parlormaid had appeared at the door again. "If you please, Mrs. Sarah, it's the new maid," the woman said hesitatingly.

"Has she broken more dishes? These Irish girls cannot pick up a plate without dropping it."

"The wine cellar. Thomas found her in the wine cellar," Mathilde said.

There was a brief pause. Levanah saw mistress and

maid exchange a long look. Then Sarah Varney said, "Has Thomas dealt with it?"

"As you would wish, Mrs. Sarah."

"I'll come down later. Levanah, my dear—such a pretty name, don't you think Mathilde?—you must be tired and hungry and longing to see your room. Mathilde will take you up, and you can unpack your things. This is a big house, so don't be afraid of disturbing anybody. The library is next to your bedroom. Borrow whatever books you choose."

It was evidently a dismissal for the night. Resisting an impulse to bob a curtsey Levanah followed Mathilde into the hall again and up the stairs to the upper landing. As they rounded the curve she glanced down through the balustrade and saw that Sarah Varney had come out into the hall and stood, the dark red folds of her gown billowing over the carpet, her black head bent in thought.

"This is your room, miss." The maidservant pushed open the door and stood aside. "The bathroom is just down the hall and the library is here."

"Mathilde is a French name, isn't it?" Levanah inquired.

"Yes, miss."

"But you're not French?"

"By descent only, miss"

"Have you been with Mrs. Varney for a long time?"

"Since her childhood, miss. Mrs. Varney was born in Martinique and raised there. She married off the family plantation."

"I see. Oh, but this is a very handsome room!" Levanah looked round at the brocade hangings and carved furniture with pleasure.

"It's well enough," Mathilde said grudgingly. "It belonged to Mrs. Varney's parents. The master left it to Mrs. Sarah, but she's never been keen on it. She and I—we both like the country better."

"Then why doesn't she sell?"

"Terms of the Will, miss. Mr. Varney had a sentimental fondness for the house. Shall I have a tray sent up for you? Mrs. Sarah likes to dine late and alone."

"Yes, thank you. I don't eat very much."

"You're too thin, miss, if you'll excuse my saying so," Mathilde said. "A young girl needs nourishment. Janet will bring something tasty."

"Is that the Irish girl? I hope she doesn't drop it."

"Janet is from Cornwall, miss. A good worker but a little simple-minded."

"Are there many servants?"

"Just myself and Janet and Thomas, miss. The cook doesn't live in."

"I see. Thank you." Levanah nodded smilingly and turned to her unpacking as Mathilde went out.

There was ample room for her clothes in the capacious wardrobe. The picture, the crystal, and the little carving she left in the suitcase. At the moment she was only feeling her way into the household and had no desire to reveal any of her own private concerns.

The windows of the room looked down into a tiny yard and beyond its walls were covered sheds and narrow alleys. Far off she could hear the sonorous hooting of ships' sirens down the river. The gas jets made pools of gold in the darkness.

She suspected that the district had once been an elegant residential area but had, over the years, deteriorated. A house as large as this needed a big garden, but this was cramped in a wilderness of stone and brick. She let the heavy curtains fall into place as the door opened again and a plump girl came in with a tray.

"Your food, miss." The girl set down the tray and turned a pale, round face, remarkable only for its lack of intelligence, toward Levanah.

"Are you Janet?" Levanah asked.

"Yes, miss. I'm Janet."

"Thank you, Janet."

"Yes, miss." Janet backed three steps, then went stolidly out, setting each foot down firmly as if she were planting it.

Levanah sat down to her supper. Chicken breasts in mushroom sauce, delicate spears of asparagus, and a raspberry tart thick with cream were attractively arranged on dishes patterned with tiny golden birds. There was coffee in a tall silver pot. Evidently companions were well fed at Varney House. Unexpectedly she discovered she was hungry.

Her meal over, she opened the door to the landing again. The house was silent and reminded her of the quietness of Kingsmead, but after a moment she became aware of a difference in the quality of each silence. Her own home had the timelessness of centuries in its walls. This house with its thick carpets and heavy drapes seemed to muffle sound deliberately.

She opened the adjoining door and jumped slightly as Sarah Varney's voice came to her from the depths of a wing-backed chair.

"Exploring already, my dear?"

"You said I could borrow a book if I wished."

"Yes, of course I did. There are many from which to choose." She waved her hand about the packed shelves. "Are you found of reading? My late husband was very studious. Some of these volumes are old and quite rare."

"They look very interesting," Levanah said politely. Her eye had been caught, not by the books, but by a lamp on the desk. Its base was carved into the shape of a woman with many arms, each arm enclosing a gas jet.

"I see you are admiring Kali," Sarah Varney said. "We bought her in India, and I had her made into a lamp."

"Kali?"

"Goddess of Destruction. Her hair is twined with snakes, you see."

"Yes. Yes, I see."

The figure was of ivory, yellowed with age and cool to her fingers when she touched it.

"The other lamp is a Dugda Buddha, used in certain blood and fertility rites. We bought that in India too." Sarah Varney rose in a graceful, flowing movement. An emerald on the index finger of her left hand gleamed in the light. She moved without haste to the shelves and ran her nail along the spine of some books with a little, rasping noise.

"Do you like romance?" she inquired. "But all young girls like romance, don't they? Let me see. We have Ouida—rather florid in style, but she tells an excellent story. Or do you prefer poetry?"

"I don't mind," Levanah said.

"Perhaps you were not interested in reading after all. Perhaps you merely wanted a peek into the library?"

"Mrs. Varney, I—"

"Sarah. It's so pleasant to be called by my Christian name. And you are free to go where you please, my dear. I want you to feel completely at home here.

Wander where you please, except in the basement. The servants like to keep their own quarters private. Ah! here are some ladies' journals. These will provide you with some light reading. Now, have you everything you need?"

She spoke solicitously, the emerald gleaming on her narrow, olive hand.

"Yes, indeed. Janet brought a delicious supper." Levanah accepted the magazines. "She didn't drop anything, either."

"Drop anything?"

"Like the Irish girl," Levanah said.

"Of course." The olive knuckles relaxed. "Poor Biddy! I had high hopes for her but she has proved most unsuitable. She is in the habit of flirting with every male she meets! I trust you don't have the same habit."

"I don't think so," Levanah said in bewilderment.

"But a sweetheart? Surely there is someone at home for whom you have a *tendresse?*"

"There isn't anybody," Levanah said firmly.

"Untouched." The long fingers patted her cheek. "Charming, quite charming. Run along, my dear. In the morning you must write to your aunt to let her know that you have arrived safely."

"Good night." Clutching her magazines, Levanah accepted her second dismissal of the evening. As she glanced back, Sarah was leaning over the lamp, tracing with her finger the convolutions of the snakes in the head of the many-armed goddess.

The tray had been removed, the bedclothes folded back, and a stone hot water bottle placed between the sheets. There were biscuits and a jug of lemonade on the table.

Levanah, having paid a brief visit to the cavernous bathroom where the water had been pleasantly warm in the round, poppy-patterned basin, took off her clothes and hung them neatly over the back of the chair.

The long mirror on the wardrobe door reflected her nakedness. She was too small and too thin, with none of Mary's pretty curves. The purple crescent was a dark stain on her thigh. She grimaced at her own face, at the beaky nose in the narrow cheeks, the slanting amber eyes, the uncurling red hair that dipped in a fringe above her sandy brows.

After a few moments she grew weary of contemplating her own plainness, and wriggled into her nightdress. The figure in the glass turned from nymph to angel, red hair haloed by the gaslight.

She climbed into bed, curving her toes over the stone hump of the bottle, plumping up the pillows, and opening the magazine. Aunt Leah never subscribed to magazines, and she had a pleasant half-hour reading advice to ladies on how to beautify their complexions, how to refuse an invitation gracefully, how to choose a servant wisely. There were advertisements for corsets, for health salts, and for shoes with high heels.

Her lashes drooped and the magazine slid down to the thick carpet. Against the closed window the curtains hung heavily and the gaslight cast shadows across the ceiling. The silence of the house folded each room in secrecy.

A clock, striking loudly, woke her from a confused dream of Aunt Leah. In the dream her aunt had stretched out many pairs of arms, and on each finger of each hand gleamed a moonstone ring.

She sat up against the high pillows, threads of the

dream still tangling the edges of her mind, and listened. The sound had ceased. It had not, she thought mistily, sounded much like a clock at all, but more like the tang of metal on metal.

She pushed back the covers and padded over to the window, drawing back an edge of the curtain. Fog swirled beyond the pane and the moon was hidden, but the faint hissing of voices came up from the yard below.

The sash window slid up a couple of inches without noise. She crouched at sill level, her ear to the cold, stifling, yellow air.

"Must you make so much noise?" That was Mathilde's voice, but low and uneasy.

"I let the shutter clang too loudly." A man's voice, discreetly hushed. Levanah guessed that it belonged to Thomas, the manservant.

"Be silent, both of you. The Master dislikes uncontrolled noise and undisciplined conduct."

That was Sarah Varney's precise, unaccented voice.

"The fog is getting thicker, Mrs. Sarah." Mathilde's voice again, concerned and chiding.

"We will be inside again soon, so let's not fuss," Sarah Varney's voice said.

The fog lifted briefly, and for an instant the figures below were revealed as they moved slowly across the yard. Straining her eyes, Levanah discerned shapes but not features. Four cloaked shapes with hoods drawn over their heads against the cold. Sarah Varney, Mathilde, the manservant, and a smaller figure who walked in the midst of them as if she walked in a dream.

It was a glimpse only and then the fog closed in again, and a door closed somewhere, the voices and footsteps muffling into blurred whispers and shuffles. It was colder than Levanah had realized. She closed the window and let the heavy curtain fall back into place.

After a moment she stood upright and went over to the door, opening it and peering out into the corridor. The lights had been dimmed but it was still possible to see, when she looked over the banisters, that the hall was empty, the doors closed.

She hesitated, wondering whether or not to risk going downstairs, when a door at the back of the hall opened. She stepped away from the rail and watched as a tall man emerged. Tall and black-haired, he was a stranger to her, and something in his bearing told her that he was not a servant. From above it was impossible to see his face, but he wore a dark cloak as the others had done, its pointed hood folded back over his shoulders. His hands, emerging through the side slits in the garment, gleamed whitely. A ring on the index finger of his left hand flashed fire as he raised it. Then he entered one of the lower rooms and the door swung shut behind him.

A cold draft flickered the gaslights and ruffled the pile of the thick carpet. Levanah was suddenly glad that the man had not looked up and seen her. It was so cold where she stood that the flesh shriveled on her bones as if she were growing old in a few seconds.

In terror of something she couldn't understand, she turned and went swiftly back into her own room. The bed was warmer, but she burrowed deeper into the covers, wrenching up the heavy quilt until it almost concealed her.

Out of its depths her amber eyes peered, bright and suspicious as the eyes of a fox. The room was pleasant and luxurious, but there was safety in her cocoon of sheets and quilt. Just before she slept she heard a ship's siren hoot dimly somewhere beyond the fog.

Chapter IX

Leah, drinking her morning tea, glanced through the newspaper. Her eyes scanned the close-printed columns with academic interest. Nothing that happened on the outside world meant as much to her as the events within her own family, but it was necessary to keep abreast of the news. However, the information in this morning's edition was as uninteresting as ever. Funds to aid the victims of the San Francisco earthquake were still being begged months after the event. A woman had tried to make a speech in Parliament Square demanding the right to vote, and been hauled off by policemen. A girl, believed to have been Irish and unemployed, had been fished out of the Thames. 'Suicide,' Leah thought, 'is ultimately so weak-willed.'

She put the newspaper down, finished her cup of tea, and rose, smoothing her skirt over her hips. It would be pleasant to drive down into the village to inspect the flower arrangements for the New Year

Services at the church, but there were the menus to be discussed with Cook, Mary's new dress to be altered, gifts for the orphans at Maidstone Foundlings' Home to be wrapped, and Teddy had declared he would like cheese soufflé for lunch.

Her brows creased as she thought of Teddy. Although she would not admit it, his coming home had been a disappointment. He had expressed what Leah considered an inordinate amount of disappointment over Levanah's absence. "A Falcon earning her living as a paid companion! Aunt Leah, what possessed you to allow such a thing?"

He had grown and filled out during his first term at University. She had to look up at him now.

"Levanah has been a very foolish, disobedient girl," Leah had said. "She was becoming quite a bad influence on Mary. And she was very discontented. At least she has an opportunity to make a life for herself."

"Her life is here, at Kingsmead with us," Teddy said.

"My dear Teddy, Levanah will not always live at Kingsmead," Leah said. "She may marry one day."

"As her mother never did," Teddy said.

Startled, she looked at him. Her nephew, although the most good-natured of young men, was not given to deep or analytical thoughts, which made his occasional penetrating remark all the more surprising.

"You know about Beth? About my sister?"

"I've known for some time that she was never married and that she killed herself just after Levanah was born. The parents of one of the boys at the school had heard about the case. Does Levanah know?"

"I believe so."

"It was very good of you to rear her," he said. "We owe you a great deal, Aunt."

He did not, to her relief, mention Edith or Cal. She would have found it painful to have to explain yet again why she had cut her sister out of her life.

"Levanah will enjoy her taste of independence." She had changed the subject adroitly. "It is Mary who worries me. She needs to get out more. I look to you to encourage her a little. She has missed you a great deal."

"She seems content with Miss Bishop's friendship," Teddy said cheerfully. "Those two are as thick as thieves."

Leah, thinking of that remark, frowned. Teddy had sounded completely unconcerned, and, far from resenting the teacher, he had escorted both her and Mary to the local festivities.

The school had been closed for a month over Christmas, which meant that Charlotte Bishop had had a great deal of spare time, most of which had been spent with Teddy and Mary. The young woman, Leah decided irritably, lacked tact.

She sighed and then stiffened slightly as voices sounded from the courtyard. Mary and Charlotte Bishop were riding their bicycles across the cobbles. Mary's purchase of the gleaming machine had annoyed Leah intensely, but she had said nothing. She had even held her peace when Mary had come in wearing one of the new divided skirts.

'Better divided skirts and a bicycle,' Leah thought, 'than blasphemous orgies in that wretched cottage.' She composed her face into a smile as the two of them came in.

"It's such a fine day, Mother, that we thought we'd

take a spin along the London road," Mary said by way of greeting.

"Must you use slang, dear? Good morning, Miss Bishop."

"Good morning, Mrs. Simmons." The teacher shook hands briskly.

"It is all right for me to go, isn't it?" Mary asked.

"I suppose so, but it would be polite to find out Teddy's plans for the day," Leah said.

"Teddy is going to Maidstone to see some friends there," Mary said.

"Miss Bishop, would you excuse us for a moment?" Leah asked.

"Certainly, I'll wait in the courtyard," the young woman said promptly.

Leah closed the door on her retreating back and turned to face her daughter. Mary's face bore the faintly mutinous expression that often settled upon it these days.

"We wanted to make an early start," she said.

"You have the entire day ahead of you," Leah said. "Doesn't it seem a little selfish of you not to allow your cousin some part of it."

"But Teddy has made his own plans," Mary argued. "He really isn't interested in what Charlie and I do."

"Such a ridiculous nickname! That young woman is positively insinuating herself into the family."

"You don't like her because she's my friend," Mary said sullenly. "You don't want me to make any friends. You never did!"

"That is absolute nonsense," Leah said wearily. "I encouraged your friendship with Miss Bishop. I regarded her as a sensible, healthy-minded girl, but when Teddy came home—"

"Stop pushing Teddy at me!" Color flamed in

Mary's white face. "He's not the least bit interested in me, and I've told you over and over that I'll never marry him."

"You never make the smallest effort to attract him," Leah chided. "That blue dress with the little fur jacket suits you beautifully, and you've worn it once since I had it made for you. How can you expect anybody to look at you twice when you make such a perfect fright of yourself?"

"All you can think about is me finding a husband!" Mary flashed. "Well, I might not want to find a husband at all. And if I do, it'll not be Teddy, so do leave well alone!"

"I don't understand you," Leah said helplessly. "I've always done my best for you. You know that! And yet you constantly defy me, over and over. I cannot understand you."

"If you've finished," Mary said stiffly, "may I go now, please? Charlie and I have a considerable distance to go. We thought we'd have lunch along the way and then turn back."

"Unchaperoned," Leah said in disgust. "In my young days no girl went unchaperoned in a public place."

"Which didn't prevent both your sisters from bearing bastards!" Mary flamed.

Leah's hand struck her daughter's cheek hard. For a moment they glared at each other. Then Mary swung on her heel, walked out and slammed the door. Leah sat down, staring in a kind of horror at her tingling fingers. Mary was her own child, the sweetly pretty girl she herself had always wanted to be, the one blessing of her failed marriage. All her life she had been obedient and gentle, until she had been corrupted by Levanah and Cal. Well, Levanah was out of the way for a long time, Leah hoped. But Cal Falcon still lived at Whittle Farm. Cal Falcon should never have been born at all. He had been born out of her husband's trust and her sister's shame.

Edith's face rose up in Leah's mind, not haggard as it was now, but serenely beautiful as it had been when she was a girl. Paul Simmons had admired Edith, but he had married Leah, and then betrayed her. And Edith had stayed on in Marie Regina, flaunting her bastard. Beth, who had also borne a love child, had paid the price by committing suicide and would burn in hell forever. Edith was still alive, still breathing.

'I will make her leave,' Leah thought. 'I will drive her away if it's the last thing I do.'

She kept the picture of Edith firmly in her mind as she went out to order the trap harnessed. Teddy had talked, a little wistfully, of thinking about buying one of the new motorcars. Leah hoped fervently that he would reconsider. She hated the smell and the noise of the things even more than she loathed the shiny, two-wheeled machines that Mary and Miss Bishop rode about so shamelessly.

It was a cold, clear morning with a fine golden haze over the countryside. The pale sunlight gleamed on the spire of the church and the roofs of the houses. Snug in its hollow between river and graveyard, Marie Regina dreamed into the New Year.

Leah drove over the bridge past the hill on which the ruins of the monastery brooded. Her mouth was firmly set, her eyes implacable. She could not remember the last time when she had stopped at Whittle Farm.

The latch opened smoothly, and she stood within the yard. The stones were weed-free and the net curtains across the windows were clean. She frowned a little. One of the servants had mentioned that the Whittle maids had given notice some time back.

The front door was slightly ajar. For a moment she hesitated. Then she walked forward quietly, pushed the door wider, and went into the narrow hall. The parlor and dining room were, she knew, on the left. On the right, a short corridor led to the big kitchen. She could see that the kitchen door was partly open and the sound of voices issued from it.

She went noiselessly to the door and looked in. The large room was clean, fragrant with the scent of baking bread, warm with fireglow. Two people were sitting at the table, drinking tea. The boy Cal had his back to her and was hunched, peasant fashion, with his elbows on the table. Cousin Wenna was at the end of the table, her profile toward Leah's view, her brown hair drawn into a heavy bun. Her flushed cheeks, the laughter lines at the corners of her eyes, the swell of her breasts, above the apron tied about her waist, all were imprinted with new meaning on Leah's mind.

"—hoping to persuade Edith to have her hair styled," Wenna was saying. "If she puts on a little weight, why it will take years off her."

"She looks better already," Cal said. "Everything looks better. You'll never know how grateful we are to you."

"Dear Cal! Your friendship has made such a difference to me," Wenna said.

His hand left the cup he was holding and moved to cover the square capable fingers of the woman. In the tableau there was a warmth and an intimacy that told its own story.

Silently Leah backed away and went into the yard

again. She moved cautiously as if a sudden jerk might break her into pieces. That Cousin Wenna and Cal Falcon should be on terms of such intimacy was a fact that struck her with the force of a blow.

She was conscious of such violent anger that her temper with Mary faded into insignificance. Cousin Wenna had been a young widow when she had come from the farm in Wales to make her home in Marie Regina. She had been glad of the opportunity to teach at the Manor School. She had been grateful for Leah's friendship, so grateful that the idea that she might crave a home of her own had never entered Leah's head.

But to defy the unwritten rule and go to Whittle Farm, no doubt with the object of seducing Cal. A woman of forty and a boy! It was absurd and obscene, almost as shocking as the notion of Cal and Mary making love.

She had mounted to the driving seat and was returning along the road, though she had no memory of having turned the horse and trap. In her mind a series of ugly scenes unfolded as if she were watching a play. Cousin Wenna, sly-eyed and big-breasted, leaning white and wanton over the boy. Cousin Edith, unaware of the snake in her alcoholic Eden, smiling at the two of them sitting, dressed and prim, in the new-scrubbed kitchen. Terrible scenes that sprang from Leah's own years of frustrated continence.

A figure was moving about on the hill. Her eyes had always been sharp and she had no difficulty in recognizing her sister. The scene in her mind changed. Now the boy and the woman enjoyed clandestine embraces while Edith, unsuspecting, walked on the high hill.

Leah stopped the trap and, climbing down, began

to mount the slope. At this time of the year the clustering apple trees were bare, the long grass frost-rimed. The wind cut keenly through her black garments and hood. She had worn black for nearly twenty years, not out of mourning for the husband who had betrayed her, but out of hatred for him.

Arrived at the top where the ruins of the monastery untidied the skyline, she paused, hand to her side to stifle a stitch, and looked about her. Edith seemed to have vanished for the moment, and then she saw her again, sitting on a fallen block of masonry in the shadow of two standing walls.

"Edith! Edith, I have to talk to you." Leah raised her voice slightly, and Edith turned her head toward her.

With a little shock of jealous rage, Leah saw that her sister did, in truth, look very different from the distraught woman who had hammered on the front door of Kingsmead so short a time before. Edith had always had a beautiful bone structure. Today the wind had whipped color into her high cheekbones and her eyes had regained some tinge of their Madonna blue.

"Leah." She acknowledged her sister's presence with a brief nod but made no attempt to rise.

"Edith." Leah strode over and stood, looking down at the younger woman.

"You don't often walk up here," Edith said. There was a faintly ironic inflection in her voice. It increased as she said, "I'm quite sober, you know, if you have anything particular to say to me."

"I hope I may be allowed to greet my sister when I please," Leah said calmly, sitting down by Edith.

"After nearly twenty years this sudden yearning for my company is a little—strange," Edith said.

"It was you who came first to me," Leah said. "I'm not blaming you. It pleased me that, even after everything that has happened, you still came to me for help when you saw what was happening. It proved, I think, that you still regard me with a certain respect."

"You sent Levanah away," Edith said. "Wenna told me she'd gone to London."

"About Cousin Wenna," Leah began. "Do you remember when we were girls?"

Edith interrupted. "Do you remember our London season, when we were presented at Court? Do you remember the dress I wore? Bustles were coming in then and mine was of cream lace with tiny blue flowers, and I had three ostrich feathers in my hair. I was greatly admired."

"Were you? I don't recall those days very clearly," Leah said briefly.

"But you were not so greatly admired, were you?" Edith said. The blue eyes gleamed spite for a moment. Then Edith laughed softly. "You never did have many beaux, did you? Poor Leah! how you must have hated sitting with Mam while I waltzed past."

"And in the end you never married at all," Leah said.

"Only because you did everything in your power to prevent it," Edith said. She sounded, not resentful, but wearily amused. "You took Paul away from me and wed him yourself. I think that was why I allowed him to seduce me. I took him back again."

"He didn't stay very long," Leah said.

"He gave me a child," Edith said. "You'd have had Cal off me too when he was a baby, wouldn't you? Just as you took Levanah when poor Beth killed herself. It would have suited you very well if I'd died as well, and then you could have reared my son as one of your possessions. But I didn't die, and because you couldn't have my son you cast him out. You tried to make him ashamed he'd ever been born."

"Your son is a bastard," Leah said coldly.

"So is Beth's child, but Levanah was reared as a little lady at the great house, wasn't she? And a fine bitch she proved, didn't she?"

"I can't deny it," Leah said.

"So you'll not get my son," Edith said. "He's a man grown and a good worker, and a proud man, too, for all that you despise him. And so you may rest content with Teddy and Mary."

"Cal is, as you say, a man," Leah agreed. "There's another who's noticed that."

"Your daughter will have to look further than her own half brother for a mate," Edith said, with an air of triumph.

"I was speaking of Cousin Wenna," said Leah.

"What of her?"

"She's down at the farm now," Leah said. "While you stroll about up here, dreaming of past gaieties, Wenna Davies is down there with your son."

"I know," Edith said calmly. "I've high hopes in that direction."

"Edith Falcon, have you completely lost your senses?" Leah demanded.

"Wenna came to us when we were in great trouble," Edith said. "She's been very kind. Cal—he needs kindness as we all do. You never understand that."

"I'm not speaking of kindness," Leah said angrily. "I'm speaking of Cousin Wenna who's forty if she's a day and your son, holding hands, joking together."

"She'll make him a good wife," Edith said placidly.

"I'll not allow it," Leah said. Her eyes were cold as the wind that swirled the grass at their feet.

"You cannot prevent it," Edith said, rising slowly and pulling her hood more securely over her silver-streaked hair. "I won't make old bones, Leah. I've been drinking for years out of loneliness and despair, but since Wenna came to see us, I've not been so unhappy. She'll make Cal a good wife and she's not too old to have children who'll live at Whittle Farm. Generations of Cal and Wenna's children, Leah, living at Whittle Farm."

"You bitch!" Leah said.

"Go home and look to your own child," Edith said scornfully. "While you run to me with tittle-tattle about my son, the whole district is whispering about the unnatural friendship between Mary and that Bishop woman!"

Behind Leah's eyes something exploded. The wind, the grass, the ruins were misted with red and her heart beat rapid drumbeats in her ears. Her hand closed on something rough and hard. Edith's face rose up out of the encircling mist, and then was gone.

Leah was shaking so much that her legs buckled beneath her, but the mist was clearing, her heartbeats steadying. She went to her sister and knelt down, her hand reached out to touch the bloodied mass of pulped flesh and bone. The jagged stone lay near Edith's head. Leah could not remember even picking it up.

"Edith," she said, but her sister's mouth gaped silently.

It was not possible that a moment ago she had been alive, and now was dead. People couldn't die between one heardbeat and the next.

She stood up, aware that the hem of her skirt was soaked from the melting frost. After a moment she began to run, clumsily, her hair escaping in wisps from its chignon.

"Looked half-demented, poor creature," Jake said later, describing it to a fascinated circle of his customers at the inn. "Just driving from Maidstone I was, minding my own business, when down the hill she comes. 'Come quickly!' she says to me. 'There's been a terrible accident. A stone has fallen on my sister and she's hurt bad.' Of course I outs of the wagon and runs up with her, don't I? And there's Miss Edith laying there. Once glance and I can tell she's gone, but Miss Leah is tugging at my coat saying, 'She can't be dead. She's my sister.'"

"I heard as how there was bad blood between them when Miss Edith was alive."

The speaker, a comparative stranger, having lived in the village for only about five years, received a concerted glare.

Then Jake said reluctantly, "Well, there's no use pretending they were close friends. Miss Leah being so religious and Miss Edith having a love child—not that I'm saying a word against young Caleb, mind! He's a fine young fellow and that farm's a credit to him. But there's no denying Miss Leah resents him, and no denying that Miss Edith sometimes took a drop too much."

"Miss Leah's had a lot of grief," another said.

"Aye! that's true," Jake agreed. "Her husband running off, her brother being killed when his horse reared, poor Miss Beth—"

"A lovely girl," said Tom Stone, staring into his tankard. "A lovely girl."

"But strange," said Amos. "A strange girl."

"A tragic girl," Jake said with an air of finality. "And now, poor Miss Edith. And Miss Leah hoping to mend the breach between them both, hoping for a reconciliation."

"Is that a fact?" Tom asked.

"A fact, or I may be struck where I stand!" Jake vowed. "Miss Leah told me that she was on her way to see Miss Edith at the farm when she caught sight of her up on the hill. She turned back and was halfway up the hill when Miss Edith saw her. She moved away, Miss Leah says, and then the stone fell from the wall."

"I've said it before, and I'll say it again," David Jenks said. "Those ruins are a public danger. Someone ought to do something."

"Nobody's been hurt up there before," Amos objected. "A chance in a million, I'd say."

"At the moment of reconciliation," Jake said.

"Poor Miss Edith!" someone said.

"Her skull cracked like an eggshell," Amos reminded them with gloomy relish. "The Coroner said her bones were very brittle. Poor Miss Edith!"

"And poor Miss Leah," Jake said. "She blames herself, I'm afraid. She feels that if Miss Edith had not been startled by seeing her, she would not have moved away. Fate is an odd thing."

"And Miss Edith was such a very pretty girl," said David Jenks. "The prettiest of the three sisters. These younger Falcons are nothing to her. Even Miss Mary is nothing against what Miss Edith once was."

"Charlotte Bishop wouldn't agree with you," Amos said.

"Now that's enough of that," Jake said sharply. "I'll have no talk of that kind in here, if you please."

There was a general mumbling and shuffling of feet, but Amos changed the subject. "Mrs. Davies helped with the funeral arrangements, I'm told. A nice lady that. My little granddaughter can write as pretty as a picture now, and she was reckoned to be backward for her age."

"Mrs. Davies will have more on her mind than the teaching of children before long," Tom said.

"Many funerals lead to a wedding," Jake said.

"Stranger matches have turned out well," Amos said judicially.

"He has the farm and there's a piece of land up in Wales that goes to Mrs. Davies when her old mother dies," Tom remembered.

"A wedding," said Jake, with an air of putting an end to the discussion, "should cheer us all up."

Chapter X

"Is everything well with your family?" Sara Varney asked, glancing across to Levanah, who sat reading a letter.

"My aunt has sent news," Levanah said, looking up. "Her sister has died."

"Another aunt?"

"Aunt Edith. She, that is to say . . . she and Aunt Leah never got on together very well. But Aunt Leah is very upset by her death."

"I hope it was not a long illness," Sarah said in concern.

"An accident. There are the ruins of an old monastery overlooking the village," Levanah explained. "A stone fell from them and killed her."

"How terrible! Does this mean that you will require some time off in order to attend the funeral?"

"The funeral is tomorrow," Levanah said, "but Aunt Leah says there is no need for me to attend. I wonder if I ought to go into black."

"My dear, surely not!" Sarah exclaimed. "You were not particularly fond of this aunt, were you?"

"I scarcely knew her," Levanah said honestly. Her eyes had returned to the elegant copperplate writing.

'Not all my tidings are gloomy,' Leah had written. 'You will be surprised to hear that Cousin Wenna Davies and Caleb Falcon are to be married very quietly after a suitable period of mourning has elapsed. The disparity in age will cause comment, I fear, but Cousin Wenna knows her own mind. She will not, of course, continue to teach at the Manor School. I hope that you will make yourself useful to Mrs. Varney and not give any cause for complaint.'

Cal and Cousin Wenna to be married was such an incredible piece of news that Levanah found it difficult to assess her own reactions. She had always hoped, without putting the hope into words, that one day Cal would look at her as if she were beautiful. Cousin Wenna was old. The idea of her as Cal's wife was so ludicrous that Levanah set it aside to be considered later.

"Will you be wanting anything done in town this morning?" she asked her employer.

"Let me think." Sarah tapped her teeth with the handle of her teaspoon. "You could call at the wine merchants' for me. They have some very good Burgundy in, and I'd like to order a dozen bottles. Oh, and I need some tapestry silks. That pearl-gray shade and another skein of the aquamarine."

"Shall I go now?"

"Yes, my dear. That would be very good of you."

Working for Mrs. Varney, Levanah thought as she went to get her hat, was in many ways not like working at all. Her employer was unfailingly polite and sweet-tempered, and Levanah's duties were so light that she sometimes wondered why Sarah needed a companion at all. All that she was required to do, apart from running errands, was to read aloud for an hour or two every day while the older woman worked at her tapestry, and do a little dusting from time to time. For part of every afternoon she was left to her own devices while Sarah rested, and at ten o'clock Mathilde or the stupid Janet would bring up hot milk and biscuits, and her employer would bid her a cordial good night.

There had been no repetition of the mysterious activities she had glimpsed on that first night, and she had never again seen the tall stranger in the black cloak. There were times when Levanah was half-inclined to believe that she had dreamed the whole thing.

The house itself was large, silent, and luxurious, but apart from the unusual lamps in the library there was nothing mysterious or bizarre about it, unless one counted the small number of domestics kept, and the scarcity of visitors. Levanah, however, coming from Kingsmead, where visitors were also rare, discounted such a circumstance as unimportant.

She let herself out into the quiet courtyard and went briskly down the road. The houses at each side were tall, terraced buildings that might once have been elegant but were now undeniably shabby, like women past their prime.

She turned at the end of the road into the main thoroughfare, wrinkling her nose at the usual scents of fish and meat, and fog, and rotting vegetables that drifted from the direction of the river. She had begun to find her way about the city now and liked it less at each excursion. "Witch's Dower" lay like a jewel in her memory.

'One day,' she promised herself as she stepped along the hard pavements, 'I'll go back. I'll take possession of what is mine, and I'll pay Aunt Leah back for driving me away.'

She ordered the Burgundy, acquired the tapestry silks, and went on walking along aimlessly. Sara Varney never expected her to return at any stated time. Indeed, she had made it clear that Levanah was to please herself by exploring.

"And then you can come back and tell me about it," Sarah had said. "I am such a stay-at-home myself that I look forward to amusing bits of gossip."

Not that Levanah had brought back much in the way of gossip, but she had seen one of the members of the royal family driving past, had watched a fight between two street traders that had ended with grapefruit being hurled about the street, and had stood on tiptoe to see a well-known music hall comedian perform an impromptu turn for the benefit of some people waiting to attend a matinee.

Today she stopped in front of the plate-glass window of a shop displaying the latest in toques. Her own clothes were distressingly youthful, and she craved something with a bird of paradise on top that would give her an air of elegant sophistication. There was, however, nothing on the waxen heads to bring any enthusiasm to her eyes, and she turned away indifferently to glance in the next window, where some swathes of golden brown velvet drew attention to a sparkling necklace and some bracelets.

She moved closer, flattening her nose against the glass. It was not the jewelry that had caught her attention, but a framed picture leaning against the stand. It was simply the picture of a willow tree, its branches drooping over greenish water. It didn't look much like any tree she had ever seen growing, but when she stepped back it was like every willow she had ever imagined, its trunk proudly enduring, its branches heavy with grief. Across the corner of the painting the name Shaw was slanted. Inside the shop an elegant lady, who looked more like a rich customer than a salesgirl, minced forward.

"The picture in the window? Is it for sale?" Levanah asked.

"The Michael Shaw painting? Yes, miss."

"How much is it?"

"One hundred guineas, miss." The elegant lady allowed herself a glance of faintly patronizing amusement at Levanah's modest costume.

"This Michael Shaw," she persisted, "are there other paintings by him?"

"I believe so, miss," the other said, "but I don't think you'll find any at less expensive price. Most of his work is in galleries."

"You wouldn't know where he lives, I suppose?"

"Why, I'm not certain, miss. I think he lives abroad, in Paris mainly."

"He's a—distant connection of mine," Levanah said, wondering if the other believed her.

"I believe he does have a studio in Albemarle Street, miss."

"Albemarle Street. Thank you."

"You'll not be buying the picture then?" There was a slight sneer underlying the words.

"I have one already," Levanah said. Her voice was gentle but something flashed at the back of her amber eyes, and the salesgirl found herself opening the door as meekly as if she had made a profitable sale.

Albemarle Street was too far to walk. It would be necessary to take a cab, and even when she arrived he might not be there, or it might be the wrong Michael Shaw.

But this last possibility she discounted. There had been something in the quality of the painting in the window that reminded her of the painting she owned herself.

However, she had no intention of rushing off to Albemarle Street until she had decided what to do when she got there. This Michael Shaw might not be her father, and if he was, she had already waited nearly eighteen years to find him. A few more days wouldn't hurt. She intended to use them in order to think and plan, for there were questions to be asked.

It was almost lunchtime. Sarah Varney and Levanah had the meal together. The evening meal Levanah ate alone in her room. Mathilde had told her the mistress preferred to dine late. Very late, the girl assumed, for after her own repast she sat with Sarah, reading or playing chess, until the hot milk and the biscuits were brought in. The tapestry silks having been approved, the meal proceeded in its usual leisurely fashion. Sarah Varney ate fastidiously, flicking in stray crumbs from the corners of her mouth with the tip of her tongue, constantly dipping her fingers into the little bowl of rose-scented water at her place. There was a languor about her movements that hinted, not of weariness, but of power held in check.

"You're a strange girl," she said idly, breaking into Levanah's account of her morning's expedition.

"Because I like bird-of-paradise hats?"

"Because you talk of ordinary things and, all the time, extraordinary things are going on behind your eyes," Sarah said. "You speak very little of your family. One might almost suppose you to be indifferent to them."

"My aunt and I don't get on very comfortably," Levanah said.

"In her letter to me, Mrs. Simmons spoke of you as a difficult girl," Sarah said. "I took that to mean she didn't understand you. I find you charming, well mannered, and discreet."

"Thank you." Levanah gave her employer a faintly suspicious look.

"I am having some guests to stay," Sarah said, apparently changing the subject. "Only for a day or two, but it will mean extra work for you, I fear. I am so unused to entertaining that I shall require your help."

"Yes, of course."

"You haven't asked me who is coming," Sarah said.

"I was remembering how you'd praised my discretion," Levanah said.

"*Touché!*" Sarah drank a little of her wine and laughed. "In fact, four of my guests will only be coming for the evening. They reside in London already. The other four will be staying—old friends of mine whom I knew out in India. You will like Professor and Mrs. Manning very much. Mrs. Ganton is the widow of my husband's old general. She and her daughter, Eulalia, will also be staying."

"Is it a special occasion?" Levanah ventured.

"I think you might call it that," Sarah reflected. Indeed, I think you might."

Her light eyes were thoughtful, her lips curved in a smile. A moment later she gave her black head a small shake, drained her wine, and drifted upstairs. The girl Janet, silent as usual, came in to clear the table, and a few minutes later Mathilde, wrapped in the black sealskin coat she wore for her afternoons out, put in her head at the door to say that Mrs.

Sarah was resting and that she herself would be back again at five.

"And I've got all the greens to do and the bottles to sort," Janet muttered, breaking her silence.

"Won't Cook or Thomas help you?" Levanah asked.

"Cook's gone home—her sister is sick—and Thomas had to go to the toothpuller," Janet said.

"And left you with all the work? What a shame."

"Biddy would've helped," Janet said sullenly. "She was a willing one was Biddy."

"The Irish maid? The one who was dismissed for dropping things?"

"Biddy never dropped nothing," said Janet. "She was here and then she wasn't here. That's all I know and I don't ask questions."

"But didn't you see her go?"

"Here and then gone. I never ask questions," Janet said virtuously.

"I'll help you sort the bottles," Levanah offered.

"Mrs. Sarah wouldn't have it."

"Mrs. Sarah needn't know, and Mathilde and Thomas won't be back until teatime. Come, I'll help you."

Janet would have protested further, but Levanah had risen and was leading the way toward the baize-covered door. She had, mindful of her instructions, never ventured into the servants' quarters, and she descended the stairs with eager curiosity.

The basement was the cavernous, gloomy area she had expected, its windows below street level, its walls decorated in a dull cream that had yellowed in places. A fire burned in the grate, but the lamps were lit against the gloom of the winter afternoon.

"You shouldn't be here, miss," Janet said nervously from behind her.

"Get on with the greens," said Levanah sharply. "Where are those bottles that have to be sorted?"

"In the back kitchen, miss. The wine bottles go into the rack outside the cellar door, and the others go into the bin. Thomas sees to them then."

Levanah went through to the outer kitchen and frowned at the pile of empty bottles. For a lady who never entertained Sarah Varney got through a great many bottles of wine. Levanah pursed up her mouth in Aunt Leah's fashion, and then smiled wryly. She'd forgotten the servants, who probably took advantage of their easygoing mistress to help themselves to the contents of her wine cellar.

"It's the new maid ... Thomas found her in the wine cellar." The remembered words came back to her. So did the swirling fog, the clang of metal on metal, the whispering voices, the small figure moving dreamily among other cloaked figures.

Janet was cleaning the greens, her round face heavy with concentration. Levanah closed the connecting door and looked around.

The door to the wine cellar was locked. She made a face at the padlock and looked down with distaste at the dusty rack. The only other door in the back kitchen led into the yard. She stepped out, glanced up at the other windows and the high walls that cut the yard off from the neighboring alleys, and shrugged. There was nothing here to engage her attention. Nothing except a square iron shutter set into the wall. She stared at it, puzzled, for it seemed to have no connection with the back door. For a moment she hesitated and then, approaching the shutter, ran her nail experimentally around the edge where the iron fitted into the brick. Her nail was impeded by something. A faint click as the hidden latch lifted and the shutter swung outward.

She was looking, not into the back kitchen, but down a narrow sloping passage, scarcely wide enough to admit a grown man. It evidently ran between the kitchen wall and the outer wall and ended in a flight of stone steps.

She made her way cautiously into the darkness, her fingers scraping against the brick walls, her feet slithering on the steps. At the bottom a door with a bolt on the outside barred her path. Her hands lifted and slid it from its socket.

The room within was large and low-ceilinged, its floor covered with thick carpet, its walls hung with muffling velvet. Light came from a lamp burning on a small table in the middle of the room. She took it up and circled slowly, her eyes going from the reversed crucifix to the golden chalice. There were stools about the room. She counted twelve, and against the wall under a black canopy towered a high-backed chair of carved wood, its seat upholstered in black. From the ceiling hung other lamps, and against the further wall black candles waited in serried ranks to be lit. The whole place smelled of some sweet, heavy stuff that spiraled up from a brazier glowing faintly near the table.

Excitement gripped her. There was something here that called to her from across the centuries; something which she thought she had never known but which some part of her had never forgotten. She was shivering a little and the lamp in her hand cast blurred shadows against the dark hangings.

There were black cloaks hanging on a row of pegs near the big door. The door itself could, Levanah noticed, be bolted from either side. It could repel in-

truders or delay pursuit. Above the high chair hung a
double-edged sword. She stood on tiptoe, her fingers
grazing its hilt, and felt a tingling shoot down her
arm into her shoulder.

There was a rustling from behind the hangings, a
light footstep, and then Sarah Varney parted the
heavy velvet and came in, her loose red gown a glowing splash of color in the lamplight.

"I wondered how long it would take you to find this
place," she said, smiling.

"It's a chapel for witches, isn't it?" Levanah said
slowly.

To her own surprise the appearance of her employer had not frightened her. It was all of a piece
with the events of the afternoon.

"'Witch' is such a childish, medieval word," Sarah
said. "And most of their activities are so futile. We
are concerned here with— But come! You try to tell
me. What impressions do you receive from this place,
my dear?"

Levanah stared round, her eyes narrowed. "Power,"
she said at last. "I can feel power here."

"Power for the taking, my dear," Sarah nodded.
"The power that can destroy, bound in your own
hands, for you to unleash as you choose."

"If the Master agrees," said Levanah.

"What do you know of the Master?" Sarah questioned sharply.

"Only what I've read," Levanah said blandly.
"There has to be a Master, doesn't there?"

"The physical embodiment of the power we cannot
see. As above, so below."

"Is the power always evil?" Levanah asked.

"In itself it is neither good nor bad," Sarah said. "It
is how it is used that counts."

"And you use it . . .?"

"To obtain dominion," Sarah said. "We are too much at the mercy of fate, tossed here and there by circumstance, sending up our futile little prayers to a deity who no longer cares. How much better to reach out and take what one wants. All one has to do is join the service of the Master."

"I see," said Levanah.

She was not sure that she saw anything at all, but the conversation had taken on an unreal, dreamlike quality, and behind it lay very deep and strangely familiar ideas.

"What will happen to me now?" she asked, and thought of that small figure moving among the cloaked figures.

"That depends on you," Sarah said lightly. "It depends entirely on you. Nobody can be forced against their will."

"Is that why you advertised for a companion?"

"It was a desperate remedy," Sarah admitted. "One of our group died last November, and we were not up to full strength. The prospect of training a young girl appealed to us as a likely solution."

"But why me? You must have had other replies."

"Your name intrigued us," said Sarah. "Levanah is a moon title, an odd name for a Christian child. We made certain inquiries into your family background."

"And discovered one of my ancestors was drowned as a witch in the seventeenth century?"

"And another is said to have drunk human blood and murdered children."

"Charles Falcon," Levanah said, "but I'm sure that's just a story."

"Even in the wildest story there is a basis of truth," Sarah said calmly. "And then your immediate history was interesting. A love child whose mother killed herself—that is a romantic and tragic beginning, if you please! And your aunt, despite her careful phrases, was so anxious to be rid of you."

"She dislikes me," said Levanah, "because of this." She set the lamp on the table and pulled up her skirt to expose the purple crescent on her thigh.

Sarah bent closer to examine it. When she stood erect her face bore a quiet triumph.

"The Master marks his own," she said, "and how have you served him up to now?"

"I can make candle flames go up and down," Levanah said eagerly, "and I have a little nature god. I call him Lob. And I can brew tisanes and poultices."

"Amateur jiggery-pokery!" Sarah said in scorn. "A convinced Christian could do as much."

"There was nobody I could ask," Levanah said.

"No need to ask," said Sarah. "We know and gather in our own."

"To what end?"

"To serve the Master and take from life everything we desire. Tell me, have you never hated?"

Levanah thought of Aunt Leah.

"I see that you have." Sarah nodded her black head again. "Are you content to brood vaguely on the wrongs done to you, or will you take steps to avenge them? There is no compulsion."

None, save the memory of Biddy, who had gone into the wine cellar by mistake, and of voices and figures in the swirling fog.

"I would like to have the power," she said slowly.

"As to that, you have it already," Sarah said. "We will teach you how to release it, control it, and direct it."

"Against anybody I choose?"

"If the group agrees. We work together, many minds being more powerful than one. You'd best go out the way you came in."

"Janet—"

"Is happily cleaning turnips. Put the shutter back quietly. I'll bolt the door from this side and go back through the wine cellar."

She made a jagged, flashing symbol in the air, her emerald ring glowing on her finger.

Levanah took a last look at the high carved chair above which the double-edged sword slowly turned in the draft from the narrow passage. Then she went up into the yard again, remembering not to clang the shutter as she fitted it back against the space in the brickwork.

The bottles hastily sorted, she went back through the kitchen where Janet was industriously scraping, and up to her own room.

The little carved figure was still in her locked suitcase. She drew it out and stared at it, but it seemed clumsy and childish now, and its essential innocence had nothing to do with the rich images that crowded her mind.

Cal had made it for her, but then Cal had seen and admired Mary, and now he was to marry Cousin Wenna.

First there was Aunt Leah, and then Cal and Wenna, and then? There were so many people she knew and not one of them held her in real affection. Tears pricked behind her eyelids and then she arched her red head, reminding herself that witches never cried.

Chapter XI

'It is incredible,' thought Levanah as she glanced round Sarah Varney's luxurious drawing room, 'how ordinary the occasion seems.' Of the people gathered there only Sarah herself, in a loose robe of emerald silk, struck an exotic note. The rest of them would have been picked out as typical representatives of the leisured and professional classes. Professor Manning had a small pointed beard and was not quite as tall as his wife. Mrs. Granton had a languid manner and the slightly yellow complexion of one who has spent years in the tropics. Her daughter, Eulalia, was a plain, dumpy girl of about Levanah's age. The other four guests, who would not be sleeping at the house, were gentlemen. Two of them apparently shared a flat together, the one being so much plumper and pinker than the other that Levanah had the uneasy thought that he probably fed off his companion. The third gentleman had the air of a prosperous rake; the fourth was so insignificant that Levanah was certain she would never be able to pick him out in a crowd.

They had smiled, bowed, and shaken hands as Levanah was introduced to them. Their names she had heard mumbled and whispered as if some conspiracy of secret identities existed. A light meal of pâté, chicken salad, and candied fruits had been served by Mathilde and Thomas, and now the company sat about in the long drawing room, talking idly and sipping liqueurs from thick, greenish glasses with wide, snake-patterned stems.

"Janet will be going up to bed soon," Sarah remarked to nobody in particular. "Mathilde will give her a mug of hot milk."

"And the rest of the staff?" Mrs. Granton asked.

"Gone home. I told them they could leave as soon as we started the meal."

"Dear Sarah! So considerate!" Mrs. Granton leaned over and patted her hostess's arm. On her thin yellowish forefinger an opal sparkled, milky blue with gleams of gold.

They all of them, Levanah noticed, wore a heavy ring set with a large stone. Even the men wore them, and, glancing toward Mathilde and Thomas, she saw that both of them had slipped on rings, Mathilde's being a sapphire and Thomas's an onyx stone. She looked down at her own narrow hands and thought of the moonstone that the girl in the portrait had worn. There had been a gentleness in that ring that matched the dreaming eyes of the girl.

"So you are to become one of us," the little professor said, sitting down beside her.

"Yes, I believe so. I don't know," said Levanah carefully, "very much about it."

"Then you have many pleasing and instructive surprises ahead." His eyes, bright behind rimless spectacles, twinkled at her. "Sarah is an admirable woman. Place yourself in her hands and you will prosper."

"I understand you knew her late husband."

"An excellent fellow. Rather given to the more spectacular forms of esoteric practice, table-rapping and so on. But well-meaning and an amusing sort. We were very upset for her when he died."

"Was he—one of you?"

"The outer fringe only," said the professor. "More of a game with him. No dedication. Sarah now is the moving spirit, the presiding genius among us. This house of course is quite perfect for our meetings. It is a great pity that we cannot come together more often, but we have our own lives to lead."

"And the Master?" Unconsciously Levanah lowered her voice.

"He will be at the ceremony," Professor Manning said. "He comes late and leaves when the dawn begins."

"I see," Levanah said.

"Ah, my dear child, there are many things you don't understand"—the professor beamed—"but all in good time. Make haste slowly."

"Levanah, my dear, would you like to lie down for a while and rest?" Sarah asked. "The ceremony is long and tiring and we ourselves need to prepare for it."

"When shall I come down?"

"Eulalia will come up and tell you. Oh, there's a dress on your bed. Do put it on, there's a dear," Sarah said pleasantly.

The others were still talking together when she went out, but glancing back she surprised a cheerful wave from Professor Manning. It was, she thought, so ridiculous to imagine that in a little while they would all go down into the big cellar with the velvet hangings. It was surely a joke, a nonsense dream that she had exaggerated into reality. And there was no compulsion. At the last minute she could refuse, and then what would happen? An accident? The suicide of a lonely girl? She knew that she had already seen too much to be allowed not to become part of it.

"She's an unusual child," the professor said approvingly. "Are you sure she is right?"

"The final decision will be for the Master," Sarah reminded them, "but I've no doubts in my own mind. She carries the mark."

"Which can mean nothing at all," said Mrs. Ganton.

"Or can mean a very great deal," said Sarah. "She is full of resentment against her family. And she has the power—embryo, as yet, but with training—" She broke off, spreading her hands in unspoken anticipation.

"It is not solely with a view to her training that she has been chosen," said the rakish-looking gentleman.

"Of course not, but I anticipate no difficulties on that score," Sarah assured him.

"The girl has the promise of beauty," Mrs. Manning said. "That hair and those strange yellow eyes, a striking combination."

"Her family are not likely to make trouble, are they?" one of the others asked. "You mentioned she was a connection of young Lord Falcon."

"A cousin on the wrong side of the blanket," Sarah said. "Nothing to fear there. They're not likely to find out anyway. The oath is not lightly broken."

"If she agrees to take it," Mrs. Ganton said.

"She will take it." Sarah spoke with lazy confidence, her pale eyes serene.

In her room Levanah took off the light green dress she had worn at dinner and slipped over her head the

loose white gown she had found thrown across the
end of her bed. The gown had a medieval air, its
cowl neck folding into a hood, its wide sleeves dipping into points, its full skirt confined by a narrow
sash. The dress was embroidered with little silver
stars, each star centered with a pearl.

The glass showed a slim, ethereal being, shimmer-
ing misty white. There was, she thought, something
bridal about it. For an instant the dream image of Cal
stood beside her and then was gone.

She had come, she thought, a very long way since
the day she had disobeyed Aunt Leah and gone to
the old cottage. It was odd, but she couldn't remember how she felt before she had learned the meaning
of the crescent moon on her thigh. It was as if she
had been born knowing there was a power in her that
she could use. To use it for evil would be wrong. The
part of her that still remained childlike knew that
well and, staring at her bridal image, she felt
threatened in a way she couldn't understand. Then
she set her mouth firmly, combing her hair with her
fingers. When she had paid back all those who had
ever hurt her, she would use her powers for good. She
would serve this mysterious Master for as long as it
suited her, and then she would spend the rest of her
life in doing good works.

She sat down in the armchair, leaned her head
against the cushion, and closed her eyes. She drifted
into a half sleep, the fringe of her mind conscious of
the silk billowing about her legs and the glow of the
fire, the center of her mind dwindling down into a
narrow tunnel along which she walked, evading the
hands that clutched at her, trying not to see the faces
leering out of the dark.

A clock chimed the hour and she woke with a start,

blinking at Eulalia Ganton, who stood in the doorway. The dumpy, plain-faced girl wore a black cloak,
its hood pulled over her head. In Levanah's sleep-
blurred vision she seemed to have grown taller and
slimmer, and the black candle in her hand cast a
greenish light on her face.

"We are ready," she said, and even her voice had a
new authority.

Levanah rose, her hands moving instinctively to
pull up the hood of her own gown. Then, slowly as if
it were still part of her dream, she followed the other
through the silent house.

The door to the wine cellar was open now. Eulalia
passed through, holding her cloak clear of the stone
floor, her candle casting gleams of light across cob-
webbed bins and wooden racks of bottles. Another
door stood ajar at the far end of the cellar and from
within came a confused humming sound like the murmuring of bees.

"Wait here," Eulalia said, and pushed through a
heavy curtain that shielded the inner room from view.

The noise ceased, and a white smoke drifted
toward her mingled with some heady perfume that
teased her senses.

Eulalia came back, her hood tossed over her shoulders, her cloak unfastened to reveal a tightly fitting
red gown. She took hold of Levanah's hands, gripping
them tightly, and they walked together into the candlelight.

Levanah's first impression was of smoke spiraling in
columns. The stools were occupied, the figures who
sat there being robed in black and masked in scarlet.
The carved chair was empty, but the sword that hung
above it was gone. Despite the heat from the lamp

and the candles and the glowing braziers there was a
coldness in the air that struck through to the heart.

The tallest of the masked figures had risen and was
approaching. She recognized the emerald on the olive
hand, the black hair that was not coiled now but
hung in twisting ringlets like the snakes of Kali.

"Child of ignorance, do you seek knowledge?"
Sarah's voice had changed and deepened.

"She seeks knowledge," said Eulalia.

The others had risen from their stools and ad-
vanced a step.

"Child of weakness, do you seek power?" Sarah
asked.

"She seeks power," said Eulalia.

"Child of light, will you go forth into the
darkness?" Sarah asked.

"She will go forth into the darkness," Eulalia said.

At each question and answer the figures moved
closer.

"Give her the oath to read," Sarah said.

Parchment crackled in Levanah's hands. Writing,
black and angular, leaped up at her.

"Read it aloud," said Sarah. "As you read it so you
are bound."

Levanah took a deep breath and read steadily, her
voice clear and toneless in the dizzying fumes.

"I, Levanah Falcon, of my own will, do bind myself
to obey the laws of the Kingdom of Edom in the
habitations of hell. I swear to take what I need from
those who are not my brethren, and to pay for that
which I take in the performing of such service as the
Master will require of me. I swear never to reveal the
names of my brethren, nor the place or content of our
meetings. If I fail in this, may my own children

destroy me root and branch and my soul find no rest between sky and earth."

"Will you sign the pact?" Sarah spoke directly to Levanah, and the girl nodded. The words she had just read were as unreal as everything was becoming.

Her wrist was taken and held firmly. There was a flash of steel, a burning pain, and blood dripped into a small cup. One of the masked figures, recognizable as the professor by his beard, bound the cut tightly with black silk.

Sarah took Levanah's index finger, dipped it into the cup, and indicated she was to make a mark upon the parchment. It seemed inevitable that she should draw the outline of a crescent moon.

Somebody motioned her to one of the stools and she sat down, aware that her legs were shaking. The others, except for Sarah, had also backed to their seats. Sarah stood before the table, her hands lifted to shoulder height, and began to chant. It was in a tongue that Levanah had never heard before, a slurred liquid stream of syllables. Now and then she paused, and the others, rocking back and forth on their stools, emitted a long drawn-out hiss.

Sarah began to speak in English, her voice rising and falling rhythmically.

"We seek the one who comes in the guise of the Master. We who serve await the Master. We who wait invoke the Master. We who invoke crave the Master."

Her voice was becoming shriller, the hissing responses more charged with venom. The smoke from the braziers was so thick that Levanah could scarcely see through it. There was a humming in the air, like the humming of bees. It came, she assumed, from the throats of those who swayed upon their stools. She couldn't remember their names any longer or distinguish one from the other, and the lights from the lamps and candles were confusing her eyes.

She closed them briefly and opened them upon a long drawn-out hiss. The high carved chair was no longer empty. A tall figure robed in black now sat there, the face covered by a black mask, the head surmounted by silver antlers. Between the black gloved hands the double-edged sword was delicately balanced.

The others had risen and were advancing. Sarah's voice rang out strong and clear, "Welcome to thee, Grand Master of the Order of the Habitations of Hell. Welcome."

"Welcome" was echoed by the others.

Levanah had moved forward with them and now, through the slits of the black mask, she could see eyes watching her intently. For a moment fear shuddered through her, and then she raised her head proudly and stared back.

"Master, this is our new sister in death. This is Levanah," Sarah said.

"Let her approach."

She was being guided through the swirling columns of smoke, being pushed to her knees. The sword swung to within an inch of her throat and light flashed along the blade. She blinked involuntarily and then fixed her eyes upon him again.

"Let her drink," said the Master.

A chalice, gleaming gold and filled to the brim with some dark liquid, was being offered to her. She accepted it and drank, wrinkling her nose at the sweet pungent taste. The others were grouped now in a semicircle behind her, their voices humming still.

"She is welcome," said the Master.

The chalice was empty, and the sword had been withdrawn from her throat. She was sleepy and content and the shadowy smoke no longer menaced her.

They were moving in a circle, against the sun, prancing on their toes, their fingers hooked against their temples, their throats swelling in the wordless chant that was both strange and familiar.

Now they were moving faster, so fast that it was like flying through the air. She laughed in the joy and freedom of it, her hood falling back, her yellow eyes gleaming. Whirling faster and faster, black cloaks spinning, candles and lamps forming one great haze of light.

The dance ceased and she no longer stood upright but lay upon the thick carpet, legs and arms wide. Sarah bent above her, a dagger in her hand, and in her ears was the soft ripping of silk. The white dress parted, hands tugged at her underclothing, perfume teased her nostrils. This had nothing to do with Lob, or the crystal, or the portrait of a girl with a moonstone ring. There was only the perfume and the faces in the smoke and Sarah's hands stroking, stroking. Tremors of desire feathered her nerves and then the Master came, catfooted, his cloak flung back to reveal nakedness erect with anticipation, the antlers gleaming still above the black mask, and she was pressed down in pain and cold and an unbearable, mounting excitement.

At Whittle Farm, Cal woke briefly, murmuring Wenna's name. She had not yet given herself to him and he dreamed of her constantly, her body ripe and warm in his mind. She was, he thought sleepily, a wonderful woman. In a way she was like the mother he had dreamed about. His own had been too strange and too sad. It had often seemed as if he were the parent and she the child. Her drinking bouts had become more frequent as he grew to manhood as if she saw in his growing a reflection of her own lost and wasted youth.

"Your father was Paul Simmons. Your father was my sister's husband," she had told him.

That had been when he had returned to the farm after they had seen the face distorted against the glass of the cottage. She had been waiting for him, her hair hanging in wet tangles about her haggard face.

"Mary is not for you," she had said. "She is your half sister. Paul loved me first. He wanted to marry me, but Leah had control of her own money, and she bribed him with that. He left us both in the end, both expecting his child. I don't know if he's alive or dead. I don't care. I care about you, Cal. I care about your future and I don't want you to be hurt. Don't blame me, Cal."

He hadn't blamed her, and he felt no interest in, or bitterness against, the father he had never seen. Mary ... but he closed his mind against thoughts of Mary. She was, by all the laws of God and man, not for him. It was a cruel shame, for she was an enchantingly pretty thing, but they were both young and would get over it.

His mother had scarcely drawn a sober breath since her confession. And then Cousin Wenna Davies had walked into the yard, and life had become warm and comfortable. She managed him and scolded him and joked with him and set everything to rights. Even his mother had perked up and begun to eat a little and comb her hair, and once Cousin Wenna had made her laugh out loud and he realized what a lovely girl she must have been.

It had been sad that she should die in such a fashion. A million-to-one chance the Coroner had said. Yet, at the graveside, he had felt a certain relief. Now there would no longer be that tug in him between irritation and pity, no longer the silent shame of avoiding the glances of those who had seen her staggering on the hill. He had looked up and met Wenna's sleepy green eyes, and even in the midst of his regrets a new excitement had stirred.

"People will say I'm too old for you," Wenna had said. "They will say I married you for the sake of the farm. It isn't so, but you must be ready for gossip."

"I've never troubled about what folk say," he retorted.

"Then you show good sense. I have given in my notice to Cousin Leah. I suppose Charlotte Bishop will take over."

"Will you invite your mother to the wedding?" he inquired.

"She won't come," Wenna said. "She's never left the farm or been on a train in her life, and she's too old to begin now. I left Wales twenty years ago, my dear, and it's never a good idea to look back."

She was certainly the right sort of wife to have, Cal decided, turning over and punching the pillow into a shape that more closely resembled Wenna's breast.

Leah stood on the gallery at Kingsmead, her nightgown covered by a shawl, her plaits coiled under a nightcap. In the hall below, the lamps burned dimly. Oil lamps were out of fashion now, but she liked their soft glow. Teddy had talked of having gaslights installed. Gaslights and motorcars and bicycles! The

world in which she had grown up was fast vanishing,
and with it was going her own sense of security. She
had always been mistress of the circumstances thrust
upon her, even when her husband had betrayed and
deserted her.

Now she had the feeling that events were rushing
ahead out of her control. Teddy had shown no more
than a cousinly interest in Mary, and Mary had
grown hard and defiant, and spent all her time with
Charlotte Bishop. And Edith's death—Leah thought of
it firmly as an accident—had merely precipitated the
marriage between Wenna and Cal. She had accepted
the match with outwardly good grace. Wenna would
be married from Kingsmead at Easter, to silence
amused tongues. Mary was to be bridesmaid, and
Leah hoped that she had recovered from her infatuation for Cal. They had not met since the revelation
of their kinship. Mary spent all her time with the
schoolteacher these days, aping her friend's brisk
handshake and hearty stride. Leah's mind flinched
away from the implications of that friendship, and
fastened instead upon Levanah.

She had hoped, when Levanah left, that out of
sight would be out of mind. It had proved otherwise.
The girl refused to be forgotten. Some part of her
strange, passionate nature had embedded itself in the
very atmosphere her aunt breathed. Kingsmead was
full of a resentful, living presence.

The great house was silent now, the servants sleeping in their quarters behind the kitchen, Mary tucked
up in her own bed. At this hour Leah wandered
alone, unwilling to sleep, moving from room to room
while the shadows of those who had gone before
leaned from the whispering tapestries.

She stared down restlessly into the great hall. It had been built as the heart of the house, intended for a large family. It seemed such a long time since there had been children running through the hall. She remembered Teddy, who had been so bright and sturdy and never given any trouble, and Mary, sweetly obedient in her starched pinafore. Behind them, in her imagination, tagged the thin little figure with the slanting yellow eyes and the smooth, light-red hair. Levanah had always been in the way even then.

Leah's mouth tightened. Best for them all that Levanah should stay in London for as long as possible, and that Mrs. Varney should instill in her the virtues of dutiful obedience and respectable conduct.

As she turned back, the pictures along the back of the wall gleamed faintly in the light from her candle. The past stared at her out of generations of Falcon eyes. From low-necked crinoline, starched cravat, Regency stock and Tudor ruff their heads rose proudly.

All her life she had treasured the knowledge that an unbroken line of ancestors stretched behind her as owners of Kingsmead. There had been, in the past, too much marrying of cousins and that had weakened the stock. But neither she nor any of her siblings had married a cousin. It would be quite safe for Mary to marry Teddy.

The eyes of one of the portraits gazed at her and through her with a peculiar intensity. Leah paused unwillingly, lifting her candle to illuminate the slanting yellow orbs and smiling lips and long red hair. Catrin Falcon, wife of Sir Robert Falcon, swum as a witch in the early seventeenth century, judged innocent but buried outside the churchyard just to be on the safe side. But the eyes and the hair were Levanah's and the smile was mocking, and the smoke from the candle swirled up into the darkness like incense.

Chapter XII

Levanah stared at the gray façade of the house. She had taken a hansom cab to Albemarle Street, and now, standing at her destination, a qualm of misgiving shook her. She had assumed that an artist would live in Bohemian squalor, but Albemarle Street was evidently respectable and the building pointed out to her as Michael Shaw's residence was an elegant Georgian edifice.

She had dressed with care for the interview, in coat and skirt of soft green wool, banded in peacock blue at the hem. A matching ribbon trimmed her hat and ruched the frilled neckline of her white blouse. Under the brim of the hat, her red hair fell in a curve of softness against her pale face.

This, then, was the house where lived the man who might be, almost certainly was, her father. A small item in the newspaper a few days previously had mentioned the return from Paris of "the distinguished artist, Michael Shaw." She had chosen to come this afternoon, partly because she despised herself for delaying further, partly because a letter from Aunt Leah had arrived that morning telling her that Cal and Wenna had been quietly married the previous day. Levanah had not expected to feel such a stab of loneliness, as if something within her had been betrayed.

Standing on the pavement was, however, accomplishing nothing. She mounted the steps firmly and tugged at the doorbell. A few seconds later a maid, in starched cap and apron but with a flowered muslin gown instead of the usual black, opened the door, and looked an inquiry.

"Is Mr. Shaw at home?"

Even as she spoke Levanah regretted not having provided herself with some kind of visiting card. It was not likely that a man as busy as Michael Shaw would see casual callers without an appointment. The maid, however, held the door wider, asking, "What name shall I say, miss?"

"Levanah. Levanah Price."

"If you'll wait here, miss." The maid showed her into a small, white paneled room leading off the narrow hall and went up the stairs.

The room into which Levanah had been shown contained only a loveseat cushioned in blue, a bookcase filled with books, and a carved figure of a girl with head upraised as if she listened for something. The ivory statue looked old and peaceful and some of Levanah's own nervousness began to evaporate as she studied it.

"Not an original, I fear," said a voice from behind her. "This was made in ivory about a hundred years ago from a bronze found in the ruins of Pompeii. Why do you imagine she listens?"

"For the wind heralding the moon?" Levanah guessed.

"Most young ladies would have said she listened for her lover. Your answer was more perceptive. Turn about, my dear, and take off that ugly hat."

She obeyed slowly, facing him, seeing for the first time the slim, spare figure, the narrow dark face and curling silver-black hair of the man Beth had loved. A faint frown indented his brow and then was gone.

"You will have been told before," he said, "that your hair is pale Titian and your bone structure exquisite. You want to sit for me, of course. Many young girls come here hoping I will employ them to paint their portraits. Most of them have prettiness with no character. Occasionally one meets someone with both, and for that reason I see everyone who calls here. Do you like tea?"

She nodded, and he smiled and ushered her out of the room and up two flights of the close-carpeted stairs. The apartment into which they emerged evidently covered the entire second floor, for it stretched its carpets interminably to the boundaries of white-washed walls against which canvases were stacked. There were large windows with slatted blinds at them instead of curtains, and a sloping skylight through which light streamed down onto an easel. There was a dais near the easel on which vivid cushions were piled, and several couches and cane-backed chairs and a long table, but the effect was tranquil and pleasant rather than cluttered.

The little maid came in with tea and bobbed out again. Levanah sat primly on one of the cane-backed chairs and watched Michael Shaw pour the amber liquid into the cups. His hands were well shaped and moved surely, concentrating on their task, and making of it a small ritual. To her he seemed both old and young, the lines on his face recording sorrow, his movements brisk, even jaunty.

"Your name intrigued me," he commented, handing her a cup. "It's a most unusual one."

"Levanah? My mother wished me to be called that."

"She has imagination."

"Had. She died when I was a few days old."

"I'm very sorry." He gave her a compassionate glance.

"My surname isn't Price," she said abruptly. "It's Falcon. I'm Levanah Falcon."

He set his cup down carefully in the saucer and gave her a long searching look. Then he nodded.

"I knew there was something about the eyes," he said half to himself. "Where do you fit into the family?"

"Beth Falcon was my mother," Levanah told him.

"Then she married? But that means you are younger than I supposed."

"I'm eighteen. My mother never married."

"No, of course, she could not have done. Your aunt told me of Beth's death—why, it's eighteen years since." He was still looking at her, sorting years in his mind.

"She killed herself," Levanah said harshly. "She cut her wrists and bled to death. I was a baby in the cradle. She killed herself and bled all over the carpet. Perhaps you can tell me why she did it."

"Killed herself? Had a child?" he whispered.

"The day I was born," Levanah went on relentlessly, "Beth sent something through the post. I think she sent it to you. A week later she killed herself. Perhaps you know why."

"You're saying I am your father," he said.

His face had paled and his eyes were suddenly haunted by some private anguish.

"She had no lovers except an artist who stayed at 'Witch's Dower' for one summer," Levanah said. "His name was Mr. Shaw. He painted a portrait of her, just her face completed and a ring."

"A moonstone ring," he said. "Her mother had left it to her and she always wore it."

"Why did you desert her?" Levanah asked in a tight, tense, little voice. "Why did you leave her to bear a bastard and then kill herself? Why? Didn't you love her at all?"

"I loved her more than anything else in the world," he said.

"Then why didn't you go back to her?" she demanded. "Make me understand it."

"How can I?" He made a little gesture of despair. "I don't understand it all myself. You're so young—the same age as she was. I wish you could have seen her as I saw her then. She was small, with a long tail of hair the color of honey, and eyes—I can't describe her eyes."

"You painted them," she reminded him.

"No painting could do justice to them," he said. "They were so many shades—blue, gray, green, according to her mood."

"You painted her as beautiful," she said.

"I don't know if she was beautiful or not," he said. "She was thirty years younger than me, and yet there were times when she seemed much older and wiser, as if she knew, deep down, that she would never make old bones. I was on holiday when I came to Marie Regina. My bank had allowed me an extended holiday for health reasons. I'd always wanted to paint, to devote my life to painting. The holiday gave me an opportunity to find out if I could ever be anything more than a dabbler."

"And yet you stayed at 'Witch's Dower.' "

"It was her property. I met her by chance—or perhaps nothing is by chance—but she offered to let me stay at her cottage and I promised to paint her portrait, for she wouldn't accept any rent."

"You seduced her," she accused.

"Everything is black and white at your age," he said sadly. "Try to understand. I was wed when I was a young man, and Susan was bright and pretty. By the time I met Beth my wife was no longer bright and pretty. She had given up trying to please me years before. She nagged instead, incessantly, on and on and on, and flew into tantrums if the slightest thing went wrong. I stayed at the bank because she wanted me in a secure position. I tried to please her, and I did it out of kindness at first, but the years went by and kindness became duty. And then I took a painting holiday and met Beth."

"She loved you." Levanah said. "She loved you and you went away and left her. How could you?"

"I had no legal reason for a divorce," he said wearily. "I loved Beth but Susan had that piece of paper that acknowledged her as my wife in the eyes of society. I was 'respectable,' and Beth was so very young. I thought it was more honorable to leave, and give her the opportunity to meet somebody else who was free to offer her marriage. I had no idea she was with child either then or later. I went back to my secure position in the bank, back to Susan."

"But my mother sent for you! On the day I was born she sent for you. The postmistress told me she posted something in an envelope—"

"The moonstone ring," he interrupted. "We made a bargain. If she ever needed me desperately she was going to send the ring to me, care of the bank. I received it."

"And ignored her plea." The flaming patches of scarlet in her cheeks contradicted the ice in her voice.

"I sent the ring back to her in a letter saying I would be with her within a few days."

"Why not at once?"

"Because Susan had just been killed in a carriage accident. I'd been away from work seeing to the funeral arrangements. The envelope with the ring in it was given to me when I went into the bank. I wrote to Beth that same day, telling her what had happened, planning to be with her as soon as possible. I was in a position to offer her marriage, you see."

"But you never went to Marie Regina," she accused.

"There was no point." His face, worn and haggard, revealed his age. "A letter came from Mrs. Simmons."

"From Aunt Leah?" Her head went up like a fox sniffing hens.

"I'd put my home address on my letter to Beth. Your aunt must have seen it, for she wrote to me at home. She told me that Beth had died a few days before. A sudden chill, she said."

"My mother killed herself," Levanah repeated. "She bled to death all over the carpet. I never learned about it until later, but when I was small I went into the upstairs sitting room once, and the carpet was stained with blood for a moment and the room was very cold."

"Beth sometimes saw beyond things too," Michael Shaw said. "She had a mark on her thigh like a crescent moon. A witch mark she said it was, but if she were a witch it was a gentle one."

"I have the mark too." She pulled up her skirt to show him.

"I need no proof that you're Beth's child, and my daughter," he said.

"Am I like her?" she asked.

"Thinner," he said critically, "and your features are sharper. Beth was—softer. She gave in too easily."

"If a man loved me," she said with sudden fierceness, "I'd not let him go. I'd kill him first."

"And not yourself?"

"That was weakness," Levanah said, "and I am strong."

"I believe you are." He looked at her consideringly and asked. "Of what are you thinking now?"

"Of my Aunt Leah," she said softly. "She wrote to you, lying about my mother's way of dying, not telling you about the baby."

"I never knew I had ever fathered a child," he told her. "Susan was barren, and since I heard of Beth's death—I went abroad almost at once. I had no responsibilities, a little money from the sale of the house to live on, and so I traveled."

"And became famous."

"Well known among connoisseurs of art," he corrected. "I won't paint vapid society beauties, genteel vases of flowers. I exhibit very little and the Academy regards me as too avant-garde to be hung, but I make a very profitable living, and I sell a great many pictures abroad."

"You never married again?"

"After Beth?" He shook his head.

"You really did love her, then?" She was conscious of the old familiar stab of loneliness.

"So much," he said, "that even now I sometimes think I see her in a crowd of people or walking down the street just ahead of me, with that tail of hair bouncing against her back. And then she turns and it's a different girl, a stranger I never met before."

"You ought never to have left her."

"I know that now. I knew it even before Susan was killed," he said somberly.

"My mother never received that letter," Levanah said. "I'm quite sure it was kept from her. She waited, and when she didn't hear, she killed herself."

"But she would surely have waited more than a week."

"I can find out." Her young lips thinned. "Aunt Leah will know. She will know because she has to be the one who stole the letter. That was how she knew your address."

"And never told me about the child. My own daughter, and I never knew she existed!"

"You should have gone to Marie Regina. You should have gone to pay your respects."

"At first I couldn't have endured to return," he said. "Later, a few years later, I did visit her grave. There was nothing of her there, so I rode on without seeing any of the family. Not that I was ever invited to Kingsmead, you understand. Beth's brother, Lord Falcon, did come to 'Witch's Dower' to see if I was a suitable person for her to know."

"My Uncle John." Levanah nodded. "He was thrown from his horse and killed the day before I was born. Aunt Edith died a few weeks back—a stone from the old monastery ruins fell on her."

"And your Aunt Leah?"

"Is still very much alive," she said grimly, "and has a great deal of explaining to do."

"Did you come to London especially to find me? You're surely not alone!"

"I'm staying with friends," she evaded. "Will you come back with me to face Aunt Leah, to ask her why she kept your letter from my mother?"

"It might have been mislaid in the post," he objected. "I can't believe that your aunt could have tampered with somebody else's mail."

"She never told you about me, did she?"

"That's understandable," he said. "She must have felt great bitterness against me for having disgraced her sister. Perhaps she felt she could rear a child with more success than an artist with no settled home. Perhaps she felt she was acting for the best."

"You're a very forgiving kind of person, aren't you?" she said with disapproval.

"I have not lived for sixty-seven years without learning that we are all human," he said. "It is only myself I find hard to excuse. It was an offense against love to go on living with a woman I didn't love. If we could call back time we would surely alter it."

"But if Aunt Leah did take the letter," Levanah said eagerly, "she ought to be punished."

Michael Shaw rose abruptly and began to pace the studio, his head bent, his eyes fixed on the vivid carpets.

"She has to be punished," Levanah repeated, and she too rose and went to him, tugging impatiently at his arm. "She kept us apart, you and me. She has to be punished."

"But, it's not for you to decide that," he said, stopping short and looking into her upturned face. "It's not your right."

"It was my right to have a father," she said sullenly.

"And that you did not is as much my fault—"

"For which you have been punished," she interrupted. "Aunt Leah has not."

"Your aunt brought you up, and very well, from your manners and appearance. You owe her many thanks for that."

"I've repaid her with sufficient gratitude," she said briefly. "Won't you come with me?"

"I'll not go back," he said at last. "I'll not soil your mother's memory by seeking revenge."

"You talk as if she'd been a saint!" Levanah exclaimed. "She was only a silly girl who let a married man get her with child, and didn't have the courage to make him leave his wife."

He said nothing but went on staring at her.

"Why don't you answer me?" she demanded. "Why don't you say something?"

"I was thinking," he said at least, "that you are not, after all, very much like your mother."

"You painted such a beautiful picture of her," she said softly. "How will you paint me?"

"I won't," he said curtly. "I've changed my mind."

"Because I'm not as pretty as you thought?"

"Because there is something in you I can't fathom. If I painted you it would be revealed, and I don't want to know what it is."

"Then you won't help me."

"If you need money or advice or friendship, you are more than welcome to everything I have."

"I've managed for eighteen years without your money, advice, or friendship," she said coldly. "I can manage for the next eighteen years without them. Goodbye, Mr. Shaw."

Anger and pride took her swiftly down the stairs into the street again. On the pavement she stood for a moment, wondering if he would follow her, but the door she had just banged remained closed. Her father was not going to help her. The temptation to curse him ran through her like desire, then the impulse died, and she crammed her hat on her head and walked slowly down the road past the elegant houses with their closed doors and blank, indifferent windows.

Michael Shaw sat down again in one of the cane-backed chairs. For the first time he felt his actual age, limbs aching, head tight-banded with weariness. His eyes pricked with tears he had shed many years before, and into his mind drifted, not Beth as he had last seen her with her body still fragrant from his love, but bleeding, dying. Suicide was a way out he had never considered for himself. It seemed incredible that Beth should have chosen it.

Then he remembered her more clearly, her moods that even at their gayest were tinged with shadow, the wild abandon with which she had explored the secrets of love, her misery when he had told her that their affair must end. It was conceivable that in such a mood she might kill herself, especially if she had just had a child. Women, he had heard, were often strange at such times. And he had a daughter! He sat, reflecting on the fact. It was odd, but he could summon up no particular affection for her. Beth's child should have been soft and sweet, not thin and sharp with hard yellow eyes. He hoped her aunt had been kind to her, not made her feel the stigma of bastardy too acutely.

He had said he would not paint her, but shock and sorrow were flowing into his fingertips. It had been thus ever since Beth's death, the loneliness and the intolerable aching splashing onto the canvas.

The canvas on the easel was blank. He had returned from Paris with no clear ideas for a subject. Now he moved to his accustomed place beneath the skylight and let his fingers obey the instincts of his brain. Swiftly the outlines took shape. A girl with yellow eyes stood beneath a crescent moon and watched a falcon rising into the dark night. The bird's wings were tipped with silver and in its beak it held a moonstone. By the time the light began to shift the main picture was blocked in. His hands and head ached and his mouth was dry, but there was a mist before his eyes and even the knowledge that his work was good could not stifle the regrets that filled him.

When the maid came up to remind him that it was time for him to eat she found him staring out into the dusky street, and though he answered her in his usual pleasant manner she had the idea that he was not really aware of her at all.

Levanah took an omnibus back to her employer's. She had gone out with the excuse that she intended to buy a belated gift for Cal and Wenna. She would tell Sarah that she had been unable to find anything suitable. She wanted not to have to think too deeply about anything for a while. The meeting with her father had upset her more than she was willing to admit. Some childish part of her had hoped for an emotional reconciliation such as she had read about in the novels that she and Mary had borrowed from Maidstone Library. She had hoped for an ally against Aunt Leah. It would have given her tremendous satisfaction to have confronted her aunt with her father at her side.

But he had been too gentle and forgiving, too lost in his dream of a dead love. An unaccustomed pity twisted her heart. He had been lonely for so long, she guessed, that he no longer realized his need for company. Had she been softer in her manner, more like her mother—but Beth had been cheated of her love and died.

'That won't happen to me,' Levanah decided, her mouth thinning into a straight line. 'I'll find out what I want and take it.'

A gentleman across the aisle glanced at the demure little figure and met coldly hostile eyes as she turned and stared at him.

"Yellow eyes," he would tell his wife later. "Slanting at the corners and blank. Like the eyes of a fox. Gave me quite a nasty turn it did, those eyes boring through me, and the young lady so respectably dressed! One never knows who is going to rub shoulders with you these days."

Levanah, unconscious of the man's startled face, was thinking of Aunt Leah. That proud, possessive bitch who would have her day of reckoning soon. The final truth about Beth's suicide would have to be told, then would come the punishment.

'I would like,' the girl thought savagely, 'to take away from her everything she values, and then to see her die, very slowly, very painfully.'

Her mouth curved into a smile, though her eyes remained blank and bright. The horses drew up with a jangling of harness and Levanah alighted from the omnibus and walked sedately along the road, the spring sunshine glinting on her hair.

Chapter XIII

"Someone had to take the trouble to find out if you were all right, so I volunteered."

It was Teddy who spoke. Sprawled in an armchair in Sarah Varney's sitting room, his long legs stretched across the hearthrug, his air one of unself-conscious ease, he had made himself completely at home within ten minutes of his ringing the doorbell.

"I can scarcely believe that you're here," she said with real pleasure. "It seems so long since I was at home or saw anybody from Kingsmead."

"I'm in town for a few days visiting friends, seeing a couple of shows. Those Gaiety girls are quite good!"

"I'm sure they must be."

"Not that I've lost either my heart or my wallet in that direction," he grinned.

"Aunt Leah will be glad. She always hoped that you and Mary—"

"Mary declares she will never marry anybody," Teddy informed her. "She goes everywhere with that

Charlotte Bishop. Both of them on bicycles, with divided skirts and collars and ties, calling themselves 'new women'!"

"How are they all?" she inquired, surprised at her own eagerness for news.

"You know that Cousin Wenna Davies has married Cal Falcon?"

"Aunt Leah wrote and told me about it."

"As you know, we've never been encouraged to be friendly with Cousin Cal, but one can't help admiring the way he runs Whittle Farm, though why he chose to marry a woman twice his age I can't imagine!"

"Are they happy?" she asked, pleating her skirt between her fingers.

"They seem very well suited," he said. "I paid them a courtesy call at Easter. You know that Aunt Leah had the reception for them at Kingsmead? Naturally a very quiet one with Aunt Edith Falcon so recently buried, but since then there haven't been many visits. Do you know that Cousin Wenna is expecting a child?"

"She's too old," Levanah said blankly.

"She's only just past forty," said Teddy. "A fine-looking woman, too. She stayed on as teacher for the time being until a new one can be found to take over, but she's living at the farm, of course. Miss Bishop has taken over the apartment over the school."

"And the cottage? 'Witch's Dower.' It's my property you know. My mother made a Will before she died leaving it to me."

"Aunt Leah mentioned it, and Cousin Wenna said she was seeing to the upkeep of the place. I've not been there myself."

"It's so odd," she said, "to see you here, sitting opposite me and talking."

"It's even odder to be visiting you in the middle of London. I still don't know what possessed you to leave Kingsmead."

Looking at him with affection, she thought there were many things her cousin would never understand. He was a throwback to some healthy, good-humored, incurious Falcon ancestor who accepted life as it came and never probed into the perplexities of human behavior.

"I wanted some independence," she said, knowing he would accept what she chose to say. "Aunt Leah thought I was getting above myself and being a bad influence on Mary—"

"Oh, surely not!"

"Anyway, she agreed to my earning a living, and here I am!" She spread her hands wide and gave him a small smile with a hint of courage.

"I admire you tremendously," he said with enthusiasm. "Not that I approve of my cousin's working, mind, but it shows character."

"It's scarcely working," she protested. "Sarah Varney is a widow and likes young company, that's all. I help her with her correspondence and her entertaining, read to her, play chess. It's a very easy job, I have plenty of free time, and Sarah is charming."

"What a delightful recommendation," Sarah said lightly from the doorway.

She had returned from one of her rare excursions into town, and was more conventionally attired than usual in a walking dress of wine velvet and one of the new wide-brimmed hats trimmed with gray ostrich plumes.

"Sarah, may I present my cousin, Lord Edward Falcon?" Levanah said.

"You must be Teddy." Sarah came forward with

outstretched hand. "I'm very happy to receive you, milord. Levanah has told me a great deal about you."

"Including the fact that I had no desire to have my cousin take a situation, but am delighted her life is spent in such pleasant pleasures?" he smiled.

"You are quite the diplomat," Sarah said. "I am happy to have found Levanah, I may tell you. I couldn't wish for a more congenial companion than your cousin."

"Diplomacy isn't in my line," Teddy said, his eyes admiring the tall, supple figure and blue-black chignon of the woman whose slim, olive hand was still imprisoned in his. "As soon as I come down from 'Varsity I shall take over the management of my estate."

"Ah, yes! Kingsmead, isn't it? I don't know Kent at all." She withdrew her hand gently. "Has Levanah given you some tea? Or does a young gentleman require something stronger on a fine June day?"

"Mathilde brought tea and some cake," Levanah said. "You didn't want anything else, did you, Teddy?"

"I'm not a drinking man," he said, "unlike one or two of my ancestors!"

"Ah, but in such an ancient family one is practically obliged to have colorful ancestors," Sarah said lightly. "I suppose many of your own were adventurous and buccaneering."

"I don't know. My Aunt Leah would know more about that than I do. She's always been very interested in family history. I believe she had a brother who went out to Australia but we lost touch with him years ago."

"And do you intend to travel?"

"England is good enough for me," Teddy said easily. "I shall be content to live at Marie Regina for the rest of my life."

"An idyllic existence. You're a very fortunate young gentleman."

"I wondered," Teddy said, "if it might be possible for me to take Levanah to the theater one evening? Oh, you too, Mrs. Varney. I shall be delighted to escort you both, of course."

"I'm afraid that I am not an ardent devotee of the theater," Sarah said, "and my health does not permit me to go out in the evening. But you may certainly take Levanah. I see nothing improper in that, and she will be delighted to have an evening out. I'm afraid I am sometimes dull company."

"No, indeed," Levanah began, but Teddy was saying eagerly, "I have two tickets for the musical play at the Royal Court for tomorrow evening, if that isn't too short notice?"

"I'd like to come," Levanah said, "if you don't mind, Sarah?"

"Nonsense! You must run along and enjoy yourself." Sarah gave her most brilliant smile as Teddy turned to go. "At seven o'clock then, cousin? We can have a bite of dinner before the show if you like."

"I'll make sure she's ready. Ah, Mathilde! Bring Lord Falcon's hat and gloves, if you please. Do you keep your own carriage in town?"

"Lord, no!" Teddy looked horrified. "The fellows would rag me to death if I did. My aunt keeps the old coach in the stables at Kingsmead, but it's my conviction that motorcars are the things of the future. I intend to buy one."

"But not to subject poor Levanah to such an experience!" Sarah exclaimed.

"I'll hire a private carriage for tomorrow evening," Teddy promised.

"Not that I'm being overscrupulous, I hope," Sarah was saying as she walked with him into the hall, "but your cousin is very young, and I do feel in some degree responsible for her."

Levanah sat down again in the drawing room. It had jolted her a trifle to see how handsome Teddy had grown. He looked older than his years and he had evidently found her attractive.

"A very personable young man," Sarah said coming back into the room. "Stupid, of course, but most English aristocrats are somewhat bovine. You must make yourself look very fetching for the theater tomorrow. That pale green moiré of yours would look charming. The one with the knot of silver ribbon on the shoulder. I will lend you my velvet cape."

She rang for more tea and went on talking about clothes.

The following evening Levanah, feeling unfamiliarly smart in her one grown-up evening dress, a silver ribbon in her hair echoing the one on her shoulder, sat primly in the dress circle of the theater and stole occasional glances at her companion.

In evening dress, with opera cloak and top hat, her cousin looked, she thought, really rather splendid. Several young ladies in the audience were glancing at her with envy. It was a new and heady sensation. This was, she realized, the first time she had ever been escorted in public by a gentleman, the first time in her life she had ever sat in a theater. The red and gold draperies, the tiers of monogrammed seats, the displays of flowers in the foyer, the shiny, embossed program—all excited and interested her, but she resisted the temptation to wriggle around in her seat and sat quietly, Sarah's cloak folded back across her seat, the opera glasses clutched in her hand.

They had dined at a small restaurant where the manager had greeted Teddy as a favored customer and had kissed Levanah's hand with great ceremony. Now, as the frothy, tinsel-tinted play reached its final curtain, she brought the palms of her hands together with enthusiasm.

"Good, wasn't it? Those chorus ladies were little stunners, weren't they?" Teddy discarded his air of sophistication.

"It was lovely," she breathed. Something starved in her nature had responded to the music and the glitter.

They stood for the Anthem and then filed out with the rest of the chattering throng into the main foyer. 'It was,' Levanah thought, 'almost as interesting to watch the audience as it was to watch the actors.' There were several elderly gentlemen with girls much younger than themselves, a family group with one plain daughter, and several unattached gentlemen hurrying to the stage door.

"Johnnies!" Teddy whispered in her ear. "They take out the chorus girls."

"And drink champagne from their slippers. I've read about it."

"Our cab should be here in a minute." He took her arm and piloted her to the entrance, beyond which a striped awning protected the crowd from the breeze. Gaslight flared on the jeweled dresses and top hats, the darkly gleaming cabs and white-maned horses with patient eyes, the boys in cloth caps and frayed trousers who offered their services as guides, the flower sellers in their striped shawls and cherry-trimmed hats. It was gay and noisy and vulgar and innocent, and a world away from a black-draped altar and a circle of hissing, hooded shapes.

A woman passing along the pavement had stopped abruptly and was staring at them both. Levanah stared back, lifting her small chin slightly. The woman was obviously a streetwalker. Her dyed red hair and heavily rouged lips proclaimed her profession. She was past her prime and, judging from the tawdriness of her gown, had fallen on hard times. Yet there was something disconcertingly familiar about the vivid blue eyes set between spiky black lashes, as if Levanah had seen them once in a dream and then woken into forgetfulness.

"Teddy, I think this is our cab." She dragged her own eyes from the woman with difficulty and spoke serenely, ignoring the uneasy thumping of her heart.

As they climbed up into the interior she could not resist glancing back and saw that the woman was still staring at them. Teddy had evidently noticed nothing, for he went on chattering about the evening, regretting the fact that he was leaving town again so soon.

"But I'll come and see you again as soon as I can, and I'm sure that Mrs. Varney will give you leave to come home for a week or two in the summer."

"I'm sure she will. No, don't get out. Sarah gave me a key so that I could let myself in. Thank you for a wonderful evening."

"We must go out again very soon." He leaned over and kissed her cheek before she stepped down from the cab. She gave him a brief wave and then hurried up the path under the archway.

The house was silent, lights dimmed, doors closed. On this night there were no house guests and no immediate sign of her employer. She took off her cloak and went down the back stairs into the kitchen. As she had expected, the door to the wine cellar was unlocked. She went through to the inner door and stepped within the heavy curtains into the temple.

As usual, a small lamp burned on the altar below the carved chair. Levanah threw a pinch of incense into the brazier and watched the white smoke wreathe up into twisting spirals. The familiar heavy perfume drifted to her nostrils as she took her place on the stool.

For nearly a week she had pushed a trouble below the surface of her conscious mind, had refused to admit that any trouble existed. Now, after the pleasant, ordinary evening, it was no longer possible to ignore what had begun as suspicion and was now hardening into certainty.

"There you are, dear child." Sarah glided through the aperture in the curtain, genuflected to the empty chair, and came over to Levanah. "I have been inspecting some of the vestments for wear and tear. Mathilde will have to exert with needle and thread. Did you have a pleasant evening?"

"Very pleasant."

"But a trifle dull, like your admirable cousin?" Sarah yawned delicately. "I find goodness so—unimaginative. But we daughters of darkness must not separate ourselves entirely from the common herd. Your family will be pleased to learn you are being well treated."

"I don't think that anybody except Teddy cares very much," Levanah said with a flash of resentment.

"But the brethren care," said Sarah. "They care very deeply what happens to you and the child."

Levanah sat very still for a moment. Then she said dully, "So you have guessed."

"I am not unintelligent," Sarah said gently. "And it

was clear to me from the beginning that you were a favored person."

"Favored!" Levanah gave an angry little laugh. "I've no wish to bear a bastard!"

"Of course you haven't," Sarah agreed. "It would be a burden and a social embarrassment."

"Then will you help me to get rid of it?" Levanah asked eagerly.

"Not so impulsive!" Sarah chided. "When will it be born?"

"Next February, I think."

"And you are a healthy girl who will probably give birth easily. The Master will be delighted. It is becoming increasingly difficult to obtain newborn infants."

"For what purpose?" But even as she asked the question, Levanah guessed the answer.

"There must be sacrifice, my dear. We are pledged to bring offerings to the Most High. Even Christians declare that the seed of their faith is nourished by the blood of its martyrs. Shall we believe less than they believe?"

"It is the Master's own child. His own child!"

"The Master is not sentimental about anybody's offspring," Sarah said, looking amused.

"It would be—"

"Murder? Your early training still influences you from time to time. It's only natural, but you must remember your vow of obedience, my dear. And it's not as if you wanted the child. You just asked me to help you to get rid of it."

"I know." Levanah bit her lip, not certain if she could analyze her feelings about an unborn shapeless mass and a baby that had drawn breath.

"There will not even be need for you to be present

at the ceremony, nor even for you to lay eyes on the infant at all," the other said soothingly. "And you need not fear that it will suffer. I myself have a great aversion to suffering."

Levanah was silent, head drooping.

"You would not wish to offend the Dark Ones, would you?" Sarah asked.

"No, of course not."

"If the sacrifice disturbs your natural instincts, it will be all the more pleasing to them," Sarah said. "And afterward, who knows what rewards they will shower upon you?"

"That first night I came," Levanah said slowly, "was that a sacrifice too?"

"The Irish girl?" Sarah shook her head. "Mathilde foolishly left the door unlocked, and the silly chit wandered in. Thomas found her on knees babbling an Ave Maria. We calmed her with laudanum, and later, after the Master had arrived, certain steps were taken."

'Into the river probably,' Levanah thought, and shivered.

"But you need not concern yourself with such matters," Sarah said. "We will arrange everything for you, and your family will never know. Pray about it, child. The Dark Ones will give you guidance, and when the Master and the others come for the meeting next month we will make plans."

She patted Levanah's shoulder and withdrew, the train of her scarlet gown hissing across the carpet.

The girl rose from the stool and went over to the great chair, leaning her hands on its carved arms and gazing up at the sword as she lowered herself to her knees. There was no answer here, no comfort, only an empty chill that ran along her nerves.

She wondered, not for the first time, who the Master was. His identity was concealed beneath the cloak and mask and horns. If anyone in the Lodge knew his name they had not revealed one hint of it to her. And now he was the father of her coming child. Just as Beth had borne a child out of wedlock so she, Levanah, would bear one too.

But Beth's child had been conceived in love. Her own was the fruit of—she could not think of a word that would define those hours that climaxed the Temple rituals. She knew only that it was not love, but more a kind of hatred.

And Beth's child had lived to grow up. Aunt Leah had at least reared and educated her. The child she was to bear would not live beyond a few hours or a few days. It would be laid upon the altar and its throat slit as if it were a cock or a kitten.

Something inside her swelled in mute protest. It was not love for the babe. It was more a feeling of possession toward the unknown life springing inside her. Life ought not to be denied. Stronger than the Oath she had taken was the desire to preserve that which she had created.

She sat back on her heels and began to think. If she returned home it would be, not to confront Aunt Leah with questions about her mother's death, but to ask for shelter and forgiveness. Aunt Leah would shelter her and forgive her and never let her forget for one instant how much cause she had to be grateful.

And Teddy? Thinking of her cousin an unaccustomed tenderness colored her mind. Teddy was kind and decent and unsuspecting, and he would be hurt when he learned what had happened. He would never dream of paying court to her again, and she had enjoyed his companionship at the theater.

The idea of begging help from her father was discarded as soon as it arose. Michael Shaw was too wrapped up in dreams of what he had lost to be of any practical use. And it made no difference where she went or what she did. The other brethren would find her and the child, and there would be no mercy for her disobedience.

It was as if, in seeking knowledge that would help her to destroy, she had walked unwittingly into a trap from which there seemed no escape, unless . . . she found the courage to fight fire with fire. Slowly, her eyes fixed upon the hanging sword, she rose and backed away. Ideas were seething in her mind and she needed time in which to decide, privacy in which to make her plans and find the ruthlessness necessary for their completion.

She went upstairs again, not forgetting to lock the door, and found Sarah waiting for her in the library.

"I see you have decided," she said, glancing up from her desk.

"It would be ungrateful of me to refuse to give sacrifice," Levanah said blandly, "but I can't pretend—it is not an easy choice to make."

"Your feelings do you credit. We are, after all, only human."

"I sometimes wonder if the Master is," Levanah said.

"Oh, he is human enough. He is a most respectable gentleman," Sarah said lightly.

"As we all are," the girl said with equal lightness. "Would you mind if I went to bed now? I am weary."

"Of course not, dear child. Run along and enjoy a good night's sleep."

"Good night, then." Levanah made the secret gesture used among the brethren at parting and went into her own room.

Lying in the big bed, the curtains drawn back from the window to reveal the night sky, she gazed into the blue-black gloom beyond the glass and thought of all that had to be accomplished. The Lodge must be destroyed, for she believed she had learned sufficient from the brethren for her purposes, and she had no intention of becoming their slave.

The child would have to be born and given out to someone to be decently reared. It was a pity in a way that she would not be able to keep it, but she had no intention of ever revealing to Teddy the existence of a baby. When the child had been born and adopted, she would return to Kingsmead. Aunt Leah must be forced to tell the truth. Cal must be punished for having forgotten her so quickly. Michael Shaw—she could not think of him as her father—was already in Paris again, immersed in his work. For the sake of the mother she had never seen, Michael Shaw would be left unpunished.

She rolled over onto her stomach, folded her hands and began to say her prayers.

"Master of Darkness, Lord of the Habitations of Hell, Regent of the dark side of the moon and of the chaos that lies beneath the earth . . ."

Her whisper trailed into silence. Other words were rising in her mind.

'Now I lay me down to sleep, I pray the Lord—'

She had learned them when she was very little, before she had discovered she was evil and a witch, but it was such a long time ago that she had forgotten how the rest of it went.

Chapter XIV

She had crept out earlier in the day and bolted the door that led onto the yard. Now, a street dress under her black cloak and hood, the pearl that had been her gift from the Master gleaming silvery white on her forefinger, she sat in her accustomed place, mouthing the chant, watching the incense swirl up into the shrouded gloom. If she could find the courage! Under cover of the loose sleeves of the robe her small hands were clenched, and little drops of perspiration glistened along her hairline.

"Something troubles you, Levanah."

The deep voice jerked her back to awareness of her surroundings. The dark eyes glinted through the slits in the mask.

"Your thoughts are elsewhere tonight," the Master said. "Your mind is not upon what you are doing."

"I am a little tired," she faltered.

"It is more than that," he persisted. "There is a resistance in you tonight. I feel it like a barrier.

Remember that sacrifice should be willing sacrifice. Yet something holds you apart from us."

The eyes bored into hers, the voice lulled her into a waking sleep. The others were looking at her with curiosity.

Levanah stood up, emptying her mind, willing the frantic beating of her heart to subside.

"I am troubled," she said clearly. "Am I permitted to confide in the brethren?"

"By all means. We stand as your family," the Master said.

"There is something I must show you. May I leave the circle for a few minutes? It's very important," she pleaded.

"Very well, if it is so important, but I dislike any interruption to the ceremonies."

The moment for which she had nerved herself had come and could not be avoided. She forced herself to move without haste, to genuflect and make the sign of friendship. That sign was in itself a betrayal, but she had no more compunction about what she was going to do than she would have had about destroying a pack of rats.

Beyond the curtain that shielded the main body of the temple from where the robes were hung, she took a lighted candle from its socket, laid it to the oil-soaked rag she had hidden under the edge of the carpet, and stepped quickly into the wine cellar, locking the door behind her. A candle burning near the foot of the stairs provided her with the flame she needed to ignite the oil-soaked casks of wine. They flamed up more quickly than she supposed they would, and at the same moment she heard confused voices beyond the inner door.

She stumbled up the steps, locked the door that led

into the kitchen, paused long enough to scatter a shovelful of burning coals over the rush matting, and ran up into the main hall, pulling off her robe as she went. She had hidden a carpetbag under the stairs that day. It contained the picture of Beth, the crystal, and the little wooden Lob, and these were, she thought, snatching up the bag, the most precious things she possessed.

As she wrenched open the front door, smoke billowed around the edges of the baize-covered door. She had not expected the fire to take hold so quickly.

As she ran through the courtyard into the dark street she remembered that poor, stupid Janet was asleep somewhere in the house. A pang of conscience smote her and then she dismissed the girl from her mind. When a pack of rats was being destroyed the fate of an innocent white mouse was of little moment.

She walked fast, the cowled neckline of her tweed dress pulled over her head. Once she glanced back and saw an orange glare fan out across the dark sky. Then she hurried on, the ticket she had bought the previous day and the money she had saved from her salary tucked between her small breasts.

At the railway station she evaded the sleepy-looking porter and curled up between two large packing cases. It was quiet and warm in her hiding place, but she felt too alert to sleep. The wine and the oil would by now surely have aided the fire to complete what she had begun. By now they would surely be dead and past their power to harm her or her child.

The Master, Sarah Varney, Thomas, Mathilde, the Professor and his wife, the two gentlemen who shared an apartment, the insignificant gentleman, the rake, Mrs. Ganton and Eulalia. She ticked them off one by one. Twelve people.

'I have just murdered twelve people,' Levanah thought. Surely she *ought* to feel something! Shame or grief or horror or even triumph. But she felt nothing at all except a vague sense of satisfaction at having completed a task. The whole episode had about it the quality of a dream.

The first train to Wales left at six o'clock. She had never been to Wales before, never seen the mountains from which the first Falcon witch had sprung. Cousin Wenna's mother still lived up in the hills.

'My own grandmother's aunt,' Levanah thought. 'Why, she must be as old as time.'

Old or not, she had a tiny farm where Levanah could hide, and the old woman could be bribed or threatened into silence. She could have the child there and there would be somebody to take it off her hands, and then when it was over she would go back to Kingsmead and the reckoning could begin.

'Twelve people,' she thought again. 'One for each month in the year.'

She was abruptly and completely and dreamlessly asleep, her cowled head leaning against the packing case, the distant sound of shunting engines making no more than a vague accompaniment to the harmony of her slumber.

It was a weary, crumpled Levanah who alighted from the buggy cart in which she had made the last part of her journey. It was a hot sunlit afternoon and a faint haze lay over the yellow corn. She had glimpsed the grayish brown ramparts of the castle and a curve of blue water and then they were climbing out of the town, above slate roofs and steeply twisting streets. On the left a red-brick building with adjacent playing fields was pointed out by the driver as the Grammar School.

"Got to pay to go there, unless you pass the Scholarship," he told her. "You'll have finished with schooling though, I take it?"

"I'm visiting a relative—Mrs. Evans."

"Old Mrs. Catrin Price that was? Well, now, I knew when I picked you up there was something familiar about your face. They say she had red hair when she was a girl. About a hundred years ago, I'd reckon." He chuckled at his own joke.

"But she's still alive?," she questioned anxiously.

"Spry as a two-year-old," he assured her cheerfully. "Tom-Color-the-Sheep does the farmwork now, what there is of it."

"Tom-Color-the-Sheep?"

"On account of he put some dye in the dip years back, to spite his dad for giving him low wages. Bright red those sheep came out of that dip!" He chuckled again, slapping his knee with his hand. "You'll be a great-niece or something to Mrs. Catrin?"

"Great-great niece."

"Now there was a sister once who died young, they say."

"That sister's daughter was my grandmother."

"So there's the connection. Mrs. Catrin had a daughter herself once. Married late she did, and Wenna was born, oh, it must be forty years ago. She wed a young fellow who was killed in the quarry, and after that she went into England. Must be twenty years since I've seen Wenna."

"She married again," Levanah said briefly.

"So Mrs. Catrin was telling me. She was invited to the wedding, but she wouldn't go, of course. Too old and set in her ways to jaunt off on trains. 'Saron' is up that short lane, just past the chapel. Built last year the chapel was, and we've had a good selection of preachers since. Will you be church or chapel now?"

"Neither," she said flatly.

The driver gave her a tolerant look as he pulled on the reins and watched her climb down into the road.

"Mrs. Catrin was never one for chapel going either," he commented. "Shall I come to the door with you?"

"No need." She cut short his desire to be a witness at the family reunion. "Thank you for the ride."

"I was coming this way." He flapped the reins, gave her a friendly, slightly puzzled nod, and hunched in his seat again.

The yard was swept clean save for some grains being pecked up by a fat, lazy-looking hen. A dog barked furiously somewhere out of sight, and then a tall woman, only slightly bent with age, came around the corner of the small stone house and stopped short.

"Were you wanting something, miss?" she inquired.

"Are you Mrs. Evans—Catrin Price that was?"

"I'm Catrin Evans, Miss—?"

"Falcon. Levanah Falcon."

The old woman's sun-seamed face creased into a smile displaying an excellent set of porcelain teeth. She was neatly dressed in an ankle-length skirt and long-sleeved bodice of brown wool and had a red scarf tied gypsy fashion over her white hair.

"Levanah! Why you'll be Beth's daughter!" she exclaimed.

"You knew her?" For an instant Levanah was confused.

"I never met her, but my daughter Wenna keeps me up to date with news of the English relatives. Well, come in, do. No sense in standing in the hot sun!"

She bustled open the front door and led the way into a large whitewashed room, which stretched to the back of the house and was evidently the sole living area, for a caldron of what smelled like broth hung on a chain over a crackling fire, a newspaper was folded on the seat of a rocking chair, and a tray of buns was cooling on the back windowsill. There were some geranium plants also on the windowsill and a large, colored print of King Edward hung over the fireplace.

"Come in and sit down. The other chair is more comfortable. You'll have a nice cup of tea in a minute. And how are they all in England? Wenna has not written since her marriage, but she is busy, I suppose, between the farm and the school. You'll have some drop scones after your beef broth? It's lucky I keep the big bed in the spare room aired and made up. For twenty years I've been expecting a visitor and now one arrives!"

The voice, lively despite its age, ran on serenely. Levanah felt herself relaxing into it. A small gate-legged table was set up next to her chair and to her surprise she found herself eating heartily. Not until she had drained a second cup of tea did Aunt Catrin come to the matter in hand.

"Wenna said in her last letter that you were in London, working as a companion to a lady there. Has she given you a holiday, then?"

Levanah hesitated. The events of the previous months had become more unreal than ever during the long train journey north. It was impossible to tell the whole truth, but the old woman's eyes, though kindly, were shrewd, and part of the story would have to be told.

"I left my place of employment," she said at last.

"There was ... there was a terrible accident late last night. A fire. I managed to get out and I ... I must have wandered. The next thing I can recall is getting on a train. I slept most of the way here."

"Was anyone hurt in this fire?" Aunt Catrin demanded.

"Mrs. Varney, my employer, was in the wine cellar, I think. It's all so confused that my head aches when I try to remember."

"Perhaps you had a blow on your head."

"I rather think I must have done," Levanah said. "But it's all very hazy."

"I see." The old woman gave her a long look and then settled herself in the rocking chair. After a few moments she said, "But why did you come here? It would have been more natural for you to go to Marie Regina."

"I can't. I can't go back there yet."

"Why not?"

"I'm expecting a child," Levanah said. "I can't tell them at home. I can't possibly tell them."

"And so you came here to me? Why to me?"

"I thought I could hide here until after it's born. Then I could have it adopted and go home."

"But they'll surely inquire your whereabouts before then!" Aunt Catrin exclaimed. "And then the fire ..."

"Don't you see? They'll think I was burned up in the fire and not look for me. I can go back after the child is born."

"Telling them you lost your memory after a blow on the head, I suppose? That's a very foolish idea. A wicked one, too, causing them grief when there's no cause. Why not tell them the truth?"

"If you won't let me stay here," Levanah said sullenly, "I'll go somewhere else."

"Now wait a minute! Let me think. You cannot go wandering the country at your age!" The old woman leaned her chin on her hand and frowned into the fire. When she looked up again her eyes were sharp.

"This fire . . ." she said. "Child, have you anything on your conscience?"

"Only the child." Levanah's eyes were soft and clear. "I allowed myself to be seduced. He promised to marry me, but he has a wife."

"Did your employer know?"

"I was going to tell her," Levanah said. "I expected to be dismissed at once, so I packed a few things. And then the fire broke out and I was running. I'd had it in mind to come to you, and I suppose with the shock . . ."

"And the blow on your head."

"Yes, that too. I simply got on the train and came here."

"Where am I supposed to hide you while the rest of your family believes you were killed in the fire? It won't do, cariad. It won't do at all."

Levanah's fingers clenched on her cup. She had pictured Aunt Catrin as old and frail, and easily persuaded, but this woman was disconcertingly acute.

"I'm in your hands," she said meekly. "But don't tell Aunt Leah or the others about the child. You don't know what it would be like! She was forever telling me how wicked my mother was to bear a child out of wedlock."

"It won't be the first time that a member of this family has dropped a hedge get," Aunt Catrin said. "If my own sister hadn't lain down under the apple trees for a passing tinker, your own grandmother would never have been born. These things happen."

"Aunt Leah wouldn't think of it like that," Levanah said.

"I think the best course to take," Aunt Catrin mused, "is for you to write to your Aunt Leah at once. Tell her you traveled up yesterday to spend a month with me. She will assume you left before the fire started."

"She will write and tell me about it, and then I will simply delay my return until after the child is born! Nobody will travel all the way up here to see me. It's quite perfect!"

"It's very far from perfect," Aunt Catrin said severely. "I resent being dragged into your affairs, but you are my niece's granddaughter, and I owe the Falcons nothing. I reared Margred after my sister died and she went into England and married her grand-cousin and never came home again. My own girl went into England and never came back, though she sends me money from time to time. But I owe the Falcons nothing."

"So you'll help me?"

"The fire ..." The old woman's mind had returned to its original worry. "How did it begin?"

"Mrs. Varney drank sometimes," Levanah said, her voice reluctant. "She used to invite friends down into the wine cellar, late at night. I never went there my-self, but I used to hear them ... singing."

"And the father of your baby?"

"I don't want to think about him. He knows nothing of the child. I'm very tired and I don't want to talk about it." Her voice was ragged with the threat of hysteria.

"Then we won't talk of it."

Aunt Catrin rose and opened one of the two doors leading off the main room. "Your grandmother slept here when she was a child. She was actually born in that bed, and her mother died there. I've been expecting a visitor for twenty years, ever since Wenna left home."

The room was square and whitewashed, with a flowered carpet on the floor and an embroidered motto in Welsh hanging over the bed. The room smelled faintly musty and she stepped across to the window and opened it. The air was sharp and fresh, and she breathed in deeply, letting the tension drain out of her.

She would write to Aunt Leah, telling her she was holidaying in Wales. It was unlikely she would be questioned about the fire. Nobody could have survived such a holocaust, and there was little risk of anybody's having seen her getting on the early train.

'That part of my life is behind me,' she thought. 'I can stay here quietly until the baby is born, and then I'll go home, and Aunt Leah can begin to fret because I'll not rest until I've learned the truth about my mother's suicide.'

"I can heat some water in the tub for a bath for you," said Aunt Catrin. "We've no bathroom here, but the well's sweet and there's an earth closet next to the barn."

"A wash-down will be fine," Levanah said sweetly. "You mustn't think I intend to be a burden on you while I'm here. And I can help you and I've money to pay for my keep."

"Save it for the babe," the old woman advised. "I can manage well enough. I've managed alone for the past twenty years. You'd not think I was eighty-four, would you?"

"No, indeed," Levanah said truthfully.

"Well, I am," Aunt Catrin said proudly. "Eighty-

four years old, and never been out of Wales in my
life. I went to Chester once, years ago. Not on a train,
but by stagecoach. Rattled my bones to bits, and
when we got there, it was nothing but hard pavements and noisy English visitors. I vowed then I'd
stay where the Good Lord planted me. I reared your
grandmother and wed a good man for all that he
came from the south, and was past forty when I bore
my own child. And now she's wed to another English
cousin, and my man is buried here, and there's space
beside him for me when my time comes. And that
won't be for a long while!" she finished fiercely.

"I'm sure it won't," Levanah said soothingly, wondering if the old woman was always so garrulous.

"I still have some schoolbooks that your grandmother had," Aunt Catrin said happily. "You'll be interested to see them. She had a very pretty hand and
she could read better than the minister."

"Is it true," Levanah interrupted, "that the first
witch ever born in our family came from here?"

"Old tales," Aunt Catrin said. "I never knew how
much to believe. But it's true that my mother and my
sister and Margred too bore the crescent moon on
their thighs."

"So did my mother and so do I," Levanah said.

"Then there may be truth in it. I mocked when I
was younger, but now that I am older I don't mock at
anything," Aunt Catrin said. "If you'd like some more
tea, just help yourself. I like to keep the kettle sim-
mering and the soup too. A basin of hot soup with a
crust of fresh bread is a very comforting thing indeed.
Good for the baby too. When will it be born?"

"February, I think. Will it make things difficult for
you—with your neighbors, I mean?"

"I've enough Falcon blood in me not to care tuppence what the neighbors say," Aunt Catrin declared. "You have a nice rest for an hour or two now. I've the cow to milk and Toss to walk."

"Was that the dog I heard barking?" Levanah asked, sitting on the edge of the bed.

"He usually runs free, but Griff Jones's bitch is in heat and she's scarcely over her last litter yet," Aunt Catrin said. "You sleep now and you can see the schoolbooks later."

'As if I were interested,' Levanah thought, punching the feather pillow irritably as the slightly bent, tall old figure hurried out.

It was going to be a long and tedious wait until the baby was born, with only the nattering old woman for company. It was to be hoped Teddy wouldn't take it in his head to pay her a flying visit. She doubted it, but if he did she would think of something. It was odd to realize that Wenna and Cal's child would be born about the same time as her own. There had been a period when she had been jealous of Cal's admiration for Mary.

She drifted into a half sleep, shot through with vivid images. The Master, horns glinting, stood with the sword between his hands and beat time with a cloven foot, as the others circled about him. Mary danced with Cal until Charlotte Bishop rode up on a bicycle and snatched her up behind. Wenna danced with Cal then, and Aunt Leah whirled past with Teddy. Only Levanah danced alone, round and round, while the sword flashed in her eyes.

She heard herself cry out into the wind, "But I have no partner!" and the music played more loudly, the dancers whirled ever faster, and Aunt Catrin was calling, "Wake up, cariad! You're riding the nightmare!"

"I was dreaming." She sat up, blinking to bring the lined, old face into focus.

"And sweating something terrible. All this riding about in trains is very bad for the health. And now there are motorcars too, if you please. Filling the roads with smoke, addling the brains, frightening the cattle ..."

"Have I been asleep for long?"

"More than two hours. The water is heated for your wash and I've some potato scones on the griddle."

"Did I— I suppose I was talking a lot?" Levanah swung her legs over the side of the bed.

"Muttering you were!" said Aunt Catrin. "Muttering away and not one word clear. My man was like that sometimes when his chest was bad. It was coal dust, you see. He'd worked down the mines for years."

'If she doesn't stop talking soon,' Levanah thought, smiling gently, 'I will go insane! It's no wonder I'm her first visitor for twenty years; if she talked as much to all of them they'd give the place a wide berth. And I have to endure it for months!"

Chapter XV

"I made it perfectly clear to you," Leah said, "that I will not have you running over to Whittle Farm at every available opportunity!"

"But little Giles is perfectly sweet," Mary protested.

"Giles!" Leah pursed her lips. "I cannot imagine what possessed Wenna and Caleb to choose such a rustic name! There has never been a Giles in the family. Not, you understand, that I consider Caleb to be a member of the family in any but the most limited sense. And if you are suddenly so passionately fond of children it is a very great pity that you do not exert yourself more in the direction of matrimony."

"You're pushing Teddy at me again," Mary said. "You don't accept facts, do you? He's not interested in me and I'm not interested in any man!"

"You and Charlotte Bishop make that abundantly clear," Leah said. "Your relationship is the scandal of the neighborhood."

"The neighborhood can think what it chooses,"

Mary said, flushing deeply. "My friendship with Charlie is a pure, spiritual relationship."

"Very spiritual," Leah said coldly. "Two women holding hands, riding on bicycles, smoking cigarettes! Don't deny it! Your room reeked of tobacco when I went in the other day."

"You had no right—"

"As your mother I have every right to ensure that your friends are suitable and your habits respectable. You are not yet of age."

"You never thought of that when you sent Levanah away. She was younger than I am."

"She was a bad influence."

"Everyone I like becomes a bad influence sooner or later," the girl muttered. "You would like to creep into my mind and rearrange my thoughts."

Leah straightened her aching shoulders and gazed at her daughter in perplexity. Mary had changed a great deal since Levanah's departure. Her dark prettiness had become harder and brighter. Her voice had lost its gentleness. In her striped blouse and divided skirt, a small bowler of dark green matching the boyish tie, a faint smear of nicotine on her index finger, she looked, Leah thought, a typically fast modern woman.

"I have decided," she said at last, "to take no notice of your insolence. Fortunately I've already taken steps to ensure that this unnatural friendship comes to an end. I've waited too long as it is. I admit that in the beginning I thought that Miss Bishop would be a pleasant companion, but I was deceived in her character. I was grossly deceived. However, I have now made up my mind that the association is to end."

"How? How are you going to do that?"

"I have written to Miss Bishop dismissing her from the school."

"For what reason? She's a good teacher and she's carried all the work alone since Cousin Wenna left."

"I consider her an undesirable influence upon the pupils," Leah said coldly. "I have been fortunate to engage two maiden ladies, sisters, to take over the running of the school."

"You have no right—" Mary began.

"The school was built with my money on Falcon land. I engage and dismiss whom I choose. I have chosen to dismiss Charlotte Bishop. She will have received the letter this morning with three months' salary in lieu of notice. I've also provided her with a glowing reference. She will have no difficulty in obtaining fresh employment."

"It's monstrous!" Mary gasped. "You couldn't be so cruel, so unfair!"

"If you're going to be hysterical, go to your room," Leah said wearily.

Mary burst into angry tears and fled, slamming the door so hard that the ornaments on the mantelpiece rattled. A moment later her bicycle wheels churned over the cobbles beyond the solar window.

Leah put her fingers up to her temples and willed their throbbing to cease. For months she had suffered from headaches of increasing severity that made her sick and dizzy. If the headache would only stop she would be able to cope properly with everything that was happening. Recently she had begun to feel that events were slipping out of her control.

Mary had become a rebellious stranger, Teddy was concerned only with his friends at the University, and Levanah ... when she thought of Levanah the throbbing in her head became a searing pain.

The newspaper report of the fire that had gutted Varney House, incinerating all those within, had filled her with a mixture of sorrow and relief. Levanah had been a very sweet baby and such a death for so young a girl was horrible. But Levanah was evil, with the witchmark on her thigh and lewd, pagan notions in her narrow red head. It was right that such evil should be burned out and purified.

Then had come the letter telling them that Levanah had left for a holiday in Wales on the day before the fire. And later on another letter had arrived, expressing great shock at the news of Mrs. Varney's terrible death and informing Leah blandly that Levanah intended to stay on with Aunt Catrin.

"Mam will be glad of the company," Wenna had said. "I've often felt that I ought to go back and see her myself, but now with the child coming and a husband to feed . . ."

She had glanced smilingly at Cal as she spoke, her hand unconsciously stroking her swollen belly. Since her wedding she had blossomed, becoming plumper and glossier, her green eyes sleepy as a cat's. Leah had felt fierce envy mingled with disgust. After one duty visit to see the new baby she had not been near Whittle Farm since. Not only Wenna's contentment and Cal's obvious pride in his wife and son had upset her. The old farm had been warm and gay and filled with laughter.

In contrast, the great house rang with loneliness. Her footsteps were too loud on the stone stairs and the tapestries had whispered against the walls. She would have been glad of company, but Levanah and Teddy penned home only dutiful little notes. Mary was always off with Charlotte Bishop, and there were few callers.

The rain-drenched darkness of an April night was closing in. The house was even more silent than usual, for she had given the servants the evening off to attend the Easter Dance in the Assembly Rooms at Maidstone. They would not be back until dawn, when, after a night's jollification, they would start at once on their daily duties. A cold supper had been laid for her but she was in no mood to eat. Later she would brew herself some tea in the silver teapot she had used all her adult life. Like the bunch of keys at her waist, it had become a symbol of her authority as mistress of Kingsmead. After her, who would rule? She had hoped so desperately that it might be Mary.

A loud rapping at the front door disturbed her reverie. She wondered irritably if Charlotte Bishop had come to plead for another chance. It seemed unlikely, her letter of dismissal being couched in terms that admitted no argument. She smoothed her heavy chignon and went through into the hall.

The opened door revealed a tall figure against a background of rain-swept sky and the dark encircling walls of the courtyard. For an instant she blinked in query, then the figure moved into the radiance of the lamp hung within the door and a voice said, "You haven't forgotten me, have you, Leah?"

"Grace? Grace Finn?" Her own voice was a thread of sound.

"Falcon. Grace Falcon. I was wed to your brother, remember?"

"I have spent twenty years trying to forget," Leah said bitterly.

"We have some things to discuss," Grace said.

"We have nothing—" Leah began, but she had fallen back a step and the other woman was within the hall.

"Shall we go into the solar?" she said. "What we have to talk about is ... private, don't you think?"

Leah found herself closing the door and following the other without conscious volition. In the oak-paneled room Grace had already divested herself of her shabby, fox-trimmed coat and the elaborate hat with its bunches of violets and cherries. Her hair, puffed into a frizz of curls, had been dyed to some semblance of its original red, but gray roots showed, and powder flaked the lines around the still-vivid blue eyes.

"Nothing's changed," Grace remarked. "Everything's the same here, as if time stood still at Kingsmead. You've worn well, Leah. I've run to an extra bit of fat, myself."

"What do you want?" She forced herself to speak coldly and steadily.

"To look up my old friends, of course."

"I was never a friend of yours!"

"That's true enough!" Grace displayed her excellent teeth. "You made a fool of me for your own purposes, didn't you? Using me to provide your brother with a wife and Kingsmead with an heir?"

"You were glad enough to accept the bargain."

"Because I was carrying your brother Price's child, and he'd taken it into his head to sail off to Australia. And then you came along, all Lady Bountiful and Kiss-Me-Fanny. 'My brother John is very shy and retiring,' says you. 'He's undertaken to let me find him a wife. Marry John and you'll be Lady Falcon. Make him believe the child is his, and you can live happy ever after.'"

"You could have done."

"In this great dump, built in the middle of nowhere? With your ruling the roost and giving the orders, and poor John impotent? How in hell he ever believed that Teddy was his child I'll never know!"

"You left him," Leah said. "You left him and the baby, and you ran away with *my* husband. You and Paul ran off together! Did you know that I was with child myself when you left? Did you know I had to rear my own daughter and your son, without the support of a husband?"

"You married Paul Simmons for breeding purposes and because he liked your sister Edith and you couldn't endure that she should be wed before you," Grace said. "But Paul had the last laugh there, didn't he? He left Edith in the family way too!"

"I was grossly deceived in the pair of you," Leah said.

"You never cared about either of us," Grace said resentfully. "You never thought of us as people, only as things to be used, fresh blood to be brought into the precious Falcon tribe!"

"I loved Paul!"

"You don't love folk," Grace said scornfully. "You suffocate them, Leah. You possess them! You never broke your heart over Paul when he left and I reckon you were glad to see the back of me, because then you could have your brother all to yourself again!"

"And did you and Paul live happily ever after?" Leah asked.

"He left me years ago. Ran off with a chorus girl," Grace said wryly. "I heard he died, in Rome, I think. Drink, I expect. He was a weak man at bottom. It was great sport while it lasted."

"And why have you come back now?" Leah asked. Odd to be told she had been a widow for years! Later, when her head had stopped aching, she would think about it.

Grace settled herself without any invitation in the chair by the fire.

"More than a year ago," she said, "I saw Teddy. He was coming out of a theater with a girl, and they stood on the pavement waiting for a cab, I daresay. I recognized him. He's the spitting image of Price. Did you ever hear of him again, by the bye?"

"We lost touch completely. Price was never one for writing letters. You didn't speak to Teddy?"

"Just had a good look at him, as a loving mother might. He does you credit, Leah. A fine, upstanding young gentleman."

"I believe I can manage without your approval," Leah said stonily.

"I'm giving an opinion. I've a right to do that."

"You have no rights at all! You abandoned them when you abandoned him and John."

"Teddy might not think so." The deep-blue eyes flickered slyly.

"He believes you died when he was born. You know poor John was thrown from his horse and killed?"

"I read it in the newsppaer. I was sorry about it."

"I reared Teddy by myself. He believes both his parents are dead."

"Then he'll be very pleased to welcome a long-lost mother."

"You'd not do it! You'd not dare! Why you're a streetwalker, a common streetwalker! You'd not tell him!"

"Teddy's a fine gentleman. He'd not want to see his mother in need."

"John gave you jewels when he married you," Leah said gaspingly. "You took them with you. What happened to them?"

"Your husband drank them up," Grace said. "Believe me, I'm not here to make trouble. I'd not do that for the world, but this past winter's been a hard one. My doctor says I ought to go abroad for my health—chest, you know—but where's the money to come from?"

"You dirty, blackmailing bitch!" Leah's eyes blazed with fury.

"Hard words," Grace chided. "You can forget to act the lady when it suits you. I'd not want very much."

"Not in the beginning," said Leah. She spoke slowly, almost gently, the vein in her temple pulsating under the white skin. "But you wouldn't be content with a little. You'd come back for more and more, bleeding us dry. I know it. I know people like you. Trashy guttersnipes."

"Then I'll see if my son is more generous. I'm not in good health, and I couldn't even afford a ride from the station. I walked here."

"You'll not go near Teddy!"

"Oh, but I think I will. I'm certain he'd be interested in my story. How I was seduced by your brother Price, how you bribed me to marry John and make him believe the child was his, and how—"

She broke off, her hands flung up in sudden panic.

Leah had snatched up the heavy poker and, even as Grace's words rose into panic, she brought it crashing down on the other's head. Her thick, unswept curls afforded some protection but the blow stunned her. She moaned slightly and clutched at space, her heavy frame in the gaudily cheap dress beginning to fall sideways across the arm of the chair. Leah raised the poker and struck again, hearing the sharp crack of bone, seeing blood spurt brightly from the powdered skin. The rouged mouth opened, and a thin high scream came out between the parted lips.

She had to make the dreadful noise stop. She had to restore peace to the tranquil old room so that the pain in her head would go away. She went on striking over and over and over, and then there was silence, save for her own labored breathing and the hissing of coals in the grate.

She looked dully at the poker in her hands, at her red-stained forearms, at the inert, broken thing that flopped over the side of the chair. Nausea twisted her insides and she bent over, retching, the coldness of sweat dewing her forehead.

Then there were footsteps and Levanah walked in.

Leah straightened up, the poker dangling from her clenched hand, and stared at her niece.

"You'd best put the poker down, Aunt Leah," Levanah said.

She sounded amused, and even in the midst of the unreality that surrounded her, Leah felt a faint distaste. A nicely reared young lady should have displayed horror at the scene.

"I'll get you some brandy," Levanah said, moving to the decanter. "You'd best sit down before you faint."

"I am not going to faint," Leah said, pronouncing each word slowly and carefully, but she sat down, the bloodied poker clattering into the hearth as her fingers relaxed.

Levanah came over with the brandy and gave it to her. The glass rattled against her teeth and the fiery liquid burned her throat, but the room was coming back into focus, its outlines solidifying.

"Is that how you killed Aunt Edith?" Levanah

asked. "With a stone instead of the poker? Is that how it was?"

"An accident. It was an accident," Leah said numbly.

"This was murder," Levanah said, "and they'll hang you for it. At the very least, you'll rot in prison for the next twenty years."

"You don't understand," Leah said. "You don't know—"

"I came through the back door," Levanah interrupted. "I walked from the station too, a few yards behind her. I wondered who she was and why she seemed familiar. I remember now I saw her months ago when Teddy visited me and took me to the theater. I stood in the hall just now, listening."

"Then you must realize I had to protect Teddy."

"Protect him—or yourself? What a liar you are," the girl said coolly. She was looking at the sagging figure with an expression of disgust on her face.

"So that was Teddy's mother," she said at last.

"A cheap chorus girl whom I picked up out of the gutter," Leah said. "Price never knew she was with child, and he'd never have married her anyway. He was wild, with no sense of responsibility, wanting to make his fortune in the Colonies. John was the elder, the gentle one who loved the land. He had a right to have a son, but he'd confided to me that he didn't think himself capable of fathering a child. I said I would find him a decent, healthy girl."

"And foisted his brother's child on him."

"John loved Grace and he was proud of Teddy, proud of his son! She was Lady Falcon, and she lived here at Kingsmead. I treated her like a sister."

"If that's true," Levanah said dryly, "then God help her!"

"She betrayed me," Leah said. "First Edith and then Grace—they both made a fool of me. And when Grace ran away she took my husband with her. My husband! And I reared her babe. I'm the only mother that Teddy has ever known. I won't have it spoiled and dirtied."

"So you killed her," Levanah said.

"It was an accident. I didn't mean to . . . it was an accident," Leah said flatly.

"They'll hang you," Levanah said. "They'll hang you if they find out."

"She said she'd walked here from the station. You were behind her, you said? Were you together on the train? Did she see you?"

"She got on just ahead of me when I changed trains at London," Levanah said, wrinkling her nose in an effort to remember. "She didn't see me. We walked straight off the platform without giving in our tickets. The station master wasn't around. Oh, I did see Mary and Charlotte Bishop but they didn't see me."

"Mary? I'd forgotten about her. She'll be home at any time!" Panic surged up in her again.

"They were in the gig," Levanah said calmly, "with trunks and boxes piled up behind them. They looked as if they were going away."

"To London," Leah said. "They would have been going to London. There's no train back there tonight and they'd not want to wait until morning."

"You mean they were running away. Mary finally cutting the apron strings!"

"I'll think about it later," Leah said. "I can't—cope with Mary now. I'll think about it later."

"Where are the servants?"

"In Maidstone. The Easter Dance is being held there. They'll not be back until dawn."

"We have to get rid of *that!*" Levanah said.

"We?" Leah too stared at the body.

"We'll wrap it in a sheet and put it in the back of the cart," Levanah said. "We can bury it in the woods. I'll be getting the sheet while you wash the poker and the chair cover. You'd better change your dress, too. We'll bury it with her."

"Are you saying you'll help me?" Leah whispered.

"Scandal in the Falcon family would never do," Levanah said. "I'll get the sheet."

Numbness descended on Leah again, blanking her brain. She had no mind, no will of her own, but moved to her niece's directions, her eyes unseeing, her hands lifting, carrying, cleaning.

The body was heavier than she imagined it would be. It was so heavy that sweat ran down her face into her mouth and tasted like tears. Levanah had harnessed one of the ponies to the cart, and had helped her to lift the shrouded figure into the back.

"We'll need a spade," Levanah said briskly. "After the rain the ground will be soft. It won't be long before we're back at Kingsmead. Did you put your soiled gown into the cart?"

Leah could not even remember having changed her dress, but she nodded.

"Get up, then!" Levanah's voice sounded impatient. "We'll go across the fields. It's so dark nobody will see us."

There was no reality anywhere. Even the rain fell soft and blurred, without wetting her overmuch. The spade squelching in the earth threw up clods of mud under the ghosts of dead birches.

"That's deep enough," Levanah said. "We'll put her in it. Hold your end up. The blood will seep through the sheet if you're not careful. The gown too. When it's filled in we'll drag branches over it."

The girl's voice was so calm, so confident. In the darkness the yellow eyes turned briefly toward her and glittered.

The journey back was soft and silent, the cart jolting a little over the plowed ruts. Lamps welcomed them back into the great hall, and the fire in the solar sent out a comforting glow.

"The chair cover had better be burned," Levanah was saying, thrusting it into the grate.

"It's very old, eighteenth-century. One of the daughters of the house embroidered it," Leah said.

She felt cold and stiff and her teeth were chattering.

"We'll have a nice cup of tea," Levanah said. "You must admit it was a lucky chance that made me decide to come home today. Aunt Catrin was all for me staying on with her until summer, but I thought you'd like to see me again. You've a lot to tell me, haven't you?"

"About what?" Leah, her head feeling as if it were about to float from her body, spoke with infinite weariness.

"About my mother and Michael Shaw," Levanah said. "And why she killed herself when he'd written to say he was coming. Did you truly think there would never be a reckoning?"

Chapter XVI

Reality came back in a cold wind of accusation, leveled at her from hard, young eyes. But that was not the right word. Levanah's eyes had never been young even when she was a baby in the cradle.

"I know that my father was a married man," her niece was saying. "I know that he and my mother parted, and on the day I was born she sent him her moonstone ring as a sign that she needed him desperately. And I know that he sent it back to her with a letter saying that his wife had died. I know all that, so don't bother trying to deny it."

"You are talking wildly," Leah said. "This terrible accident—"

"Murder, Aunt. It was murder, and so I shall inform the constable at Maidstone unless you tell me the truth."

She was too weary, too heartsick to lie.

"Your mother was an ... innocent," she said slowly. "There was something in her that was not balanced.

She was ... fey, they call it. To let a complete
stranger lodge on her property, to give herself to him
without question! There was no sense in it. She had
to be protected against herself. After he left, when
she discovered she was pregnant, she wrote to him. In
those days, mail was collected from the house. I took
the letters she wrote. They were never posted."

"Why? Why?"

"He could not have married her unless there had
been a divorce. My sister might have been involved
in a divorce action."

"But she was going to have a child!"

"There have been bastards in our family many
times. Such things happen. There has not yet been a
divorce."

"But he did receive the ring."

"She must have run to the village and posted it
there," Leah said. "It was a terrible time for me. I
couldn't watch her every second. My own husband
had run away with Grace. Mary and Teddy were babies, and Edith had gone to Whittle Farm to bear her
own bastard there. And then John was thrown from
his horse, right in front of Beth. She ran away down
to the old cottage and left him lying there. We didn't
find her until the next day, and you were born then.
There was so much coming and going. She must have
sent him the ring then."

"He wrote back to her. Did you steal the letter?"

"He wrote saying his wife had been killed and he
was free to come to her. If he'd come he'd have taken
her away and the baby. He'd have taken two Falcons
from Kingsmead. I couldn't let that happen. John was
dead, and Paul and Grace gone, and Edith estranged
from me, and Price out in Australia. I'd have been left
with Teddy and Mary. I couldn't allow a stranger to

take Beth away. She wasn't fit for marriage and he wasn't good enough. A strong man would have left his wife."

"But you would have stopped that. You did stop it. He never knew she was with child!"

"I was clever," Leah said. "I told her that the ring had been returned from his bank with a letter saying he'd died three weeks before. I said that as soon as she could travel we'd go for a holiday, up to Aunt Catrin in Wales. She'd never been there. She never asked to see the letter. Beth always trusted people."

"She killed herself," Levanah said. "She killed herself because she thought her lover was dead."

"Within an hour of my giving her the news," Leah said sadly. "I left her alone to have privacy in her grief. She got out of bed and cut her wrists open with a little silver penknife. No balance in her nature, you see."

"And you wrote to Michael Shaw, telling him she'd died of pneumonia."

"You were only a week old. You needed a mother," Leah said. "Your father had no claim on you. You were a Falcon, like Mary and Teddy. You belonged to Kingsmead."

"And to you. Isn't that what you really mean?"

"I've always loved children," Leah said. "I was never loved as a child, you know. Not really loved, like Edith and Beth and the boys. But when I grew older I found that children liked me. I used to wish sometimes they could stay little forever, and not grow up to argue with me and turn against me. I loved you too, Levanah. But you grew up and defied me and so I had to send you away to punish you."

"It was—a useful experience," Levanah said.

"But you've come back now," Leah said. "You can

stay if you like and I'll have Mary found and brought home."

"Let Mary alone!" Levanah said sharply. "Let her lead her own life!"

"A girl of twenty!"

"Let her find out what she wants to be," Levanah said. "She might come back one day, or she might choose to live with the schoolteacher, but she has the right to choose. Where is the moonstone ring that belonged to my mother?"

Moving slowly, like an old woman, Leah crossed to the dresser, pulled open a drawer, and scrabbled at the back of it.

"They made a secret compartment in the old days," she said in a vague, disjointed fashion. "They were useful for hiding valuables. I burned the letters long ago, but the ring is still here."

It glowed faintly blue with, deep in its heart, a gleam of silver. Levanah held it on the palm of her hand. The ring on her own forefinger, the black pearl, had a sinister beauty. The moonstone was gentle. She would send it to Aunt Catrin and tell her to give it to the people at the Orphanage. That would ensure that nice people adopted the bastard she had borne.

"With any luck," she said aloud, "nobody will ever discover what happened here tonight. Unless that woman told anybody what she planned to do, which I doubt, it's likely nobody even knew she was coming here. We're quite safe, you and I."

"And you won't tell? It was for Teddy's sake that I did it."

"For the family," Levanah nodded. She was smiling as if something amused her very much indeed.

After a moment she said, "I'll live here, Aunt. You

wouldn't want me to bury myself at 'Witch's Dower,' would you? You'd not want to be alone here."

"No, I'd not want to be alone," Leah said.

"I'll go down to the cottage, of course," Levanah said pleasantly. "To keep it aired and sweetened."

"I'll not have you capering in front of heathen altars there!" Leah said, clutching desperately at the last remnant of her frayed authority.

Levanah smiled again. How innocent that little woodland god seemed now, how childishly impotent when she thought of the dark powers with which she had allied herself.

"I've grown out of such foolishness," she said gently. "We'll get along well together now that we understand each other. We'll make Kingsmead a happy place again. Teddy will like that."

"Teddy?" If her head would only stop pounding for one minute she might take in what her niece was saying.

"I've decided to marry Teddy," Levanah said. "I've decided to become Lady Falcon. When he comes home he'll fall in love with me, you know. I'm not pretty, but I have a certain something."

It was true, Leah thought. The girl was too small and too thin, her hair unfashionably straight, but there was something in the narrow face with the slitted, amber eyes that caught the attention.

"Shall we go upstairs?" Levanah asked. "I'll sleep in Mary's room tonight. You know, we ought to use the upstairs sitting room more frequently. It has a lovely view over the fields. Think how cosy we shall be, when Teddy isn't here, you and I! Sitting up there, talking over old times."

As she snuffed out the lamps and led the way back into the hall, Leah had the sensation of being watched, not by the shadows crowding the tapestries nor by the portraits along the gallery, but by the house itself, as if deep in its foundations it observed and waited. For a moment she wanted to scream out, "Let me alone! Don't judge me!"

"Are you coming, Aunt?" Levanah called.

She was on the staircase, her face shadowed, her voice gentle. Raising her arms to slip off her coat, she spread bat-shaped darkness behind her. Leah, climbing toward her, had never known the house to be so cold.

"We'll have to send the gig back," Mary was saying, shivering as the wind bellied her cape.

Charlotte, negotiating a bend skillfully, replied, "We'll worry about that when we get to London. I want to make sure we're on the boat train before your mother sends after us."

"I'll not go back," Mary said. "I'll never go back to a place where you were so unjustly treated."

"You'll be cut off without a penny," Charlotte warned.

"We can earn our living," Mary said. "We can start a café."

"A café! What put that notion into your head?"

"They have them in France," Mary said lamely.

"Run by the French! I doubt if there's scope for an English tea shop," Charlotte said, amused.

"We could open a hat shop. I like hats!"

"We'll think of something when we get there. You do have your passport?"

"In my bag. Mother had some idea of our taking a holiday on the Continent this summer. And now you and I will be there! In Paris!"

"It might be best for us to push on into Switzerland," Charlotte said thoughtfully. "We could give instruction in English, or take posts in a school. I favor the first. Independence is precious."

"Oh, it is!" Mary agreed fervently. In the darkness her blue eyes were fixed adoringly on her friend.

Wenna, having fed Giles, padded barefoot back to bed. Her baby was plump and good-tempered, with a fuzz of yellow hair and Cal's features. Cal at the moment was snoring loudly. She dug him in the back with her elbow and the snore gurgled away. Under cover of the darkness Wenna grinned. Cal was so young in so many ways that he amused her constantly. There was as much maternal tenderness as passion in her love, and there were moments when he seemed like a larger edition of Giles. Curling herself against his back she closed her eyes, savoring the warmth and the male smell of him. She would write to her mother the next day and give the old lady further news of her grandson. Perhaps one day, when there was not so much work to be done on the farm, she would persuade him to visit her native mountains. On this thought, a wry smile curving her mouth as her husband began to snore again, Wenna fell asleep.

On Saron Farm a lamp burned still in the living room. Aunt Catrin was enjoying these solitary hours by the fire when she had made a circle of brightness against the dark beyond the windows. She needed less and less sleep as she grew older, but there were times during the day when she found herself nodding off into a doze.

She was glad that Levanah had gone. The girl had been sweetly helpful during the long months of her stay, but there had been something cold and hard in the yellow eyes. And the story she had told about the fire that had destroyed her employer's house had not rung true. She had meant to ask the girl more about the accident but the yellow eyes had warned her to be silent, and she had said nothing.

The neighbors had whispered. Aunt Catrin was well aware of that fact and cared nothing for it. Folk always talked and they would have been kind if Levanah had given them any encouragement, but the girl had held aloof and been left severely alone, though her condition would have elicited sympathetic inquiries had her own manner been more friendly. But she had walked alone in the fields near the farm, and come back from her one visit into Caernarvon complaining that the town stank of slate and fish.

Aunt Catrin had planned to engage the services of a midwife, but when she had mentioned it to Levanah the girl had said, "I want no ignorant country-woman pushing and pulling at my body. You can help me, Aunt Catrin."

In the end the child had been born in less than an hour. Aunt Catrin had been shocked at Levanah's reaction, for the girl had displayed no interest in the baby at all. She had barely glanced at the tiny, crumpled face, and when the child had yelled with hunger she had said, "Dilute some cow's milk and give it that. I haven't any milk."

Aunt Catrin, who had spent the winter knitting for the expected infant, had done as she was bidden, telling herself that the girl was understandably upset at having borne a bastard. But Levanah had not seemed upset, only indifferent. She had recovered very quickly from her confinement, had given Aunt Catrin thirty pounds and instructions to put the baby into the Orphanage as soon as possible and never to tell Wenna or any of the Falcons about the baby. And she had kissed the old woman and walked off to catch her train without even a glance in the direction of the old cradle where the baby lay.

'Such a pretty baby,' Aunt Catrin thought, going over to the cradle now and peering in. 'Small but quite perfect, with dainty feet and hands. Such a good babe.'

The baby gazed up at her, awake and aware, in its eyes the tolerant resignation of a soul locked up in a child's body. The eyes were not blue and blurred, but green as grass; the hair was a soft mass of tawny strands.

Levanah had not bothered to give the child a name.

"I shall call you after me," Aunt Catrin said. "I shall name you Catrin. Catrin Falcon. That's a very pretty name. Catrin Falcon. Nobody at the Orphanage will have such a grand name."

The baby yawned, pink tongue flicking. Aunt Catrin drew the covers farther up around the tiny shoulders. Such a pity that the little thing had to go into a Home. Homes were cold, comfortless places. She had seen the inmates, wearing clogs and with their heads cropped against lice. This babe deserved more.

"If I could only keep you!" the old woman murmured. "Nobody comes to see me. I'm good for ten or fifteen years yet. I could bring you up."

She fancied the babe had a look of her sister about her. Saron had been sweet and dreaming, with the same crescent moon mark etched in purple upon her thigh.

"I *will* bring you up," she said in a defiant decision. "I'll rear you as my own, and when you're old enough I'll tell you about your grand relatives. A mother has no right to give her child away as if it were an animal. Babes are precious things, and you are my own sister's great-great-granddaughter."

In a wish of love, she stooped her big, gaunt body over the old cradle and scooped up the little, bundled form.

"Catrin Falcon," she crooned, her weatherbeaten face tender. "Cat Falcon. My kitten, my little cat."

The green eyes stared back at her wisely out of the tiny heart-shaped face. Then the sooty lashes fluttered and fell. The baby blew a small bubble as if she had just made some far-reaching decision.

"Nobody," said Aunt Catrin fiercely, "is going to give you away! You have grand English relatives and one day ... one day you are going to rise high. High as the moon, my Cat! You'll see!"

KATHERYN KIMBROUGH'S
Saga of the Phenwick Women

The spellbinding novels in the greatest series of gothic romances ever conceived.

- [ ] AUGUSTA, BOOK 1 — $1.25
- [ ] JANE, THE COURAGEOUS, BOOK 2 — $1.25
- [ ] MARGARET, THE FAITHFUL, BOOK 3 — $1.25
- [ ] PATRICIA, THE BEAUTIFUL, BOOK 4 — $1.25
- [ ] RACHEL, THE POSSESSED, BOOK 5 — $1.25
- [ ] SUSANNAH, THE RIGHTEOUS, BOOK 6 — $1.25
- [ ] REBECCA, THE MYSTERIOUS, BOOK 7 — $1.25
- [ ] JOANNE, THE UNPREDICTABLE, BOOK 8 — $1.25
- [ ] OLIVIA, THE TORMENTED, BOOK 9 — $1.25
- [ ] HARRIET, THE HAUNTED, BOOK 10 — $1.25
- [ ] NANCY, THE DARING, BOOK 11 — $1.25

SPECIAL OFFER! Buy 5 books for $5.00. Save $1.25. Buy 10 books for $10.00. Save $2.50. Get 11th book FREE!